CW00759060

KILL FOR LOVE

EMILY SWANSON BOOK 5

MALCOLM RICHARDS

StormHouse

All characters in this publication are fictitious and any similarity to real persons, alive or dead, is purely coincidental.

Storm House Books
Copyright © 2020 Malcolm Richards
Large print edition, 2020.
ISBN 978-1-9162104-8-6

All rights reserved.

No part of this publication may be reproduced, distributed, or transmitted in any form or by any means, including photocopying, recording, or other electronic or mechanical methods, without the prior written permission of the publisher, except in the case of brief quotations embodied in critical reviews and certain other non-commercial uses permitted by copyright law.

This book is written in UK English.

Available in large print from Malcolm Richards:

The Emily Swanson Series
Next To Disappear
Mind For Murder
Trail Of Poison
Watch You Sleep
Kill For Love

The Devil's Cove Trilogy
The Cove
Desperation Point
The Devil's Gate

PI Blake Hollow
Circle Of Bones

PROLOGUE

It wasn't the pain she noticed first. It was the blood. Wendy Wilson teetered on the edge of the hill, one hand paddling the air, the other clutching the back of her head, sticky red liquid oozing between her fingers. Wet soil crumbled beneath her feet as she struggled to regain her balance. Above her head, a sprawling charcoal sky stretched out as far as the eye could see. Below her, crooked trees with spindly branches sprouted from the sloping ground, while sodden, muddy fields and clusters of villages lay in the distance.

On any other day, Wendy would have marvelled at the view. She would have whispered "spectacular" under her breath, a word she'd adopted from her father.

But not today. Not now.

Having regained her balance, she half staggered, half turned on her heels, warm blood already cooling on her skin. More trees swung into view, all gripped in late November's decaying hand. Just moments ago, she'd been taking pictures of burnt orange leaves with her camera phone, some still clinging to life while most covered the ground in a mass grave. She was going to upload the pictures to Instagram, maybe even without adding a filter.

Now the pain struck; at first dull and throbbing, then instantly white hot and unbearable.

"What—" she began, as she stared at the duo in front of her. One stared at Wendy with wide, uncertain eyes, mouth hanging open, a mobile phone pointing in her direction. The other still clutched the rock in his hand, so dull and inanimate only seconds ago, now slick and gleaming with Wendy's blood.

"Wha—" she sputtered again, this time

unable to complete the word. Something was happening to her brain. It felt as if it were fading. Along with her vision.

The two stared at her, then at each other. The girl with the phone sucked in a sharp, strangled breath, her eyes glistening in the dull light. Was it fear that made her pupils shine so darkly? Wendy stared into them. Felt the world spin around her.

"What are you waiting for?" the teenager with the phone said. She was eighteen years old. Just like Wendy.

The boy with the rock blinked, as if waking from a dream. He stared at Wendy, whose vision had shifted from black to white, then red to yellow.

"Please," Wendy said. Only it came out as, "Plnngth . . ."

She raised her free hand in front of her as she staggered towards the two. Her other hand was still clutched to the back of her head. The pain in her skull was unbearable now, the blood a thick sludge on her scalp and neck.

The girl with the phone stepped back, her eyes growing wide and panicked.

"Do it!" she hissed.

"Please stop," Wendy begged. "Plnngth strmm . . ."

The boy with the rock lifted it high above his head. The girl with the phone watched, unblinking.

Wendy tried to scream. She peeled her hand from the back of her broken skull. Lifted both hands up with her fingers splayed.

The boy brought the rock down hard, hitting Wendy straight between the eyes with a sickening crunch.

The world went white. Then silent.

Wendy fell backwards, her feet slipping in the mud. The sky spun above her, grey and dirty, like cotton wool dragged through mud. Then she was falling; tumbling and flipping down the hill, arms and legs flapping. Rolling over and over.

The girl with the phone hurried towards the edge, pinched the screen and zoomed in, filming Wendy's descent. Then her body was gone, swallowed up by the undergrowth.

The girl glanced up at the boy and let out an unsteady breath. The boy tossed his arm back and threw the rock far into the distance.

"Did you get it?" he asked, bending down to retrieve Wendy's phone from the ground.

The girl slowly nodded. She turned away from him to stare at the vista, and shivered in the cold.

CHAPTER 1

It was a nice looking house for a new build. Red brick walls, slate grey roof, large picture windows with embroidered curtains. A garden with a manicured lawn and flower beds, although most of the flowers had already lost their summer blooms. Emily Swanson stared at the house through the rain-splattered glass of the driver door, then heaved her shoulders as she tucked a loose strand of blonde hair behind her right ear.

It was late Saturday morning, almost lunchtime. The suburban street she was currently parked in was quiet and still. Tall trees lined the grassy verges, their last leaves clinging to their branches. Puddles rippled on the pavements, patiently waiting for tiny rubber boots to make thunderous splashes. But there were no other people around. Only the rain and the cold, wet air.

"So, are we going in?" a deep, velvety voice said next to her.

Emily expelled another heavy breath and turned to stare at her passenger. Carter West stared back at her, a warm smile on his full lips, his curiously coloured eyes glinting despite the lack of sunlight. He had shaved for the trip and got a haircut, his mop of dark hair now short and tidy. It wasn't that Emily disliked his new look. It was that he looked like a completely different person; an impostor pretending to be her boyfriend. She winced. Boyfriend. Carter was thirty-two. She would be thirty in just a few months. Boyfriend and girlfriend were names reserved for lovesick teenagers. So what did they call each other instead? Partners? Significant others? Certainly not 'other half' or 'betrothed'—they both suggested loss of the self. And Emily had only just found herself.

"Em?"

"Hmm?"

"It's getting cold. Shall we?"

Emily returned her gaze to the house. Her stomach fluttered and flipped.

"It's going to be fine," Carter said. "So, you haven't seen each other for a few years. But you were good friends once. Good friends brave all sorts of weather."

"Do they?" Emily felt her body furl in on itself. It would be easy to start the car again and drive back to London. To forget that good friends were there for good times and the bad. The trouble was she had no idea if Angela Jackson knew anything about the bad times.

Carter sighed and leaned forward. "You can't live your whole life worrying about the past. You'll drive yourself insane."

"It's a bit late for that."

"Besides, if Angela thought badly of you, she wouldn't have asked you to come."

Emily shrugged.

"Hey."

"What?"

Carter leaned forward and kissed her, his lips melting some of the anxiety away.

"Whatever you want to do, it's your call," he said. "But I think it would be a shame to travel all the way to Somerset, only to turn around again because of a case of the jitters."

Emily leaned into him, bumped her head against his. He's right, she thought. Not that she would ever tell him that. And hadn't she made herself a promise? Eyes forward, Emily Swanson. Never look back.

"Fine. We'll go in. I need to pee anyway."

They climbed out of the car and hurried through the garden together, giggling like teenagers caught in the rain. Emily pressed the door buzzer and stepped back, a wave of anxiety washing the smile from her face. Carter gently squeezed her hand.

The door opened and there she was. Angela Jackson. All frizzy red hair and rosy cheeks, her glasses still sliding down her nose after all these years.

"Honestly, I don't know why we chose to get married this time of year," she said, grinning broadly and beckoning with a hand. "Come in, before you catch your death!"

Emily and Carter hurried over the step and into a hallway that was as bright as Angela's smile, with yellow walls and pictures of rolling, green landscapes.

Closing the door, she took their coats and hung them up, then stood and stared at Emily, her smile growing even wider.

Emily stared back. Before she could speak, Angela threw out her arms and pulled Emily into a bearlike hug.

"It's good to see you!"

Nostalgia warmed Emily's body as memories of her university days filled her mind.

Angela leaned back and laughed. She hadn't aged much; a few fine lines here and there, her face maybe a little fuller. But she was the same Angela Jackson.

"Let me look at you," she said, the intensity of her gaze making Emily uncomfortable. She had never really liked being stared at. "You look so different. So—I don't know—confident?"

Emily glanced away. 'Confident' was not a word she ever associated with herself. 'Confident' sounded like an impostor. A mask.

She smiled stiffly, scrambling for something to say. But Angela was already staring at Carter, her smile growing wider.

"This is him?" she whispered.

Carter raised an eyebrow. "This is me indeed. Carter West. It's great to finally meet you."

He leaned forward and stretched out a hand.

Releasing Emily, Angela batted Carter's hand away and drew him in for a hug. "Handshaking is for lawyers and accountants. How was the journey down from London?"

"Fine," Emily said, watching her friend. There was something beneath the friendly smiles and warm welcomes. She had noticed it as soon as Angela had opened the door; a shadow lurking in a sunny room.

"Did you take the motorway or the A303? I always find that drive much nicer."

"Except for when you pass Stonehenge," Carter said. "Traffic grinds to a halt."

Angela shot a glance down the hallway. "Well, you know us humans. We love to stand and stare at things. This way."

She led them through a doorway on the right and into the living room, which was large and airy, furnished with two plush sofas and a huge television fixed on the wall. A tall, handsome man in his mid-thirties stood in the centre, wearing jeans and an expensive-looking shirt.

"This is Trevor," Angela said, introducing them. "Or should I say my future husband?"

Trevor approached, white teeth beaming as he shook both their hands. "More like immediate future husband. It's great to meet you."

Emily smiled, noting his firm grip and expensive smelling cologne.

"Accountant or lawyer?" she asked.

Trevor opened his mouth in surprise. "Accountant. But how did you—?"

Emily flashed a sideways glance at Angela. "A lucky guess?"

"Well, it's nice to finally meet you both. Angela often talks about your university days. How long has it been since you last saw each other?"

"Eight years," Angela said. "I suppose with me travelling the world for half of that and Emily heading back to Cornwall then up to London . . ." Her smile wavered a little, and Emily was sure she was avoiding her gaze now. "Trevor, perhaps you'd like to fix our guests a drink. There's white wine in the fridge, or something stronger in the bar if you prefer."

"We brought some red too." Carter removed two bottles of Rioja from a shoulder bag.

"Looks like a party!" Trevor said, clapping his hands together.

Angela glanced at Emily. "You want to help me in the kitchen?"

Emily stared at her, then at the men. "Fine. We women can drink and serve at the same time."

Eyeing Carter, who gave a helpless shrug, she followed Angela out of the room. The kitchen was of average size, just large enough to fit a table and chairs. Aromas of roast beef and potatoes drifted from the oven. Emily had eaten breakfast at Carter's house before their journey, but now her stomach rumbled in anticipation.

Angela pulled a bottle of white wine from the fridge and filled two glasses in silence. She smiled at Emily then looked away, eight years of absence settling between them.

"Here's to old friends," Emily said, raising her glass. "It's good to see you again, Angie."

They clinked glasses and sipped the wine.

"So, how are you?" Putting her glass down, Angela opened the oven door and checked on the beef.

"Oh, you know," Emily replied, watching her. "I'm fine."

"Just fine?"

"Good, actually. It's been a while since I've been able to say that, but yes, things are good."

"I'm happy to hear it." A ripple travelled across Angela's brow. She was definitely avoiding Emily's gaze.

"How about you? You're getting married. That's exciting."

"I suppose it is. I know Trevor isn't the kind of man you probably pictured me with, but he's good and kind, treats me with respect and fully supports my endeavours. What more could a woman ask for?"

Some help in the kitchen, Emily thought. She smiled and took another sip of wine. "And you're teaching at good old Quantock University. How did that happen?"

"Oh, you know. After travelling the world for so long, I just wanted to come home. A job was going at Quantock, so I thought why not apply? I've been there four years now. I know it doesn't sound very ambitious, teaching in the same department where we both studied. But I like it. Teaching teachers is fun."

"Vice Chancellor Eriksson still in charge?"

"God, no. He left a few years back."

"So, there's some justice left in the world."

"Too right. That son of his—Damien—he finally got caught dealing drugs on campus. Now we have Vice Chancellor Ford. She seems decent enough, actually cares about her staff and students."

"That's great," Emily said. "I'm happy for you."

"How about you? Enjoying London?"

Emily's fingers tightened around the wineglass. She watched Angela set the plates on the table, then return to the counter to pull cutlery from a drawer. She did it all without making eye contact.

"It's been an interesting few years. If you told me four years ago that I'd be working as a private investigator, I would have said you'd lost your mind."

Now Angela did stare at her, eyebrows fully raised. "I've been wanting to ask you about that . . ."

Here it was. The dreaded question. One

that Emily was desperate to avoid answering at all costs.

"You always loved teaching," Angela said. She had grown very still. "It was your passion."

"Yes, it was." Emily's eyes found the floor. She felt her body furling again, like a dying petal.

Angela let out a sad, heavy sigh. "I know what happened, Em."

Emily's heart crashed against her chest. The truth was that no matter how much she tried to change, no matter how much she moved further away from the past, it would always be there, trailing behind her like a sick puppy. She tried to look up and found that she couldn't.

The car's just outside, she thought. She could grab Carter, turn around and leave. Never come back. Pretend Angela Jackson didn't exist. It would be easy.

"It must have been terrible for you," Angela said. "To lose a student like that. Some of these children we work with, they're so troubled. Damaged. We do our best to help, but sometimes we still lose them. Salacious gossip and accusatory newspaper headlines don't make it any better, either." She heaved her shoulders and smiled warmly. "I'm sorry you had to go through that, but I'm glad you survived. Most people wouldn't have."

Emily was still staring, mouth open, her breath thin and shallow.

"Thank you," she whispered.

Angela shrugged. "Pass me those napkins, will you? Anyway, I'm glad you've found something new and exciting. Something where you still get to make a difference."

"I'm not sure I do. Unless you count spying on people suspected of insurance fraud as making a difference. It's not exactly what I signed up for." She watched Angela fold each napkin carefully, corner to corner, smoothing out the creases, before laying them at each table place.

"I thought being a private investigator would involve solving cold cases and finding missing people, that sort of thing."

"I wish. But it's my own fault. I was given a case earlier this year. A big one. I may have broken a few codes of practice to get to the truth. Now I'm back on the insurance fraud beat until I prove I can follow the rules."

"Why doesn't that surprise me? You were always so headstrong. And all that business before graduation . . ."

Emily smiled. "I like to think of Becky Briar as my first official missing persons case."

"And my only one, thank goodness." Angela laughed. But then she stood there, staring into space.

"Something's bothering you," Emily said. "Pre-marital jitters?"

Angela looked up. Let out a sad sigh. "Have you heard about the local girl who's missing?"

"No, I haven't."

"Wendy Wilson. Eighteen years old. She's a student at Quantock. Not in my class, she's an English major. She disappeared a few days ago. Went out with a friend and never came back. Her friend says Wendy left her to go and meet a boy. It was the last time anyone saw her."

A strange itch had started in the middle of Emily's chest.

"Was Wendy popular?" she asked.

Angela moved to the counter and picked up her wineglass. "Not really. She was harmless. Practically invisible from what I've heard. Not like Becky Briar. Not like her."

They were both quiet, remembering their final weeks of university, when a fellow student teacher had vanished from the face of the earth. The only difference was that no one had liked Becky Briar. She had been cruel and manipulative, hurting others for her own gain.

"Are you in touch with anyone from back then?" Angela asked.

Emily quickly shook her head. "Just you."

Angela looked up, deep lines creasing her brow. "The thing about Wendy Wilson—the friend she was with on the day she disappeared—it's Bridget."

Emily stared at her. "Bridget? As in your little sister?"

"Except she's not so little anymore. She's eighteen, in her first year at Quantock. Majoring in English, just like Wendy."

"She must be worried sick about her friend."

Angela swallowed a large gulp of wine and stared at the floor, her eyes dark and troubled. "You'd think so, wouldn't you?"

"What do you mean?"

"Nothing. It's just, well, ever since Dad died last year, Bridget gets overemotional at the slightest thing. But with Wendy missing, you'd think the two of them weren't friends at all."

"I'm sorry about your dad," Emily said. "I didn't know."

"It was a heart attack. One minute he was here, the next. . . With Mum gone years ago, I always thought I'd at least have Dad there on my wedding day. Now it will just be Bridget. We're all the family we have left." Angela shook her head as she stared at Emily. "I'm worried about her, Em. Something isn't right."

"People react to bad news in different ways," Emily suggested.

"I hope that's all it is. And I hope they find Wendy soon. Especially with the wedding two days away. Sorry, that sounded more selfish than I intended."

"No one would want this hanging over their special day."

Angela set down her glass. "I'm glad you're here, Em. We should probably go rescue your boyfriend. As much as I love Trevor, small talk isn't his forte."

The itching in Emily's chest began to spread as she followed Angela from the kitchen and back towards the living room. What had Angela meant? "With Wendy missing, you'd think the two of them weren't friends at all."

Was she saying that her sister Bridget didn't seem to care?

The men were in the living room, Carter nodding and smiling in all the right places as Trevor relayed tales from the world of accountancy. Seeing Emily, he flashed her a smile and raised an eyebrow.

"Lunch is almost ready," Angela announced. "Let's move into the kitchen. And Carter, I want to hear all about your furniture making."

"Are you sure about that?" Carter said.

Angela laughed, any trace of concern now vanished.

Just like Wendy Wilson, Emily thought.

CHAPTER 2

The hotel stood at the edge of Taunton's town centre. It was a Victorian era building with just a handful of guest rooms, which meant it was peaceful and quiet. The room itself was large and comfy, with high ceilings and sturdy radiators to fend off the cold. Emily had been awake for an hour. Having already showered and dressed, she now sat at a cherry wood desk, green eyes effervescent in the slice of winter light that had slipped through a crack in the curtains. In her hands was a mug of bitter instant coffee, which she sipped as she stared at the blank screen of her laptop.

Behind her, Carter lay flat on his back and

half buried beneath the sheets, his mouth slightly open as he slumbered. Sleep was still a work in progress for Emily, but she had managed a few hours until her mind had woken her with a barrage of thoughts about yesterday's visit to Angela.

The four of them had enjoyed an afternoon of eating and drinking that had spilled over into the evening. For Angela and Emily there had been several years to catch up on, with certain events subtly skirted around, while both Trevor and Carter had been subjected to a barrage of getting-to-know-you questions. Emily's first impression of Trevor had been dubious at best. But Angela was right about her husband-to-be. He was pleasant and friendly, held eye contact, and listened intently when others spoke. When he stared at Angela, it was with love and adoration, not ownership. But in spite of all the frivolity, something had been lurking beneath the afternoon's conversations; a silent undercurrent of unease shifting between Emily and Angela.

Wendy Wilson. She had not been talked

about again after their conversation in the kitchen. Emily had wanted to ask more, but despite Angela's clear angst, she had remained tight-lipped. Which was understandable; the missing girl was casting a long shadow over Angela and Trevor's wedding day.

But it was more than that. What Angela had said about her sister, Bridget—something wasn't right.

Switching on her laptop, Emily sipped more coffee, then clicked on a web browser and typed 'Wendy Wilson' into the search bar. A moment later, she was scanning the latest updates from a local Somerset news site. Police were still making door-to-door enquiries, the story said. Anyone with information pertaining to Wendy's whereabouts should contact Crimestoppers. There was no mention of a search party. No scouring of nearby woodland and fields. Emily frowned. If Wendy had been just a few years younger, the story of her disappearance would have reached the national newspapers. But she was eighteen years old. A legal adult. And legal adults could disappear whenever they felt like it.

Leaning back, Emily drained her mug and exhaled deeply through her nose. She had encountered enough missing women in the past few years to know that the majority did not disappear of their own volition. She leaned forward again, clicked through to another story. This one contained a school photograph. Wendy Wilson, eleven years old, pretty and awkward-looking, her eyes barely meeting the camera's gaze. There was a quote from her parents, describing Wendy as a quiet and thoughtful girl—even though she was now a young woman—who was enjoying her first year at Quantock University, and who was making new friends after a difficult childhood plagued by illness and isolation.

She's vulnerable, Emily thought. Quiet and trusting. Eager to please. Which made her a prime target and an easy victim.

She glanced over her shoulder at Carter, who was still lost in sleep. Setting the coffee mug down, she ran her fingers over the keyboard, searching for more stories. There was no mention of what had happened prior to Wendy's disappearance. Only that she'd been out with a friend that afternoon, then had gone to meet a boy. A boy Wendy's family knew nothing about.

Two friends. Wendy Wilson and Bridget Jackson.

Emily didn't know much about Bridget, only that she'd been a late surprise to Angela's parents, with an age gap of ten years between the sisters. Angela had grown up locally, just a few miles south of the Quantock Hills. Emily vaguely remembered spending a Saturday afternoon with Angela and an eleven-year-old Bridget, who had seemed more interested in her mobile phone than her boring older sister and friend.

She thought back to yesterday afternoon, to Angela's strained expression in the kitchen. Reaching for the keyboard again, she clicked on Facebook and found Bridget's profile page. Bridget Louise Jackson. Eighteen years old.

She had red hair like her sister, but where Angela's face was soft and oval, Bridget's was all cut-glass cheekbones and steely gaze. She had grown into quite the striking young woman, Emily thought. Scrolling down the profile page, she read through the typical teenage status updates—I'm so bored!—Vodka is life!—as well as more serious post shares and outcries about political scandals and climate chaos. There were photographs, too. Lots of them. Pictures taken on nights out at the student union bar. Fancy dress theme parties. Karaoke evenings. Emily scrolled back up to the top and scanned through Bridget's friends list.

There she was. Wendy Wilson.

"What are you doing?"

The voice startled her. Emily swivelled in her seat to see Carter sitting up in bed, one hand scratching at his chest hair, the other pointing at the window as he stretched and yawned.

Emily closed the laptop. "Nothing. Waiting for you to wake up."

"So you weren't working just then? Because this is supposed to be a mini-break and you said you were going to take the whole time off. I thought you were between cases."

"I did. I mean, I am," Emily said, narrowing her eyes.

Carter was still staring at her, a smile teasing the corners of his lips. Emily glanced away. When she looked back, he was still staring.

"Okay, fine," she said. "I was just reading the news, to see if I could find anything about Wendy Wilson."

Carter frowned. "Who?"

"The young woman Angela told me about. The one who's missing."

"I see . . ."

"I'm concerned, that's all. She's eighteen years old. And there's a personal connection to Angela's sister. Wendy is Bridget's friend. She was with her the day she vanished."

"Must be a worry for Wendy's family," Carter said, pulling the sheets up to his chest. "I'm assuming the police are looking into it?"

"Of course. But they're only going door to door. There isn't even a search party."

Carter's eyebrow arched even higher.

Emily stared at the closed laptop, then back at Carter. "Yesterday, in the kitchen, when Angela told me about Wendy, I said, 'Bridget must be worried.' And Angela said, 'You'd think so, wouldn't you?' As if Bridget wasn't worried at all. Don't you think that's strange?"

Carter sighed as he rubbed his chin. Stubble was already growing back. "Emily, we're meant to be having a couple of days away together. You've been working so much lately. The police are already investigating, so there's no reason for you to get involved."

"I'm not getting involved."

"You're already in research mode."

"Just reading, that's all."

"Are you sure about that?"

They stared at each other, the silence growing thick and awkward between them.

"Look," Carter said. "I know you've been trying to prove to your boss that you're worthy of better cases than the insurance fraud grind she's got you on, but I'm worried about you. You've been working longer and longer hours. Evenings and weekends . . . I'm worried you're going to work yourself into the ground. Then you won't be able to help anyone."

Emily sucked in a breath, relaxed the muscles of her jaw. "Whether or not I'm trying to get Erica to see that I'm a better investigator than she thinks I am is beside the point. I'm just curious, that's all. Don't you ever read the news and want to know more?"

"Of course. But I don't go actively investigating it. And I can't help wondering if you're trying to prove something to Erica Braithwaite or to yourself." Lines appeared on Carter's brow. His chest heaved. "Look, I get it. I really do. But I'd hate for you to burn yourself out when you really have nothing to prove. You're a fine investigator. A great one."

Emily stared at him, then down at the floor. A smile teased her lips. "That's your professional opinion, is it?"

Carter pulled back the sheets and patted

the mattress. "Come back to bed. It's still early."

"It's nine o'clock."

"We're on a mini-break. Nine o'clock is like five a.m. in the real world."

"We're supposed to be exploring the delights of Taunton. I thought we could go to the museum. It's inside a castle. They have dinosaurs."

Carter smiled. "Well, you know I can't resist a dinosaur. But first . . ."

He stared at the empty space beside him and flashed a wicked grin.

Emily's shoulders softened.

"Fine," she said, getting up and strolling towards him. "But no funny business. I've already showered."

Carter reached out a hand, which Emily clasped in her own.

"That's the thing about showers," he said. "You can have more than one."

———

By the time Emily and Carter left the hotel, the crisp morning sky had turned a dull cement grey. After a late lunch at a nearby cafe, they worked their way through the Museum of Somerset, viewing a rich collection of locally discovered fossils and artefacts, from Plesiosaur bones to impressive Roman mosaics, before visiting an exhibition of Somerset artist Doris Hatt's colourful paintings in the adjoining gallery.

As they roamed the halls, hand in hand, Emily couldn't help feeling distracted. Her thoughts returned to Wendy Wilson, then took a dive into the past, back to those final weeks before graduation, when Becky Briar had disappeared. She knew it was a coincidence that Wendy Wilson attended the same university as they had. It was also by chance that Wendy happened to be friends with Angela's sister. Yet Emily's mind was trying to connect the missing young women together as pieces of the same puzzle, even though she knew they weren't. It was just ghosts haunting her, that was all. Just like they always did.

Leaving the museum, she and Carter strolled through the castle's green gardens, following the murky waters of the River Tone. Carter smiled and gently squeezed Emily's hand.

"This is nice," he said.

Emily smiled then shivered. The temperature had dropped while they'd been inside. Rain was imminent.

"When we get back to London," Carter continued, "we should schedule some more days out."

"Schedule? How businesslike."

"I didn't mean it like that. It's just that you've been so busy lately. I feel like we're spending less and less time together, when this far along we should be spending more."

Emily shot him a sideways glance, her shoulder muscles tensing.

"That sounded needier than I'd intended," Carter said. "Honestly though, with you living at The Holmeswood and me out in West Hampstead, don't you think that—"

"It's not that far." Emily let go of his hand

and zipped up her jacket as fresh spots of rain dampened her skin.

"No, I suppose not. But don't you think . . ." Carter stared at her, then looked away again; just like he always did when he had something difficult to say.

"Come on," Emily said, quickening her pace. "It's starting to rain."

Carter slid to a halt. "What I'm trying to say is, we've been together for a while now. Don't you think it's time that we, I mean, that is, if you're feeling ready, we could . . ."

Emily's heart thumped in her chest. Despite the cold, a sudden warmth heated her body. She knew what was coming. She just didn't know if she wanted to hear it. If she was ready to hear it.

She risked another glance at Carter, saw him stammering and shifting uncomfortably.

"Come on," she said again, as the rainfall grew heavier.

She pressed ahead, Carter following behind. Leaving the river, they crossed through a cobblestone square and entered the high street. Shoppers filled the pavements, umbrellas bouncing off each other. Carter caught up with Emily and slipped his hand into hers. When she looked at him, she saw a sting in his eyes. But the moment had passed. For now.

Emily relaxed a little as they continued down the street, weaving in between the umbrellas. But then, through the crowds, she saw a familiar face. She slowed down, until she was standing outside a newsagent. Wendy Wilson's pale features peered out from the front page of a local newspaper. In bold black letters, the headline read: 'Bring Our Girl Home.'

Emily stared into Wendy's eyes. There was no darkness there. Only innocence and light.

"She'll turn up," Carter said, stroking the fingers of Emily's hand. "I'm sure of it."

Emily nodded. "I hope so. I really do."

CHAPTER 3

The wedding was held at Doone Court, a sprawling redbrick mansion situated near the edge of the Quantock Hills. It was a grand building, complete with ballroom and banquet hall, centred in resplendent green gardens and surrounded by trees. Seated next to Carter on an uncomfortable pew, Emily tried to stay focused on Angela, who wore a traditional white gown with a flowing train, and couldn't stop crying as she and a dark-suited Trevor exchanged vows. But every minute or so, Emily's gaze would wander over to the squad of bridesmaids and Bridget Jackson. She was pale and thin, her skin gleaming against the jade of her satin bridesmaid dress.

In the absence of their father, Bridget had walked Angela down the aisle. With Bridget's strange, vacant expression and Angela's tears, it felt to Emily like watching a funeral march. The rain lashing relentlessly against the chapel windows did nothing to change her viewpoint.

With the ceremony over and the happy couple pronounced husband and wife, the wedding party was shepherded over to the reception area outside the main banqueting hall, where drinks were served and the guests mingled as the newly-weds posed for photographs.

"That was nice," Carter said, an arm wrapped around Emily's waist as he sipped a glass of champagne. "Very romantic. How long do you think until we eat?"

"I told you to double up on breakfast." Emily was oblivious to the other guests, her eyes trained on the grand central staircase, where Angela and Trevor stood halfway up, while an overzealous photographer directed them from below. The bridesmaids stood nearby, waiting for their turn in front of the lens. They were all quiet, Emily noted, their mood dampened by Bridget's sullen expression. Even Angela kept flicking her gaze towards her sister, prompting both Trevor and the photographer to repeatedly call her name.

"I don't know why they make everyone wait to eat at these things," Carter said, gulping down more champagne. "What if I was diabetic?"

"You're not," Emily said. "And they're serving hors d'oeuvres."

Carter eyed the smartly-dressed waiters who were drifting through the guests with silver plates of shrimp and bruschetta. "Cover me. I'm going in."

Emily watched him dive into the throng, heading for the nearest platter. She smiled, then returned her attention to Bridget, who was now standing to one side, the same haunted expression on her face.

Despite the rain and the notable absence of the bride's father, this should have been a joyful day filled with warm memories to look back on in the years to come. Yet the heavy mood seemed to be spreading through the room like disease, dampening conversations, reducing laughter to polite chuckles, and carving a deep frown into Angela's brow. Emily watched Trevor tap her on the shoulder. Saw her blink and smile apologetically, before giving her sister another concerned glance.

It was all because of Wendy Wilson.

Carter returned, a small pile of canapés balanced in his hand and a triumphant smile on his lips.

"I come bearing gifts," he said, beaming. "Want one?"

Emily shook her head. She had no appetite. Wendy had been missing for over four days now, and the likelihood of finding her alive was almost nil.

CHAPTER 4

The rain continued to fall over Somerset.
Clouds grew thicker, heavier, the sky darker.
Seven miles south of Taunton, the Blackdown
Hills were becoming slick with mud, dirty
rivulets of rainwater running down the slopes.
The man pulled his raincoat tightly around him,
zipping it up to his neck. He stood at the edge
of a gravel stretch, peering at the land below, a
dog leash hanging from one hand, the finger
and thumb of the other pinched in his mouth.
He blew a short, sharp whistle, then called out.

"Charlie! Here boy!"

Behind him, a Land Rover growled and put
on its headlights. He turned, waved a hand and

smiled as the driver pulled away, a black and white border collie panting in the back seat.

He was alone now, standing in the cold rain. From below came an urgent barking.

"Bloody dog," he muttered.

He started forward, carefully digging his boots into the wet earth as he descended the slope. He could see Charlie thirty feet down the hill, the dog's caramel-coloured fur sodden and soiled.

"Here boy!" the man called, unable to hide the irritation in his voice. The rain fell harder, slapping against his raincoat. He continued to descend, one cautious step at a time. As he drew closer, Charlie's barking grew more intense. The animal was fixated on something, his snout diving in and out of the bracken, his front paws bouncing up and down on the spot.

The man slid one foot in front of the other, the cold seeping into his bones.

The dog stopped barking and began to whine.

"Charlie boy!" the man called, sliding to a

standstill. "Come on now. Or we'll both catch colds."

But Charlie wouldn't come. Instead, the animal continued to whine and scratch at the earth, its tail tucked between its hind legs.

"What is it, boy? Did you find a rabbit?"

Slowly, carefully, the man started downhill once more, the earth growing slicker and more precarious with each step. He was ten feet away now. The rainfall was so heavy that he had to squint. Up ahead, Charlie sat down on the wet ground and rested his head on his front paws. The whining continued as his large brown eyes fixed on the bracken in front of him.

Suddenly, the man slipped and fell heavily on his backside, sliding down another three feet. He shot out a hand, dug his nails into the earth to stop himself from going further. In warmer circumstances he would have laughed at his predicament, but now he swore bitterly as he struggled to stand up.

"Thank you, Charlie," he said, glancing

down at his mud-covered clothing. He swore again. "You're officially in the doghouse."

That made him laugh. But just for a second.

Because now that he was closer, he could see what Charlie had found.

A chill ran through the man's body, as if the rain had seeped through his skin and into his bones.

"Dear God," he gasped.

A bare foot was sticking out from beneath the fronds of bracken, the skin as grey as the sky above, the big toe broken and sticking out at an unpleasant angle.

The man tried to call Charlie, to tell him to come away, but his voice had dried into a croak. Instead, he took a faltering step closer. And realised he'd just found the missing Wilson girl.

CHAPTER 5

The afternoon reception was a sit-down affair of three sumptuous courses in the banquet hall, followed by an exhausting series of speeches made by Trevor, Angela, the best man, and the best woman, a friend of Angela's whom Emily didn't know. The wedding guests were doing their best to keep a jovial atmosphere, but by the time the evening came around, cracks were beginning to show.

Now, as a middle-aged DJ blasted out eighties classics across the ballroom, Emily and Carter stood with a trio of women who Emily vaguely remembered from her university days. She'd tried her best to avoid the old faces throughout the day, but they had finally tracked her down. Currently, Carter was busy working his magic, enthralling them with charming tales of how he and Emily had met while volunteering at a missing persons charity. But the topic of conversation was now shifting to Emily.

"Tell me all about London life!" Sally Spencer said, a broad smile on her lips. She and Emily had studied together, and now Sally taught at a local private school for girls.

Emily cleared her throat. "Well, it's busy. Loud. A far cry from country living. But it's home, and I like it."

"I'd absolutely hate living there!" Sally said, with a dramatic wave of her hands. "Me, I like the peace and quiet. Not to mention the clean air. And teaching at St Stevens certainly has its benefits."

"Ah, yes, the clean air," Carter said. "I've been breathing in deeply all weekend."

Sally's eyes sparkled as they fixed on Emily. "I heard that you stopped teaching. I was surprised, you seemed to love it so. What made you quit?"

Emily had been busy watching Angela put on a brave face as she chatted to guests on the other side of the room. Now, her gaze found its way back to Sally, who was still smiling, her eyes glittering like ice in the disco lights.

"I'm sorry?"

"I asked why you stopped teaching? There must have been a reason."

"Well, I—" Emily began. Her mouth dropped open and stayed there. She stared at Sally, saw her lips curve into a sharp smile. She knows, Emily thought. She knows, but she wants to hear me say it.

Carter leaned forward. "I think Emily realised her skills were better served elsewhere. Isn't that right?"

Emily nodded mutely.

"I see. And what is it that you do now?" The disappointment on Sally's face was all too apparent.

"Insurance fraud," Emily said. "Catching liars."

The song came to an end and the DJ started playing a power ballad, complete with big drums and airy eighties synthesisers.

Carter grinned. "God bless the eighties. Excuse me, but this is my cue to step in and ask my woman to dance."

Sally and the others tittered as Emily arched an eyebrow.

"Your woman?" she said through tight lips.

Carter winked and held out a hand. She grasped it, allowing him to lead her away from the group and onto the dance floor, where other couples had locked arms and were busy swaying from side to side and staring into each other's eyes. Emily glanced around, her face flushing.

"Sorry about the woman thing," Carter said, as they slowly turned in a circle. "I was trying to get us out of there and it was the first thing that popped into my head."

"Forget it." Emily reached up and kissed

him. "Thank you for rescuing me. You're my hero."

"Why, Miss Swanson, steady on. With all this romance in the air, you'll be giving me the wrong ideas."

Emily felt Carter's hands slide down her back.

"Careful tiger. The night is still young."

She glanced back at Sally and friends, who had already turned their attention to another face from the past. Searching out Angela again, she found her sitting at a table, deep in conversation with Bridget. Both sisters looked fraught and unhappy. Bridget tugged at the edges of her satin jade bridesmaid dress, her empty eyes staring into space.

"I feel bad for Angela," Carter said, following Emily's gaze. "And poor Bridget, having to put on a brave face while her best friend is missing."

Her thoughts drifted back to Angela's kitchen and the curious comment she had made about Bridget: "You'd think so, wouldn't you?"

"Em?"

"Hmm?"

"I love you."

"I love you, too."

Across the room, Angela and Bridget's conversation was over. Angela stood up, brushed down her gown, then headed over to her husband and his parents, who were sitting together at the wedding table. She embraced Trevor, whispered in his ear and took his hand, leading him onto the dance floor.

On the other side of the ballroom, Bridget got up and stalked away, pushing through a set of large double doors.

"I was thinking," Carter said.

"Oh, I wouldn't do that. You'll get a headache." Emily watched the doors swing to a standstill.

"You're funny. Anyway, I was thinking about you and me."

Emily looked up, her throat running dry. "You were?"

She glanced away again, her gaze landing on the bride and groom, who were dancing slowly, arms wrapped around each other. Angela's face was buried into Trevor's chest. Was she crying? Or simply trying to enjoy the moment?

"Don't panic," Carter said, laughing. "I'm not about to propose, if that's what you're worried about."

"Who says I'm worried?"

"Well, your face has gone about as white as Angela's wedding dress over there."

Emily risked a glance at him. "And I'm the funny one."

"So, like I was trying to say yesterday, we haven't been seeing so much of each other lately, and we've been together for a while now. . . So, at the risk of ruining our relationship, how would you feel about moving in together?"

The air seemed to rush out of the room. Emily's gaze shifted from Carter, to the floor, then back again.

"I—"

The words stuck in her throat. Across the dance floor, Angela and Trevor held each other, staring into each other's eyes, love shining through the worries of the day.

"I—" Emily said again, her head spinning. "I need some fresh air."

Avoiding the hope dwindling in Carter's eyes, she kissed his cheek and wriggled out of his embrace. Leaving the dance floor, she pushed through the double doors and hurried along a carpeted corridor with chandeliers hanging from the ceiling, until she reached a pair of ornate French doors. Hurrying through them, Emily stepped outside. The rain was coming down hard, battering the awning that covered the patio. Emily shivered in the cold as she sucked in deep breaths.

"Get a grip," she told herself. "He asked you to move in with him, not kill someone."

She stared out at the night, beyond the pool of porch light into the shadows of the trees. You're being ridiculous. Here's a chance at happiness and you're blowing it.

She sucked in another breath, then let it out in a steady stream. As her ears adjusted to the outside world, she suddenly heard a voice, murmuring and strained, coming through the rain.

"Don't talk to me like that!" it hissed. "He promised me."

Emily stepped forward and cocked her head. Someone was emerging from the shadows, heading for the patio.

It was Bridget. Noticing Emily, she slid to a halt with a mobile phone pressed to her ear and her bridesmaid dress swamped with rain. Her bun of dark hair was now wet and unkempt.

"I have to go," she said, and hung up.

The two stared at each other.

Emily lifted a hand. "Hi. I don't know if you remember me, but I'm Emily. I went to university with your sister."

Bridget stared at her. In the porch light, her skin was the colour of bone. "I remember. You're the private investigator."

"I suppose I am. I heard about your missing friend, Wendy. Today must have been difficult for you."

Bridget's expression remained blank. It

surprised Emily, the lack of emotion.

"Thanks," Bridget said, coming closer. "The last thing I wanted today was to be bridesmaid. But what was I supposed to do? It's Angie's wedding day."

"All the same, I'm sure your sister really appreciates you stepping up and being here for her. I'm sure she'll return the favour when you need it."

Bridget nodded, staring into the darkness. She was quiet for a long time, a frown creasing her brow. Then she turned to Emily and said, "Wendy was super nice, you know. She was a good friend. But she was too trusting."

A sudden gust of wind chilled Emily's bones. "Was?"

Bridget shook her head. "Maybe trusting is the wrong word. Gullible? I don't know. I guess no one ever taught her the difference between friends and people who just want to use her for their own good." She heaved her shoulders. "Sorry. I don't even know what I'm saying. It's been a long day."

"Yes, it has." Emily watched the young

woman. Something felt off kilter. As if they were having two separate conversations. She glanced back at the building, then stepped towards Bridget. "You were with her that day, weren't you? The day Wendy disappeared?"

Bridget locked eyes with her. She opened her mouth. Then closed it again.

"What happened?" Emily asked.

The French doors swung open and Angela stepped out, resplendent in her wedding gown, except for the frightened expression lining her face.

"The police are here," she told Bridget. "They want to talk to you."

Emily's gaze shifted between the sisters. Bridget casually nodded.

Two uniformed police officers emerged through the French doors, radios crackling as they headed straight towards Bridget. She stared at them, her eyes growing wet and glossy. She stumbled back, then righted herself.

"Bridget Jackson," one of the officers said.

"We'd like you to accompany us to the station for questioning."

"Why?" Angela asked, her hand flying up to her mouth. "What's going on?"

"It's Wendy," Bridget said. "You found her."

Her eyes went blank, like two dying stars.

CHAPTER 6

The next morning, the story of Wendy Wilson was all over the national news. Emily had slept badly, lying awake for half the night, trying to make sense of Bridget's involvement. Now she sat on the edge of the bed, her eyes glued to the television screen as she watched a breakfast news report.

"Police have confirmed the body of a young woman is that of eighteen-year-old Wendy Wilson," the news reporter said to the camera. She was standing beneath a large umbrella on a gravel parking area surrounded by trees and driving rain. "Wendy, who was a first-year English student at Quantock

University, was reported missing last Sunday after spending the afternoon with her best friend at Durleigh Reservoir, near Bridgwater. Bridget Jackson, a fellow student at Quantock University, told police that Wendy had left her at the reservoir to meet a boyfriend. Her body was discovered yesterday afternoon by a local dog walker, twenty-two miles south in the Blackdown Hills. Somerset and Avon police have confirmed that Wendy died in suspicious circumstances, meaning the search for Miss Wilson has now become a murder investigation."

As the reporter continued, the screen cut to footage of crime scene investigators conducting a fingertip search halfway down a mud drenched slope. The camera then cut to a photograph of eighteen-year-old Wendy, whose large blue eyes glittered as she smiled.

The reporter was back, her expression sad and serious. "Wendy's family has asked for privacy at this time. But they, along with Wendy's friends and the local community, must now be asking the same question: what happened that afternoon when Wendy went out with her friend and never returned? We'll have more as it comes in."

Carter, who had been busy packing, straightened up and stared at the screen. "That poor girl. I wonder what the police wanted with Bridget. I mean, she looks so harmless."

"They didn't arrest her," Emily reminded him. "It's probably routine questioning, that's all. To find out more information and to eliminate her from the investigation." She shifted on the bed, watching Carter as he continued to pack.

"What?" he asked.

"Last night, before the police came, I saw Bridget outside. She said something about Wendy that struck me as odd. She said Wendy was nice, but she was too trusting. That people she thought were her friends were only out to take advantage of her. I wonder who Bridget meant."

"Maybe she knows something about what happened to Wendy."

"If she did, she would have already told the police. Or her sister, at least."

The truth was, Emily didn't know Bridget at all, or what she might or might not do. But she knew Angela. Angela was good and kind. She had spent several years in developing countries, working with orphaned children. Emily had met her father too. Like Angela, he had been friendly and welcoming. It made sense that Bridget would be just like them.

Carter came up beside her and kissed the top of her head. "You hear anything back from Angela?"

"Not yet. But that's understandable, given the circumstances. She must be going out of her mind."

Grabbing the remote, Emily switched off the television and plunged the room into silence. Something didn't feel right. It was just a feeling, twisting in her gut, but Emily had had feelings like this before, and nothing good ever came from them.

Finished packing, Carter zipped up his bag, then stood by the bed, hovering. "I'm ready to go. But if you want to stay on for a little while, if you feel like you can help, then you should. I'll get the train back to London if you give me a ride to the station."

Guilt pinged Emily's heart; residue from last night's conversation. Which they still hadn't finished. She could stay, she supposed. But to do what? Angela wasn't responding to any of her messages. Bridget hadn't even been arrested. She could be hanging around for nothing. Besides, she was due back in the office tomorrow. And there was the question of Carter's proposal. It wouldn't be fair to leave it hanging in the air.

She reached out and squeezed his hand. "No, I'm coming home with you. If Angela needs my help, she'll call. And I'm only a three-hour drive away if she does."

"You're sure?"

Emily nodded.

Carter leaned forward and kissed her again. He stared at her for a moment, his mouth twitching. Then he said, "I'll take the bags down to the car."

When she was alone, Emily sat on the edge of the bed, her mind churning. That niggle of doubt that had been gnawing at her insides since last night grew hungrier. There was nothing she could do right now to help Angela's family. This was not her case, and she had not been invited to help. But what if Bridget knew something about Wendy's murder? Had she been trying to tell Emily last night? And what about the phone call Emily had overheard? 'Don't talk to me like that!' Bridget had said. 'He promised me.'

A thought crossed Emily's mind, one that she had previously dismissed. What if Bridget had been involved in killing her best friend? From that question came another: Why?

People didn't kill without a reason. Unless they were psychotic. And nothing about Bridget screamed 'psychopath'.

Emily grabbed her phone and texted Angela again, telling her that she was returning to London but to call if she needed to talk. Then she took the hotel room key card from the bedside table and headed out.

Halfway along the dimly lit hallway, her phone began to buzz in her pocket. But it wasn't Angela calling.

"Hey stranger, what's up? How was the wedding?"

Emily wrinkled her forehead. "Eventful. How are you doing?"

"Oh, I'm surprised you even asked," Jerome Miller said, a smile in his voice. "Seeing as you abandoned me for a romantic weekend getaway with lover boy. And what do you mean by 'eventful'? Don't tell me Carter got all gooey-eyed and proposed? Oh God, he did, didn't he? What did you say?"

Reaching the end of the corridor, Emily pushed through a fire door. "How much coffee have you had this morning?"

"Three cups. You're deflecting the question."

"No, Carter didn't ask me to marry him. He asked me to move in though."

"The sly dog! Did you say yes?"

"Not yet. Something more serious came up. You didn't see the news?" Descending the steps, Emily told Jerome about the murder of Wendy Wilson and the police arriving at Angela's wedding to question Bridget. By the time she'd finished talking, she had reached the small hotel lobby, where a young man in blue uniform stood behind the reception desk. He nodded politely as Emily approached.

"I'm sorry," Jerome said. "That's all kinds of messed up."

Emily slipped the key card onto the desk, thanked the receptionist, and headed for the exit. "Yeah, well, we're about to head back. How's it going at the office? Have I missed anything?"

"Nothing special. Although Lee Woodruff was in earlier, and I'm sure he was flirting with me again."

Emily rolled her eyes. "You two. This has been going on for months. Can't one of you make a move already?"

"I do not mix business and pleasure. And the idea of dating a private investigator fills me with paranoia."

"Um, thanks."

"Well, it's not like we would ever date, is it? That would be like dating my sister. And don't 'um, thanks' me—when you first started dating lover boy, you were running all sorts of background checks. Who's to say Lee wouldn't do the same to me?"

"Scurrilous lies," Emily said, hovering by the door. Except that Jerome was telling the truth. "Lee seems like a nice guy, not the type to run background searches on prospective dates."

"Then he's a fool. If I had the resources, it's the first thing I'd do."

Outside, the street was hues of charcoal and cement. It was still raining, although it had now eased a little. Halfway down the road, Carter was climbing into the driver seat of his car. Noticing Emily, he waved a hand.

"Anyway, the reason I'm calling is that Erica wants to see you first thing," Jerome said.

Emily's heart sank. "Do you know why?"

"A new case, I think. My guess, it's another insurance fraud."

"Well, of course it is. You'd think I would have proved myself by now."

"Except you really pissed her off with the Harris case."

"It wasn't just me. I seem to remember you were hauled over the coals too."

"And whose fault was that? Not that it matters. I'm here for a few more weeks and then I'm out. You, my friend, are stuck in purgatory until Hell freezes over. Well, must dash. The life of a temporary receptionist at Braithwaite Investigations never ends. Erica says nine o'clock sharp. I'll see you then."

Jerome hung up.

The rain already seeping into her skin, Emily scowled at the hotel. Down the street, a few pedestrians hurried along with umbrellas swaying over their heads. Carter already had the engine running, and now he stared at Emily through the windscreen and tapped a finger against his wrist.

Emily hurried towards him, that niggle of doubt still gnawing at her insides.

CHAPTER 7

Angela stood in the centre of the police station waiting area, the fingernails of her right hand clicking against her car key fob. There were a few other people sat on hard plastic seats, their expressions lined and dour. At the far end of the room, a uniformed officer sat at a desk behind a reinforced glass partition. Angela had only been waiting for a few minutes, but each second felt like an hour. The room pressed down on her. The air was thick and heavy, making her lungs work hard. It was difficult to comprehend that only twenty-four hours ago, she'd been getting ready to walk down the aisle. Now, she'd been married for less than a day and here she was at the police station, overwhelmed and running on just a few hours of sleep. What the hell was happening?

A heavy-looking door opened next to the reception area, and a plain clothed detective dressed in a charcoal suit stepped out. Bridget followed after him, flanked by another detective in similar attire. Bridget's skin was terribly pale, her shoulders slumped. Dark shadows bruised the skin beneath her eyes, which were fixed on the floor ahead of her as she was led to the reception desk. She was still in her bridesmaid dress, which was crumpled and looked horribly out of place. Angela stared at it for a moment, wondering why she had chosen jade for the colour. She lifted a hand and called out Bridget's name. The detectives looked over. The one on the left, a tall man in his mid-forties, gave her a polite nod, while the one on the right did not. Good cop, bad cop, Angela thought.

She watched Bridget lifelessly pick up a pen and sign out. The detective, who had nodded just a moment ago, smiled as Angela hurried over and introduced herself.

"Detective Sergeant Wyck," the man said in return. "This is Detective Constable Bryant."

Bryant gave a stiff nod.

"Is everything okay?" Angela asked. "Can I take Bridget home?"

DS Wyck smiled and turned to Bridget. "That will be all for now, Miss Jackson. Thank you for answering our questions. If we have any more, we'll be in touch."

It was as if Bridget hadn't heard him. As if she wasn't part of the conversation, or even in the room. DS Wyck and his partner stared at each other. Wyck smiled politely at Angela again, then both men walked away.

Angela watched them disappear through the heavy wooden door, then she placed a hand on Bridget's shoulder. "The car's outside. Let's get out of here."

Taking Bridget by the arm, she gently led her towards the front entrance. As they walked, she flicked nervous glances in her sister's direction. Outside, the rain was coming down in endless drifts. At the edge of the small parking area, a cluster of people turned to stare at the sisters.

Angela quickened her pace, pulling Bridget along. She could feel her sister's body trembling in her grip, the short sleeves of the bridesmaid dress providing no protection from the rain. Across the car park, a man had broken away from the group and was heading straight for them.

"Excuse me," he called out, waving a hand. "Do you have a minute to answer a few questions?"

Reaching her car, Angela pulled open the passenger door and bundled Bridget inside.

"Hello?" the man said, pulling a notebook and pen from inside his jacket pocket. "Can I ask why you were visiting the station today?"

He was almost at the car now and was trying to make out Bridget through the windscreen.

Angela flashed him an angry look. "No, you may not."

Pulling open the driver door, she climbed

inside and slammed it shut. She got the engine running, then drove past the man, who gave a nonchalant shrug. Manoeuvring the vehicle onto the road, she turned left, heading in the direction of Taunton's town centre.

"Who was that?" Bridget asked, her voice quiet and distant.

"I don't know. A journalist, I suppose." Angela stole a worried glance at her sister, who was staring lifelessly at the road. "Are you okay? Have you had any sleep?"

"No sleep. They had me up all night, asking the same questions over and over."

"I talked to Marc Edelmann, but he said you wouldn't let him into the interview. Dad said if we were ever in trouble, he's the lawyer to call. Why didn't you let him help you?"

For the first time since Angela had picked her sister up, Bridget turned to stare at her. "They were only interviewing me, not charging me. I didn't need him."

"All the same." The road came to a T-junction and Angela spun the wheel, heading left once more. A few people were on the pavements, umbrellas up as they battled against the rain. There were more vehicles ahead, all slowing to a halt as traffic lights turned from amber to red. "What do you want to do? You want me to take you home?"

Bridget shook her head and stared out the window. "I can't go home. I can't deal with my housemates asking me a hundred questions."

"That settles it then. You're coming back with me."

"It's the day after your wedding."

"You just lost your best friend. You've been at the police station for the last twelve hours. I think that's more important right now, don't you?"

The traffic lights changed and the flow of traffic started moving again.

"Trevor won't like it," Bridget muttered.

"Trevor will be fine. And if he isn't, well then, tough luck."

They passed through the town centre, heading towards the suburbs, where identical red bricked houses spread out in row after row. Rain splattered the car windows. The windscreen wipers squeaked on the glass as they moved back and forth. Reaching her home, Angela switched off the engine, pulled the keys from the ignition, and sat for a moment. Her chest felt tight, her breathing constricted. She stared through the driver door window up at the house, where Trevor was inside somewhere. She hadn't discussed Bridget coming to stay with them, but surely he would have realised it was an option.

They had barely spoken since last night. Angela had insisted on going down to the station, following the patrol car with Bridget inside. While she had stood there in her wedding gown, demanding to know what was going on, Trevor had stayed behind at the manor house, shutting the party down with the help of his best man. Returning home in the early hours, Angela had paced the living room floor and checked her phone every two minutes, while Trevor had slept upstairs. Their first night together as husband and wife, and they had spent it alone. But Bridget was Angela's everything. The only blood relative she had left. She had to do what was necessary to keep her sister safe.

She stared at her now. Her dear Bridget, who looked near catatonic and as white as bone.

Why had the police taken her in for questioning again? And why in such a dramatic fashion? She understood that Wendy was dead. That she had been murdered. But surely the police didn't think that . . .

No, of course they wouldn't think something as ridiculous as that! They had just needed Bridget to go over the events of that day again to make sure they hadn't missed anything. That was all. But still, for twelve hours?

Angela glanced at her sister. "Bridget?"

"What?"

Their gazes met. There was something there, lurking in the darkness of Bridget's eyes. Grief, yes. Horror, of course. But that wasn't it. There was something else. Something about the way Bridget had been behaving these past few days, before Wendy's body had been found. Angela had even mentioned it to Emily, hadn't she? Emily had said Bridget was just worried about her friend, and Angela had said, 'You'd think so, wouldn't you?' Why had she said that about her own sister?

Bridget was still staring at her, the darkness of her pupils hollow and fathomless.

"Come on," Angela muttered. "Let's go inside and get you some dry clothes."

The sisters hurried along the garden path, the rain lashing their skin. Once inside, Angela shrugged off her jacket and hung it on the coat stand. Trevor emerged from the living room, a mug of coffee in one hand. He stared at Angela, then at Bridget, his eyes widening slightly.

"Bridget is coming to stay with us for a few days," Angela said, a hint of challenge in her voice. She paused to remove her glasses and wipe rain from the lenses with her sleeve. She glanced up at Trevor again and felt a twinge in her chest. He's not the enemy, she told herself. "That's okay, isn't it?"

Trevor nodded. "What did the police

want?" The question was directed at Bridget. "They don't think you have something to do with it, do they?"

"Jesus, Trevor! Why would you even ask that?" Angela snapped.

"It's a fair question. The way they stormed into our wedding like that, it was a bit much just to question her, wasn't it?"

Angela placed a hand on her sister's back, whose eyes were now burning into Trevor's. "Why don't you go upstairs and change? There are some of your old clothes in the dresser. I'll be up in a second."

Bridget was motionless, glaring at Trevor.

"Go on," Angela said, this time more forcibly. Bridget pulled away from her, lifting the hem of her bridesmaid dress as she hurried up the stairs.

Angela waited until she heard the guest bedroom door open and shut before turning on Trevor. "What the hell are you doing? She's been awake for twenty-four hours. Her best friend has been murdered. You really think she needs you pointing fingers right now?"

Trevor shrugged. "Sorry. I didn't mean anything. I'm tired and upset. Yesterday was supposed to be the happiest day of our lives. Now it's all gone to hell."

It was true. Angela couldn't deny it. But she didn't like Trevor's tone. It was accusatory. As if Wendy being murdered was somehow her fault. Or Bridget's. She pressed her hands against her sides and sucked in a deep breath. Slowly, she let it out again.

"It's just for a couple of days," she said, trying to keep her voice calm. "She needs us right now. She needs me."

Reaching over, Trevor brushed hair from Angela's face. He said nothing, only nodded, then turned to glance at the stairs. Angela followed his gaze. That same unnerving feeling she'd felt in the car suddenly resurfaced and began to whisper in her mind.

CHAPTER 8

Monday morning arrived in a swirl of icy wind. Emily pulled up outside the grand buildings of Grosvenor Square and shivered as she pulled her coat around her neck. Angela had still not called. Emily hadn't chased her, deciding that the last thing Angela needed right now was an overly helpful friend interfering when her family was in crisis. There had been no further developments in Wendy's murder investigation as far as she could tell from the news bulletins, only that a 'suspect' had been interviewed and released without charge. Which should have brought relief, yet Emily was still plagued with unease. As she pushed through the smoked glass doors of Braithwaite Investigations, she reminded herself that discovering the truth about who killed Wendy Wilson was not her responsibility.

The reception was brilliant white, with a front desk at its centre and a waiting area furnished with a colourful collection of chairs. Jerome was sitting at the desk, his tall frame bent over a computer, the glare from the screen glancing off his russet brown skin.

"Hello stranger," he said, as Emily approached. "Finally decided to grace us with your presence?"

Emily smiled. "I missed you too. How's life?"

"Oh, you know. The life of a receptionist isn't exactly a thrill-a-minute, even at one of the country's most reputable PI firms. But I have an audition on Friday. It's for a new production of The Crucible."

"Which part?"

"John Proctor."

"Jerome, that's great!" Emily moved around the desk and gave him a hug. "I'm so happy you're auditioning again. We should go out for dinner to celebrate."

"Let's wait to see if I get the part first. But I'll hold you to dinner—and you're paying."

Emily's eyes searched the reception desk. "No coffee this morning?"

Jerome arched an eyebrow. "I'm not your servant. Besides, I made sure to drink mine before your coffee-thieving hands came in."

He lifted his hands from the keyboard and stretched out his fingers. Emily stared at the scars that still traced his skin; a permanent reminder of the case he had once helped her with.

"I saw on the news about your friend's sister. Have you heard anything more?"

Emily shook her head as she cast a glance around the room. "I feel so bad for that family. Angela just got married. But, of course, the real victim here is Wendy. I can't imagine what her parents must be going through."

They were quiet for a moment. Until Jerome cleared his throat. "Enough doom and gloom. Are you shacking up with Carter or what?"

Emily stared at him. "Oh, that."

"Well, don't sound too excited."

"It's not that. I love him. I really do. But living together, it's a big step."

"Is it, though? I mean, it's not like you've been together for five minutes. You just said that you love him. And compared to the ocean of pricks and players out there, you could do a lot, lot worse than Carter West."

Emily smiled wryly. "That can't be the reason I move in with him."

"No, I suppose not. Anyway, Erica is waiting for you in her office."

"Just what I need on a Monday morning." Heaving her shoulders, Emily squeezed Jerome's arm, then walked towards Erica Braithwaite's office. "Mind you, I suppose living with Carter wouldn't be anywhere near as horrifying as the time we lived together."

Jerome dropped his jaw. "What do you mean by that? I was the model couch surfer!"

"Sure, if you ignore leaving your dirty underwear everywhere."

Erica Braithwaite looked up from behind her desk as Emily knocked and entered. As always, she was dressed in a tailored suit, with her dark hair swept back behind her ears and the fine lines of middle-age on proud display. She regarded Emily through sharp, intelligent eyes; a gaze that Emily always found intimidating. But she had immense respect for the woman, who had single-handedly built Braithwaite Investigations from the ground up and took no crap from time wasters. She had also been the one to recognise Emily's potential as a burgeoning private investigator, and had taken her under her wing, mentoring her and honing her skills. Until ten months ago, when Emily had let her down.

"I hear Somerset didn't go so well," Erica said, nodding to the empty seat on the other side of the desk. Emily sat down and the women's eyes met.

"Well, at least the wedding went smoothly.

If you ignore the part when the chief bridesmaid was taken in for questioning."

"I'm sorry about your friends. It seems you can't get away from crime and murder." Erica's hardened gaze softened a little. She was like that; one minute scaring the hell out of Emily, the next offering her comfort. "Speaking of criminal activity, I have a new case for you."

Emily forced a polite smile as her employer pulled a file from a drawer and set it on the desk. Normally, this was the point where Erica would go over the details in brief, then send Emily on her way. But now, she simply sat there, staring at the file on the desk.

"I know I've been overloading you with fraud cases lately," she said. "Making you prove yourself after all that unfortunate business in the Chiltern Hills."

Feeling like a scolded child, Emily sank into the chair.

"But you've been working hard," Erica continued. "You've taken every case without complaint, worked overtime, and submitted exemplary reports. I have to say I'm impressed."

Emily looked up, her mouth ajar.

"Thank you," she said, gazing at the case file on the desk. Was this it? Was she finally being set free?

"Nevertheless," Erica said. "I'm not sure we're entirely there just yet. Perhaps a few more cases and we'll review the situation. In the meantime, Dennis Rogers is a twenty-seven-year-old fitness instructor who's claiming that faulty gym equipment left him with a spinal injury and unable to work . . ."

Emily kept her gaze fixed on Erica and her eyes bright and focused. But inside, she felt her heart sink into her stomach. Jerome had been right: she was stuck in purgatory until Hell froze over, or Erica finally changed her mind. She had a feeling the former would happen first.

CHAPTER 9

Bridget sat on the edge of the bed in her sister's guest room, crumpled sheets pulled around her. She was unwashed and still in her bed clothes. The curtains were drawn despite the late morning, and the air was stale and musty, irritating her lungs. Her body ached. Her mind was a maelstrom. Sleep had eluded her most of the night. When she had slept, Wendy's face had floated to the surface of her nightmares, twisting and contorting as blood seeped from her mouth, nose, and eyes. 'You killed me,' Wendy's voice whispered. 'You were supposed to be my friend.' Over and over, until the whisper became a scream. Until Bridget's eyes had snapped open and she had clamped a hand over her mouth to muffle her own terrified shrieks.

I'm going to lose my mind, she thought.

Her phone was clutched in her hand. She stared at the blank screen, then swiped a thumb across it, bringing it back to life. If only she could do the same to Wendy. Tapping the call button, she waited for the line to connect. She held her breath and began to count the rings. One, two, three, four, five, six, seven. . . A dull electronic beep sounded in her ear. Bridget opened her mouth to leave a message. But what more could she add to the fifteen messages she had already left since leaving the police station yesterday? She hung up and sat for a long time, staring into the shadows and listening to the patter of rain on the window.

Was this it? Was this her purgatory? Sitting here in the shadows, waiting for reality to completely unravel? It certainly felt like it. But she couldn't let that happen. Too much had already been lost. She redialled and waited for him to answer. This time, when the beep sounded, she left another message.

"It's me. Why won't you pick up? Please pick up! I don't understand why you're doing this. I did everything you asked. Everything. Please . . . please call me back."

She hung up again and squeezed her eyes shut, picturing Wendy lying dead on the hill, her body soaked through, half covered by bracken and wet soil. She pictured her lifeless eyes staring up at the charcoal sky, raindrops splashing on her irises. Guilt ripped through Bridget, piercing the top of her head and shredding her insides. She clutched her stomach with one hand and clamped the other over her mouth. It was only a matter of time before the police uncovered the truth. And then what? If it meant going to prison for the rest of her life, so be it. But she was not the only one who's life was at risk. She was not the only one who would be punished.

Staring at the bedroom door, she began to chew on her lower lip, gnawing away at the flesh until she tasted blood. She couldn't just sit here, waiting for it to happen. She had to do something. Now.

Picking up her phone for a third time, she skimmed through her contacts list, found another number, and tapped the call button. A moment later, a deep, thunderous voice spoke into her ear.

"What the fuck are you doing? I told you last night, you shouldn't be calling me. You know that."

Bridget's gaze shot to the door as she dropped her voice to a hush. "I know. I'm sorry. Have you heard from him?"

There was a long pause. The voice said, "I'm hanging up."

"Rick, please! Just tell me. Have you heard from Cobb?"

Another pause, followed by an impatient sigh. "No, I haven't. I don't know what the fuck he's playing at. I want my money like he promised."

"I'm starting to think this is all a lie," Bridget said.

"Bullshit. You're panicking, that's all. You need to calm down and you need to stop calling me. We both need to lie low and shut up until it's over, just like he told us."

"The police came to my sister's wedding. Did you know that? They had me at the station, questioning me for twelve hours. They know something, I'm sure of it."

"They don't know anything. You were the last person to see her alive. Of course they're going to ask questions. You knew that would happen. He told us it would. You just need to stick to the story until they leave you alone."

"But I'm telling you they know something, Rick. They kept asking me to tell them everything we did that day. Over and over, like they were trying to find holes in the story. Like they knew I was lying."

"The only way the pigs would know anything is if you fucked up. What did you tell them?"

"Nothing, I swear!"

"Good. Make sure you keep it that way.

Stay quiet and don't call me again. Understand?"

Bridget held her breath, listening to the thump of her heart inside her chest. It sounded erratic, too fast and too loud. If she stayed quiet, she would have to live with this guilt. If she stayed quiet, everyone would be protected. But how long would it be before the guilt drove her mad? What if the police came back again? How long would it take for them to break her down and make her confess everything? Because she had played her role, just as Rick had played his role, and they were both as guilty as each other.

"Do you understand me?" Rick said again, his voice low and threatening.

Bridget slowly nodded. "Yes. But I'm telling you, something's wrong. Why isn't he answering his phone? Why have neither of us heard from him?"

"Because he's staying quiet like we all should right now. I'm warning you, if you try anything stupid, if you talk to anyone about what we've done, I'll kill you myself."

"Just like you killed Wendy."

Silence filled her ear and made her skin crawl.

"Don't call here again," Rick said. The line went dead.

Bridget lowered the phone and shut her eyes. Wendy's battered face stared at her from the shadows. 'You did this to me,' she whispered. 'I thought you were my friend.'

She was going to lose her mind. Whatever happened next, she knew it was inevitable. She wondered if the police were working it all out. What if they were listening to her phone calls? Could they even do that when she had yet to be charged? There was just one piece of evidence that placed the three of them together that day at the Blackdown Hills. The video. She had already deleted it from her phone. But she wasn't the only one with a copy. He had it too. She'd sent it to him. Which meant he had all the power. Just like he had from the very beginning.

The room pressed down on Bridget. Nausea clawed her stomach. She had to make this right. She had to make it all go away. Even if it meant living with the guilt until it consumed her entire being.

Picking up her phone again, she found his number and dialled.

CHAPTER 10

Angela stood on the upstairs landing, a plate of sandwiches in one hand and a mug of steaming coffee in the other, her head cocked slightly to the left as she listened to her sister's muffled voice seeping through the closed guest room door. She couldn't make out exact words, but she could tell by Bridget's tone that she was deeply upset. It was the way the words fired from her mouth like machine-gun bullets. It was the way her sentences collided with each other, the way her voice lifted an octave, then dropped down again, before rising back up. Whoever she was talking to, it wasn't a pleasant conversation. And why would it be, considering the circumstances? Angela hovered, envy caught in her throat. Who was Bridget talking to? Certainly not Angela. She had barely left the guest room since coming back from the police station yesterday, even refusing to join Angela and Trevor for dinner. The plate of food that Angela had left outside the door had still been sitting there when she'd gone to bed.

Bridget fell silent. Angela leaned in closer, pressing her ear to the door. Then, balancing the plate of sandwiches on top of the coffee mug, she knocked and pushed the door open.

The room was dark and filled with gloom. She could just make out her sister hunched over on the edge of the bed.

"Jesus, don't you knock?" Bridget spat.

"I did," Angela said, hovering on the threshold. "I thought you might be hungry. You didn't eat your dinner last night."

She took a few steps into the room, saw Bridget drop her phone on to the bed behind her and quickly wipe her eyes.

"Well, I'm still not hungry."

"All the same, you should try to eat. You need to keep your strength up."

"For what?"

Crossing the room, Angela set the coffee and sandwiches on the bedside table. She crossed her arms and stared at her sister.

"You should open the curtains."

"No."

"A window then. You need fresh air."

"Jesus, stop mothering me!"

Angela stepped back and slipped her hands into her jean pockets. "I'm allowed to worry about you. Especially now, given the circumstances."

Bridget was silent, glaring from the shadows. Angela moved over to the window and reached for the curtains.

"I said no!"

"Just a little," Angela insisted, tugging one of the curtains. Grey light seeped in through the crack, barely illuminating the room. Angela stared at the bed, at Bridget's phone lying in the centre.

"Who were you talking to just now?"

In one fluid movement, Bridget slipped the phone beneath her pillow. "No one."

"I thought I heard you."

"I'm allowed to have friends, aren't I? Just because I'm staying with you right now doesn't mean you get to act like you're my mum."

Angela heaved her shoulders, found herself staring at the pillow. "Something's the matter with you."

"News flash: my best friend was fucking murdered!" Bridget shook her head and laughed to herself. "What a stupid thing to say."

"That's not it," Angela said. She stared at her sister's hunched form. Even in the half-light, she could see how pallid she was. As for the vitriol spitting from Bridget's mouth, it was her natural defence mechanism. It had always been that way, long before their parents had died; Bridget lashing out like a snake trapped in a corner. In normal circumstances, Angela would roll her eyes and ignore it. But this felt different. Bridget's malice was dripping with anger. Angela could feel it emanating from her body in waves. Yes, it was grief for the loss of Wendy. And who wouldn't be angry when their friend had been brutally murdered? But there was something else. It had been there, lurking beneath the surface days before Wendy's body had been found. Angela's gaze returned to the pillow and the phone hidden beneath it.

"You know you can tell me anything," she said softly. "No matter how difficult you think it might be for me to hear. No matter how bad it is. After all, we're family. We're all we have left, and I'll always be here for you, no matter what."

Bridget let out a peal of cruel laughter. "That's not true. You have Trevor. Soon you'll be making little babies together, and then you'll have your own little family, which doesn't include me."

The words were like a slap to Angela's face, making her flinch.

"You're my sister," she said. "I'll always need you."

"Yeah, well right now, I need you to leave me alone. Please."

She lowered her head, her voice cracking on that final word. Slowly, Angela crossed the room, then paused in the doorway.

"Eat your sandwich," she said quietly. "We can talk later."

"There's nothing to talk about."

Leaving the bedroom, Angela closed the door and stood on the landing, swaying slightly from side to side. Tears filled her eyes. She wiped them away, cleared her throat, and made her way downstairs.

Trevor was at the kitchen table, reading the Financial Times on his tablet. He looked up as Angela entered. Seeing her wounded expression, he stood and pulled her into his arms.

"What is it?" he asked, before kissing the top of her head. "What's wrong?"

Angela folded into him and shut her eyes, letting his touch soothe her.

"I don't know," she said.

But she knew something was wrong. Terribly wrong. She felt it deep inside her heart, like an evil spirit waking up.

CHAPTER 11

For the first time in what seemed like weeks, the rain had momentarily dried up. Above the city, the morning sky was flat and featureless. An icy breeze whistled past the skyscrapers and apartment buildings, chilling the air. Emily was on foot, ducking and weaving through heaving crowds. Her target, twenty-seven-year-old Dennis Rogers, was fifty metres up ahead, his bright red puffer jacket making him easy to spot. Emily had been watching his house for two long hours, before he had finally walked out fifteen minutes ago. Leaving the warmth of her car, she'd followed him on to Commercial Street, where she now pursued him at a discreet distance, passing by the Ten Bells pub, famous for its alleged connection to two of Jack The Ripper's victims. Across the road, shoppers and spicy food smells flowed out of Old Spitalfields Market, which had been in operation for more than three hundred and fifty years.

For someone with an incapacitating back injury, Dennis Rogers seemed to be walking freely and at a brisk pace. Hopefully, that meant this would be a quick job, over and done with by lunchtime. All Emily had to do was take incriminating pictures, but she had to time it right. Snaps of the back of his head wouldn't prove anything. She needed to get his face, which meant she needed to keep following him until the right opportunity arose.

As she followed, occasionally side-stepping to avoid an incoming shoulder, her mind wandered back to Somerset and the murder of Wendy Wilson. She pictured the young woman's body sprawled on the slopes of the Blackdown Hills. National news coverage about her murder had been scant.

Wendy wasn't a child, which meant any mention of her murder was relegated to the inner pages. If her killer wasn't apprehended soon, she would be lost in a sea of salacious gossip and more headline-grabbing crimes. It troubled Emily, how one person's death could shift more newspapers than others.

Angela still hadn't replied to Emily's text messages, which was understandable and frustrating in equal measures. Emily wanted to know that her friend was all right, yet at the same time, she was curious to know what had happened that day, after Bridget had said goodbye to Wendy. It was the investigator in her, she supposed. But it was also the night of Angela's wedding, and the way Bridget had described Wendy. It had been a cold, indifferent observation, almost scientific in its analysis of Wendy's weaknesses instead of an emotional response about a missing friend. Perhaps Emily was reading too much into it. Shock and grief made people behave in unnatural ways. And yet, the feeling that something was lying beneath the surface was still present.

Emily glanced up, suddenly aware that she'd lost her focus. Dennis Rogers was nowhere to be seen. Swearing under her breath, she sped up, dodging an incoming man in a business suit who had no intention of stepping out of the way. Shooting him a glare, she plunged deeper into the crowd, her eyes searching for the bright red puffer jacket. But all she saw were monochrome washes of greys, blues, and blacks.

"Damn it."

A crossroad was coming up. Hanbury street lay on the right, leading to bustling Brick Lane. Lamb Street lay on the left, which, according to the map on her phone, came to a dead end. Commercial street continued on up ahead, heading towards Shoreditch. Emily spun on her heels, chastising herself. This was supposed to be an easy case. She was only complicating matters by letting her mind wander.

Pushing her way to the edge of the

pavement, she scanned the traffic and the crowds on the opposite side of the street. Then she saw him, a flash of red twenty metres ahead on the other side of the road. Dennis Rogers pulled open the door of a glass fronted building and ducked inside. Above the door in large white letters was: Breathless Fitness Studio.

Got you, Emily thought.

A rush of warmth welcomed her as she entered the building. Pulling off her bobble hat, she looked around the clean, white space. A pretty young woman sat at a reception desk, talking to a pair of equally attractive gym members. A long corridor stretched to the left, where dance music filtered out from behind closed doors. At the far end of the corridor, a flash of red attracted Emily's eye. Dennis Rogers was disappearing through the door to the men's changing room.

Emily moved in his direction.

"Excuse me," the young woman at the reception desk called out. "Could I see your membership card?"

Emily slid to a halt and let out a sigh. "I don't have one."

"Oh, in that case, you'll need to sign up to use our facilities. We're offering a free fourteen-day trial right now."

"Can't I just take a look around?"

The door to the men's changing room was now shut. Dennis Rogers was gone.

"I'm afraid not," the receptionist said. "Not without signing up for the trial."

Pacing back to the reception desk, Emily flashed a wide smile. "Sign me up!"

"That's great! I'll just need you to fill in a couple of forms, and then we can book you in for your induction session."

"That's all right, I've been to the gym before. I'll just take a quick look around now."

The receptionist stared at her. "Unfortunately, we don't let anyone use the facilities without having had the induction. Health and safety and all that." She pushed a clipboard with a form attached across the counter.

Emily snatched up the pen and flashed her

another smile. "Even just to take a look around without touching anything? I mean, I didn't even bring my leotard."

———

Minutes later, Emily stood in the corner of the main gym area, energetic dance music pumping from speakers as people of all shapes and sizes used the facilities. Some members were being directed by personal trainers, while others exercised alone, their faces red and perspiring. Emily snorted as she watched one muscle-bound man lift weights in front of a full-length mirror, his face just inches from his reflection. On the opposite wall, a wide glass partition looked into the next room, where a group of twenty-somethings pedalled for their lives on spinning bikes as an overzealous instructor shouted out instructions. Dennis Rogers was not here.

As Emily waited for him to emerge from the changing rooms, she thought about the fact she did little to no exercise at all. Occasionally, when she thought about it, she would follow a Pilates video on YouTube, and she supposed she walked a lot, following 'clients' around the city, hoping to catch them in the act. Now that she had an actual gym membership, she wondered if she should actually use it, even if the thought of exercising while surrounded by pneumatic-looking men and women made her stomach knot into a tight ball.

Pressing herself up against the wall, she crossed her arms over her stomach. And saw Dennis Rogers cross the floor, heading towards a stack of free-standing weights. Now he was dressed in knee length gym shorts and a sleeveless T-shirt. He looked comfortable in the gym, and his body was toned and clearly exercised. He walked naturally, with no signs of pain or stiffness.

Emily narrowed her eyes. As she watched him pick up a dumbbell with ease, her phone began to ring loudly in her pocket.

Heads turned towards the conspicuous woman dressed in jeans and a hoodie in the corner of the room. Emily pulled out her phone and tapped a side button to silence it. She swore under her breath again, realising she'd forgotten to set the phone to 'do not disturb'. But now she was glad that she had because Angela was calling.

She glanced up, the phone vibrating in her hand. Most people had returned to their exercise, but Dennis Rogers was still staring in her direction. Turning away from him, she lifted the phone to her ear.

"Angela? It's good to hear from you. How are you doing?"

"I can't find Bridget," Angela said, her voice high and breathless. "She's missing."

"What do you mean? Missing how?"

She waited as Angela struggled to exhale. "She's been staying with me the last couple of days, ever since the police pulled her in for questioning. This morning, I took coffee up to her room, but she wasn't there."

"Okay. Well, maybe she went for a walk?"

"She knows not to go off without telling me first. She's not answering her phone, either. I've tried calling her five times. And yesterday we had a fight. She's been acting so strangely, which of course is understandable. But I'm worried, Em."

Emily glanced across the room at Dennis Rogers, who was now perched on the edge of a bench with his feet spread apart as he curled a dumbbell up and down in slow, rhythmic measures.

"You know what teenagers are like. Losing her friend the way she did, maybe she needs some time alone to think."

"Then why not tell me that instead of letting me worry?"

"She's probably not thinking straight. Grief makes people behave in strange ways."

"I know that, but—" Angela's voice trailed off. "I just get the feeling that something's really wrong. I mean, more than poor Wendy."

Emily caught her breath. So, she wasn't the only one thinking it. "What do you mean?"

"Like Bridget's hiding something."

"Listen. Give it a few hours. Maybe leave her another message. I'm sure she'll come back." Emily paused. "Have you tried her house?"

"Of course I have. Her housemates say she's not there."

"Could she have asked them to lie?"

"Why would she get them to do that?" Angela sucked in another breath and let it out. "Maybe you're right. Maybe she just needs some time. It's just that . . . oh, I don't even know what it is."

"You're her big sister, Angie. It's your job to worry about her. But I'm sure she'll turn up. Give it until tonight. If you've still heard nothing, then call me back. Okay?"

"All right. Thank you. I'm sorry I haven't been in touch. It's just that with everything going on . . ."

"You don't need to explain. Just try to stay calm. I'm sure Bridget will walk through the door any minute now."

"I hope you're right. I'll call you later, either way."

Angela hung up, leaving Emily to stare at the wall. Across the room, Dennis added more weights to the dumbbell and switched hands. As he lifted, a vein protruded at the centre of his forehead.

Emily activated camera mode on her phone and snapped pictures of him. But she felt no satisfaction at closing another case. Deep down in the pit of her stomach, a quiet dread had begun to stir.

CHAPTER 12

Angela called just after eight, while Emily was eating dinner alone, with the TV on and the volume down low. Bridget had still not come back or replied to Angela's messages. None of her friends had seen or heard from her, leaving Angela to think the worst.

With the Rogers case report already typed up and signed off, Emily had a free day. Rising early, she drove the three-hour journey to Taunton. Now, it was almost lunchtime and she was sitting in Angela's living room, as her friend paced back and forth in front of the bay windows.

"Where the hell is she? This is so unlike her. Something's happened, I know it."

Emily was quiet, watching her move up and down, noting the way she wrung her hands together and clenched her jaw in between speaking.

"I'm so grateful you're here, Em. I know it was a big ask, but I don't know what I'd do right now if you weren't here to help."

Getting to her feet, Emily went to Angela and rested her hands on her shoulders, bringing her to a standstill. Tears leaked from the corners of Angela's eyes as she buried her face into Emily's shoulder.

"You think I'm being over dramatic, don't you? That I'm worrying about nothing. But I can't help it. She's all I have left. Apart from Trevor, I mean. And she wouldn't just disappear like this. She wouldn't!"

"Then maybe it's time to call the police," Emily said. "Maybe it's time to report her missing."

Angela stared up at her with wide eyes. "No. We can't!"

She pulled away and started pacing again.

"Why not? If Bridget really is missing, they need to know."

"Because the police will see her disappearance as suspicious. They've already pulled her in for more questioning. Now they'll take one look at Bridget's disappearance and decide she's run away. They'll see it as an admission of guilt."

"Why would the police believe Bridget murdered Wendy? She was her best friend."

"Because Bridget was the last person to see Wendy alive. Because she says Wendy left her to meet a boy but she can't seem to remember his name. No one can back Bridget's story up. No one can prove she and Wendy parted ways when she said they did. Why would the police question Bridget again if they didn't suspect her story was a lie?"

Emily crossed her arms, unease creeping under her skin. "Because Bridget is the only lead the police have right now. There would be little evidence at the crime scene with all the rain we've had the last few days. Any DNA would have been washed away. There have been no other witnesses coming forward. So, until someone does, or the police find new evidence, Bridget is all they have. Anyway, what motive would Bridget have for killing her best friend?"

Angela moved closer to the windows and peered nervously out at the street. It was raining again. No one was around. "I don't know. It's just a feeling. I know I'm not making sense."

But Emily was having the same thoughts too. She couldn't stop thinking about the night of the wedding and Bridget's emotionless reaction to Wendy's disappearance. She stared at Angela, wondering if she should tell her. What if it pushed her over the edge, or made her angry enough to ask Emily to leave?

"You said you had a fight with Bridget before she took off. What about?"

"I overheard her speaking to someone on the phone. I couldn't hear what she was saying exactly, but she sounded angry. Angry and terrified. I asked her about it and she told me it was none of my business. To leave things alone. Now she's gone. Tell me that's just a coincidence."

Emily stared at her, unable to tell her anything of the sort. "So if calling the police isn't an option right now, what do you want to do?"

Angela licked her lips as her eyes darted towards an oak cabinet in the corner. "I need a drink. Do you need a drink?"

"Focus, Angie. I've driven three hours to get here. What do you want me to do?"

"You're a private investigator. I need you to find Bridget and bring her home. It's what you do, isn't it?"

"Okay. I can try," Emily said. She turned away, her mind racing. "Trevor is out right now driving around the local area looking for Bridget. You should stay here, just in case she comes back or calls. So, I'll drive up to Bridget's home to make sure her housemates are telling the truth."

"And if they are?"

"I need you to make a list of all the places

Bridget might go to. Anywhere you can think of. Places that are important to her. Places that would make her feel safe. Can you do that?"

Angela nodded, a little tension slipping from her shoulders.

"Good. Text it to me as soon as you're done, along with Bridget's phone number. Try not to worry. Between the three of us, we'll find her."

"And if we don't?"

Emily pulled her car key from her inside jacket pocket. "Then we'll have no choice but to call the police and tell them your sister is missing."

CHAPTER 13

Bridget sat bolt upright and clamped a hand over her mouth, stifling a scream. Beads of perspiration dripped from her skin and soaked the bedsheets. It took a long moment to calm herself and to remember where she was.

Yesterday, she had thrown what clothes she had into a backpack and taken a bus to Glastonbury, where she'd checked into a Travelodge. She hadn't left her sparsely furnished hotel room since. She had needed to get away from Angela's worried looks and constant questioning. From the mounting anxiety pressing down on her, and the certainty that the police would come bursting through the door at any second to take her away in handcuffs.

Climbing out of the bed, she stretched her aching limbs and opened the curtains. The rain was holding off for now, but the sky was still the colour of charcoal. She looked at the car park below and the petrol station next to it, where a tired looking woman was fuelling her car while two children bounced up and down in the back seat. Bridget's stomach rumbled as she spied shelves of snacks through the station's glass storefront. She hadn't eaten since yesterday morning. Turning back to the room, she spied a side table, where a kettle sat next to a basket filled with tea bags and sachets of coffee. Nestled in between the sachets were two packets of biscotti. She devoured the dry almond cookies, but her stomach rumbled for more.

Her mobile phone was on the bedside table. Bridget picked it up and stared at the screen. Another seven missed calls from Angela and two more voicemails. She should have felt guilty for letting her sister worry, but right now, there was only so much guilt she could bear. She would call Angela later, and tell her she needed time to herself and to stop worrying. But Angela wouldn't accept that. She would ask more questions. She would demand to know where Bridget was so she could pick her up and drive her back.

And what about Cobb? Bridget had called him another seventeen times yesterday before collapsing into a pit of exhaustion in bed. She was growing more convinced with each unanswered call that Cobb had abandoned her completely. Instinctively, she redialled his number. Her breath caught in her throat, as an automated female voice said: "The number you have dialled has not been recognised. Please hang up and try again."

Bridget stared at the phone screen. "What the hell?"

Hanging up, she redialled. But a second later, she heard the woman's lifeless tone again: "The number you have dialled has not been recognised. Please hang up and try again."

"It's all a lie," she breathed, the room closing in on her. "It's all a fucking lie!"

————

An hour later, Bridget sat on a bus travelling towards the small cathedral city of Wells. As a child, she had visited the place a few times with Angela and her father on weekend trips. Back then, she hadn't appreciated the city's breathtaking medieval architecture. Now, as she climbed off the bus and walked through the streets, she admired the history that surrounded her. Until guilt stabbed her in the ribs.

Here she was, enjoying the scenery while Wendy lay dead on a cold slab. And now Bridget was on her way to see the man who had put her there.

She had never visited Rick Frost's house before. She hadn't even known where he lived until an hour ago. A quick Google search had revealed his address. That was the thing about

Rick—he was dangerous, but he was also stupid.

Bridget stopped outside a modern terraced house and pressed the doorbell with a trembling finger. As she waited, she wondered what she would say to him. He had already threatened to kill her if she didn't stay away. But now Cobb had given her little choice. Bridget snorted. Even in Cobb's absence, he was still controlling her every move.

The front door opened and a middle-aged woman with a kind face smiled at her. Bridget asked for Rick and the woman's face lit up.

"Rick rarely has friends over, especially pretty young ladies," she said. "He's upstairs. Come in and I'll call him for you."

Bridget stepped into a carpeted hallway with flock wallpaper and stairs climbing up on the left.

"Rick! Your friend is here. A young woman!"

Rick's mother flashed a smile at Bridget, who stared back with blank eyes. Nausea twisted her gut. Her skin felt cold and clammy. She'd hoped to never see Rick's face again, but now here he was, descending the stairs, heading straight for her.

Rick Frost was in his early twenties. He was of average height and clearly worked out, his biceps bulging through his black T-shirt. His head was shaved close to the scalp, accentuating his sharp cheekbones and ice-blue eyes. His mouth was thin and curved downward at the edges. When he saw Bridget waiting in the downstairs hall, the colour drained from his lips.

Rick's mother beamed up at him and lowered her voice to a stage whisper. "You never mentioned a girlfriend."

Rick ignored her, his eyes fixed on Bridget, chilling her blood.

"Would you both like a drink?" Rick's mother asked. "Tea or coffee? Maybe a juice?"

"No," Rick said, his voice sharp and threatening. "Just go back to whatever it was you were doing."

His mother opened her mouth, then shut it

again. Shaking her head, she smiled and rolled her eyes at Bridget, then disappeared through a door at the end of the hall.

They were alone now, the two of them silently staring at each other, the air growing thick and heavy.

Rick stepped forward. "What the fuck are you doing here? I told you not to contact me. I said I'd kill you."

Bridget trembled. She tried to swallow, but her throat felt as if it were filled with broken glass.

"I had to come," she whispered. "Cobb has vanished."

Before she could say another word, Rick grabbed her wrist and began dragging her upstairs. Bridget tried to free herself, but Rick was stronger. Reaching the landing, he shouldered open a bedroom door and shoved her inside. Bridget staggered, then righted herself, in time to see Rick shut the door and lock it with a key.

They were inside his bedroom. Crumpled sheets hung off the bed and dirty clothes swamped the floor. Posters of half-naked women in suggestive poses covered the walls.

"What do you mean?" Rick said, standing in front of the door. "Why do you keep saying that?"

"Because it's true," Bridget whispered. "Cobb's gone. He can't be reached."

"He wouldn't just disappear."

"Have you tried calling him?"

"He told us to stay quiet. To lay low. He's doing the same."

"Go on. Try his number."

Rick's blue eyes flicked to the left, where his phone lay on top of a desk. Snatching it up, he swiped a thumb across the screen. Bridget waited as he tried to call Cobb. A second later, Rick's face turned a dark shade of red.

"What the fuck?"

He hung up and tried again. Bridget stepped closer, listening to the disconnect tone and the operator's recorded voice.

"I told you," she said. She felt strange

inside. Unbalanced, like the world had tilted and was unable to right itself.

Rick was staring at the floor now, his nostrils flaring and his eyes growing darker by the second. "This is bullshit! You're working with him, aren't you? You're trying to set me up, so I take all the blame."

"Don't be stupid. If that were true, why would I even be here right now?"

"There has to be another way to contact him. Another number to call."

"There isn't." Bridget held up her phone. "See? I have the same number as you."

Rick stared at the screen, then back at his own phone.

"They're different," he said.

"What?"

Bridget moved closer, staring at Rick's phone screen. It was true. The numbers were different. The world tilted even more, leaving Bridget fighting for balance.

"It's all a lie," she whispered. "All a game."

Nausea grew stronger in her stomach. The room began to swim. In front of her, Rick was unravelling. He took a large step away from her, shaking his head and dropping his phone on the floor. His hands balled into fists and he drove them hard into the wall.

"That lying fucker's ripped me off! I'll kill him. I'll fucking kill him!"

Bridget slid one foot back, then the other, eyeing the door. Rick had left the key in the lock. "We don't even know where he is. Or who he is. Don't you get it? Cobb lied to you. To us both. We've done terrible things and now we'll pay the price."

"No. There has to be a mistake. Maybe his phone lines are down."

"They're not. Cobb is gone. And Wendy is still dead."

They were both silent for a long time, staring into space, their hearts beating wildly out of control.

"You need to get rid of the phone," Rick said. "That video is the only thing that ties us to Wendy."

"I've deleted it."

"Doesn't matter. If the police get hold of

the phone, they'll still be able to pull the video from it. Don't you watch crime shows on TV?"

"Whether I get rid of the phone or not, it doesn't matter. Cobb has the video too. I sent it to him."

"Fuck! I'm not going down for this. I'm not going to prison for something that's not my fault."

Stalking towards a fitted wardrobe, Rick pulled open one of the doors and removed a sports bag from the top shelf. He moved to a chest of drawers and began pulling out clothes and dumping them into the bag.

Bridget watched him, numbness making her still. "But it is your fault. Cobb offered to pay you to kill Wendy. He didn't threaten or try to blackmail you. You didn't even think to ask for any money up front."

"Shut up."

Rick was on his knees and pulling out a cash box from beneath the bed. Flipping it open, he pulled out a bundle of notes and crammed it inside his pocket.

"You deserve to get caught," Bridget said,

her voice sounding far away. "You murdered Wendy."

"I said shut up!"

"You bashed her brains in with a rock. And I—"

Like a cobra striking, Rick launched himself at Bridget and grabbed her by the throat. He slammed the back of her head against the bedroom wall, making her vision turn white. Then Rick was choking her, his face inches from her own, his cold blue eyes flashing dangerously.

"I may have killed her," he whispered. "But you watched. You stood and filmed your friend dying and you didn't try to save her. If I go down, you're coming with me. We can rot together."

Bridget's face was turning purple. She tried to suck in a breath but couldn't. Rick leaned in even closer, until the tip of his nose touched hers. Slowly, he released his grip on her throat and pulled away, returning his focus to the half-packed bag.

Bridget slumped against the wall and

sucked in ragged breaths. Her neck throbbed. Blood rushed in her ears.

"Get out," Rick said, not even looking at her now. "I don't want to see you again. If you try to contact me or if you go to the police, I'll make sure you suffer more than Wendy ever did."

Propelling herself off the wall, Bridget dashed across the room, unlocked the door and threw it open. She staggered onto the landing then raced down the stairs, almost tripping on the bottom step. As she reached the front door, Rick's mother appeared in the kitchen doorway. Her smile was gone and her eyes were wide with fear.

"He's a good boy, really," she called out. "He doesn't mean to hurt anyone."

Bridget sucked in another painful breath and ran from the house, racing blindly down the street, the city's ancient beauty long forgotten.

She had to leave. Find a place to hide. Which meant she had to go back home and pack a bag. She just hoped her housemates wouldn't be there. Because then they would offer her sympathy and hugs, and she didn't deserve any of it.

As Bridget ran towards the bus stop, clouds burst open above her head and the rain began to fall again. Good, she thought. If only the rain could get inside her and wash away her guilt.

CHAPTER 14

Bridget Jackson's house was in North Petherton, a small town near the eastern foothills of the Quantocks, and a fifteen-minute bus ride to the university campus. It was typical student accommodation, which meant it was badly in need of repainting and repair. Emily sat in the living room on an uncomfortable armchair with a spring poking into her left buttock. Bridget's housemates sat side by side on a sofa, eyeing her nervously. Lanny Peters was on the left, a tall young woman with a shock of frizzy hair, while Julia Watson sat on the right, short and stout with piercing green eyes.

"And you're sure you haven't seen Bridget?" Emily said. "Because it's very important I find her right now, and I wouldn't want anyone who's covering for her to get into trouble."

The young women shifted uncomfortably and glanced at each other, reminding Emily how young they were.

"We haven't seen her since before Angela's wedding," Julia said, the more confident of the two. "Is she in some kind of trouble? Because if it's to do with what happened to Wendy, we don't know anything about that."

"No, we don't," Lanny said, avoiding Emily's gaze.

"And Bridget hasn't called or texted?"

They both shook their heads.

"How well do you know Bridget?"

"We've only known her since September," Julia said, Lanny nodding in agreement. "Lanny and I are both second-year education students. We've lived together since day one. Our old housemate moved out last summer and Bridget took the room. I wasn't sure about living with a first year. But Bridget pays her rent on time and doesn't like to stay out late. I don't know why she wouldn't just save her money and live at home. I would if I was local."

"We're not from around here," Lanny said. "I'm from London and Julia's from the Midlands."

"But the three of you get along?"

Julia shrugged. "We cook together sometimes. But we don't see much of Bridget on campus. Like I said, we're education majors and Bridget studies English."

Emily shifted on the seat, trying to avoid the loose spring. "And what about Wendy Wilson? Did you ever meet her?"

The young women visibly flinched and glanced at each other.

"She started hanging around the house about a month ago. She was here at least twice a week, but she's Bridget's friend, not ours," Julia said, then winced. "I mean she was. Besides, Wendy was always shy and awkward when she was over. I tried talking to her a couple of times, but she'd always get embarrassed and mumble under her breath. I could never understand a word she was saying. To be honest, I thought she was weird."

Emily raised an eyebrow. "Weird how?"

"She wasn't weird," Lanny said. "She just didn't have many friends. Bridget was always saying it. She'd tell us she was Wendy's only friend. Which is why it doesn't make sense that Bridget would . . . well, you know."

"Bridget would what?

"Murder Wendy," Julia said. "That's what everyone's saying. I mean, Bridget was the last person to see her alive, and now she's run away."

"We don't know that she's run away." Emily shifted her gaze from Lanny to Julia, sensing their horror and discomfort. She tried to imagine how it felt for them, to know that a fellow student, one who had visited their home several times, had been brutally murdered. And now their housemate was suspected by the rumour police, if not the actual police.

"And you haven't noticed any shift in

Bridget's mood lately?" Emily asked, changing tack. "Any other significant new people in her life?"

Immediately, both young women tensed, as if bracing themselves against an attack.

"Well," Julia said, wrinkling her face. "There's that Rick guy."

"I don't like him," Lanny said bitterly.

Emily leaned forward. "Who's Rick?"

"A pervert who doesn't understand the word 'no', that's who."

Lanny crossed her arms over her stomach. "He doesn't go to Quantock. Bridget knows him from somewhere else. The first time she brought him home, I was studying in my room, and I guess Bridget had gone to make a drink. Rick just walked right in and thought it was okay to . . . grope me."

Lanny's face crumpled as she stared at the floor.

"Rick thinks he's God's gift to womankind," Julia added, her face growing red. "The second time he was here, he grabbed me when Bridget was out of the room. Right between my legs. Like he had a right to do it."

"I'm sorry," Emily said.

"I told him if he ever touched me again, I'd cut his dick off."

Lanny clenched her jaw. "We told Bridget what he did to us. We warned her never to bring him around again. She shrugged it off, like we were exaggerating. But we haven't seen him since."

Emily's mind was racing. "Does this Rick have a last name?"

Neither woman knew what it was.

"How about Wendy? Did you ever see the three of them hanging out together?"

"Bridget liked to keep her friends separate," Lanny said.

"Were she and Rick involved romantically or sexually?"

Julia shook her head. "Bridget told me the only reason she hangs out with Rick is because he has a car. She's already got a boyfriend."

Emily looked up. Angela hadn't mentioned

a boyfriend. But maybe that was because she didn't know.

Julia shrugged, brushing hair from her face. "We've never met him. Bridget says he's older and that she met him on one of those online dating sites."

"What is this boyfriend's name?"

"Cobb. Which is a weird name, if you ask me. She's been seeing him for a couple of months, allegedly. To be honest, we both thought Bridget was making him up. He's never been to the house. We haven't even seen a picture of him. Even if he is real, it can't be anything serious. Bridget's never mentioned actually meeting him in the flesh."

Lanny and Julia were growing restless, chewing on their lips and glancing repeatedly at their phones.

"Is that it?" Julia asked. "Because we both have a lecture to get to."

"One more question," Emily said. "Did you ever see Wendy and Bridget argue? For example, did Wendy ever say anything negative about Bridget? Or vice versa?"

They both shook their heads.

"Bridget was always saying she felt sorry for Wendy," Lanny said. "She was always telling us Wendy had no friends and her family didn't care about her." She glanced at Julia, then back at Emily. "You don't honestly think Bridget killed Wendy, do you? I mean, I know that's what everyone's saying, but it can't be true, can it?"

Emily stood up. "Come on. I'm heading to the campus to look for her next. I'll give you both a ride."

But Lanny had grown pale and was staring at Julia. "What if it's true? What if Bridget is guilty? She could have chosen one of us instead of Wendy. I didn't even think of that until now!"

A growing unease was unsettling Emily's stomach. She stared at Bridget's housemates, who both looked scared to death. The trouble with rumours was that they spread like wildfire. It didn't even matter if facts were involved, as long as the rumour fitted the narrative that the listener wanted to hear, they would gladly pass it on to the next person, and then the next, until what started as a spark had turned into an inferno. But as much as Emily hated rumours, having once been victim to them herself, even she had started to question Bridget's involvement in Wendy's murder. Who was Rick? Why had she let such a dangerous individual into her home without a thought for her housemates? And who was this boyfriend, Cobb? She needed to find out, sooner rather than later. And she needed to find Bridget, before the rumour mill began to burn out of control.

CHAPTER 15

Ducking down behind a car, Bridget watched Lanny and Julia exit their home and enter the quiet suburban street. They were not alone. Angela's friend, Emily—the private investigator—pointed towards a silver Audi parked on the roadside. Lanny and Julia climbed into the back seat while Emily got into the front. A second later, the engine started and the vehicle drove away. Bridget got to her feet and watched the car vanish into the distance. Why was Emily here? Where was she taking Lanny and Julia?

It had to be because of Angela. The private investigator was her friend. She must have contacted Emily after Bridget ran away, and now Emily was looking for her. Pain stabbed Bridget in the chest. She still hadn't answered any of Angela's calls or text messages; much in the same way Cobb hadn't answered any of her own. Her sister was probably at home right now, sick to her stomach and thinking the worst. Bridget knew she should call to put her mind at ease. But there was no time. She needed to get inside the house, pack a bag, and go.

Glancing over her shoulder, she crossed the street and let herself in, where she locked the door and went upstairs to her room. It looked the same as she had left it a few days ago: neat and organised, except for her desk, where textbooks and papers covered the surface.

Bridget turned and caught sight of her reflection in the wall mirror. Her face was horribly pale and dark circles shadowed her eyes. Purple bruises lined her neck where Rick had choked her. She hadn't even begun to process what he'd done to her, or what he might have done if they'd been alone in the house. She would deal with it later, along with Angela and all the other urgent worries festering in her mind.

Jolting into action, Bridget ducked under her bed and pulled out a medium-sized carry case. Dumping it on the bed, she flipped the lid open and began filling it with clothes. She still didn't know where she was going or for how long. All she knew was that she needed breathing space. To be somewhere quiet, where she wouldn't be bothered by people. Because she wasn't running away for good, was she? She just needed time to think about what to do. To come up with a solution and get herself out of the trouble she was in. If it was even possible.

She froze, a pair of jeans gripped in her hand. If she ran now, it would only make her look more guilty. But she was guilty, wasn't she? She may not have picked up the rock and smashed it on Wendy's head, but she had stood there and let it happen. She had even filmed it.

"Don't go there," she whispered to the room. "Not yet."

Dumping the jeans into the carry case, she pulled open a drawer and added underwear to the growing pile. Where would she go? More importantly, how would she get there? There wasn't a lot of money in her bank account, but she would need to withdraw it all from the nearest ATM. Then what? She couldn't afford a plane ticket. She wondered if she could even afford to leave Somerset. Perhaps it was best not to go too far, in case she changed her mind and wanted to come back home. A bus ticket, then. Or a train ticket.

The carry case was almost full. All she needed to grab now were toiletries, tampons, and . . . Cobb's phone.

Rick was right. She had to destroy it.

Opening the closet door, she fumbled for the light switch and peered inside. There were a few shelves filled with books, others with storage boxes and folded knitwear she no longer wore. Pushing a pile of cardigans to one side, she fed her hand through a fist-sized hole in the wall, then fumbled around until she found the phone. Taking it out, she pressed the power button and waited for the phone to wake up. Cobb had sent it to her weeks ago. A gift, he'd said, a secret and special way for them to communicate. Back then she'd been blinded by such a surprising and expensive gift. Now that its true nature had been revealed, she wanted to throw it hard against the wall and watch it smash into pieces.

The phone was ready. Bridget flicked a thumb across the screen, scrolling through the thread of text messages in which she'd poured her heart out to Cobb. It had started so innocently. Exchanges of compliments and sweet nothings. Romantic plans for weekend getaways and exotic holidays. Then the messages had grown more intimate. Expressions of loneliness and grief, of not feeling part of the world, of being misunderstood. She'd fallen for every word. For every lie.

Bridget tapped the screen. The video was long gone, deleted after being sent to Cobb.

But the photographs she'd taken that day were still there. Pictures of Wendy, smiling and laughing, as she and Bridget had walked around Durleigh Reservoir, where Bridget had made a point of stopping to talk to other walkers or pet their dogs. 'Be visible,' Cobb had instructed. 'Make sure you're seen.' She'd copied those photographs to her own phone; evidence to prove where she and Wendy had walked that day. There were other photos that she hadn't transferred. Wendy wasn't smiling in these pictures. She looked troubled by Rick's presence. By the fact he'd driven them twenty-two miles south to the Blackdown Hills when the only place Wendy had wanted to go was home.

The nausea in Bridget's stomach bubbled up to her throat. Dropping the phone, she turned and ran for the bathroom, making it to the toilet just in time. She vomited, retched, then vomited again. When her stomach was empty, she flushed the toilet and splashed water on her face at the sink.

"I'm sorry, Wendy," she whispered. "I'm so sorry."

Her phone was ringing in the bedroom. Grabbing her toiletries and stuffing them inside a wash bag, she hurried back to the room and snatched her phone up from the bedside table. She froze as she read the caller ID on the screen: Private Number.

She didn't speak but held the phone up to her ear and listened.

"Bridget?" a rich, velvety voice said. "Are you pretending you're not there?"

The words sent shivers down her spine.

Cobb.

Something burst inside her, leaking grief and horror into her veins.

"I've been trying to call you," she sobbed. "I thought you'd disappeared."

"I've been busy," Cobb said, his tone both casual and seductive. "And we'd agreed to lay low for a while."

"Busy?" Bridget half laughed, half cried. "I did everything you told me to. Everything! You can't just abandon me like this. You can't just disappear because you feel like it!"

"Bridget, Bridget," Cobb cooed. "You're always so dramatic. Getting hysterical like a spoilt little girl."

"Fuck you! You need to help me. You need to make this all go away."

"It's a bit late for that, don't you think? It's not as if you can raise Wendy from the dead. Or put her head back together."

"Please, Cobb. Please help me."

Cobb laughed. "Oh God, are you really begging? Do you know how pathetic you sound right now? It's too late for that, Bridget. The game is over. You played your role nicely, but now I'm bored. That's right, you're boring me. You and Rick. You have nothing left to offer me, except for one last little thrill."

Bridget was trembling now, rage and grief and guilt all colliding into one furious maelstrom.

"What do you mean by that?"

"You'll find out soon enough. And you only have yourself to blame. See, I was prepared to stay quiet. To let this all blow over until you and Rick were in the clear. But you went to see him today, didn't you? I told you not to do that, yet you decided for yourself. You know that's against the rules. I decide what you do. I decide when you can eat, breathe, shit. Not you. And now I'm bored, so you and that caveman Rick get to play one last game."

"I won't do anything more for you!" Bridget cried, reaching down with her free hand to pick Cobb's phone up from the floor. "If the police come for me, I'll tell them everything I know. I'll give them the different phone numbers you've used to call me and Rick. I'll give them the text messages. I'll give them the fucking phone. I'll take you down with me, kicking and screaming all the way."

"You think you can do that?" There was surprise in Cobb's voice. "You think you're intelligent enough to beat me? To play me at a game I invented?"

"Why don't you try me? See what happens."

"You know what will happen, if you breathe

a word about me. You know the loss you'll be made to suffer."

"I don't believe you anymore, Cobb. It was all a lie. All bullshit. I was stupid enough to fall for it, and now Wendy is dead because of you."

"Me?" Cobb said, in mock innocence. "I wasn't there. I didn't touch a hair on poor little Wendy's bashed in head. You and Rick did it. I even have a video to prove it. You may not be on screen, but I can hear your voice telling Rick to finish Wendy off. Your own friend, brutally murdered on your orders."

A sliver of ice slipped down the back of Bridget's neck.

"Here's your final game," Cobb said. "It's called Hide and Seek. And I'd get going if I were you, because in about, oh, thirty minutes, the whole world will be looking for you."

"Cobb, wait!"

But Cobb had already hung up.

Bridget was frozen, the phone still pressed to her ear, realisation slowly dawning on her. Like a statue coming to life, she sprang towards the bed, threw Cobb's phone inside the carry case and snapped the lid closed. A minute later, she was racing along the street to the nearest bus stop, the case slamming into her shin.

She knew what Cobb was about to do. She knew she had to run. And now, she knew exactly where she was going to hide. She just hoped that she would make it there before it was too late.

CHAPTER 16

As Emily walked through the gates of Quantock University, a strange feeling rushed over her; a heady mix of nostalgia and deep discomfort. Her time at the university had been filled with hard work and determination, both to qualify as a teacher and to establish independence from her troubled mother. Although she had achieved both during that time, her memories were addled by the disappearance of Becky Briar in those final weeks, followed by Emily's subsequent return home to the small village in Cornwall, where four years later, her life would be ripped apart by the death of a young student.

The university campus looked exactly the same; a network of single-storey, lifeless grey buildings, with not even a hint of the lush green hills from which the establishment had taken its name. It was still raining, darkening the concrete to the colour of coal, and filling the empty quadrangle with rippling puddles. Saying goodbye to Lanny and Julia, Emily headed towards the English department.

Inside, she was greeted by a welcome rush of warmth. She walked through the main corridor, blue carpet soft beneath her feet as she passed a gaggle of fresh-faced students whose eyes were glued to their phone screens. A lecture was taking place in one of the halls on her left, and she paused to peer through the door glass, searching each row of young faces.

"Can I help you?"

Emily turned around to see a tall woman with deep brown skin and thick, black hair that was tied loosely behind her back. She wore a lanyard around her neck, containing her ID card. Alison Adesina, head of the English faculty.

"Ms Adesina?" Emily said, reaching out a hand. "My name is Emily Swanson. I'm a friend of Angela Jackson. May I speak with you for a moment?"

A few minutes later, Emily sat at a desk in a cramped office. The lecturer had a kind and intelligent face, which was now troubled by deep lines.

"I haven't seen Bridget in days," Alison said. "I couldn't tell you where she is right now."

"Were you at Angela's wedding?"

"No. We work in different departments. Our paths rarely meet."

"But Bridget is in your class?"

"That's correct. She and—" The lecturer's face suddenly crumbled. "Poor Wendy. She was such a quiet little mouse. Harmless, really."

"Perhaps you could tell me about Bridget and Wendy's relationship."

"I don't know what to tell you that I haven't

already told the police. They came by yesterday, asking questions about Wendy. About Bridget. As I told them, the two became friendly about a month ago. Before that, they barely spoke to each other. But they seemed to grow close, always sitting next to each other in lectures and in the classroom. That's why it's so hard to believe what people are suggesting. That Bridget is the one who . . ." Horror crept over Alison's features. "As for Wendy, I can't believe she's gone."

"You never saw them fight? There was no class rivalry?"

"Like I said, they seemed the best of friends."

"How are Bridget's grades?" Emily asked gently.

"Well, she's barely at the end of her first semester, but she's settling in and doing well. Admittedly, she's been a little distracted the past few weeks, but I put it down to Angela's wedding."

"And Wendy?"

Alison's shoulders sagged. "Wendy was a

different story. She struggled from day one. I'm not sure English was the right subject for her."

"Why not?"

"Well, academically she was of average ability, but she never seemed enthused by the topics we were covering, and she rarely spoke up in class. She didn't seem to have many friends, either. Except for Bridget. The first semester is always the hardest for new students. For many of them it's their first time away from home. I know that wasn't true for Wendy, that she lived locally, but it's still a big shift in mindset. You're expected to put your toys away and operate with a degree of maturity and independence. Some of these young people struggle with that at the start, especially if they're used to having everything done for them. Wendy seemed so helpless at times. Like a fish out of water. When Bridget befriended her, she seemed to quickly grow dependent, always following Bridget around like a lost puppy."

Alison glanced away, her eyes glistening.

She pulled a tissue from a box on her desk and dabbed at her eyes. "Will there be anything else? I have a lot of work to do."

Emily shook her head and thanked the woman for her time.

———

As she made a slow exit from the English department building, Emily peered through the door glass of every room, hoping to see Bridget's face. But Bridget wasn't there. Slipping into her raincoat and pulling the hood up over her head, she shouldered open the double doors and exited the building. The rain was still falling, coming down in heavy sheets. She wondered if it would ever stop, or if they would all be washed away.

She got going, heading towards the campus gates. She needed to speak to Angela, to see if she knew anything about Bridget's mysterious boyfriend, or more worryingly, about Rick. Whoever he was, he was predatory and aggressive, not someone any young woman should be left alone in a room with. Why was Bridget hanging around with a man like that? If Emily could find out his last name, she could run a search on him and discover if he had a criminal record or a history of violence.

How had Bridget met him? Her housemates had already confirmed Rick didn't go to the university. It was possible she had met him while growing up, but the idea of Bridget being friends with someone like that didn't feel right. Perhaps she had met Rick online, just like she'd met the strangely-named Cobb.

Emily slowed down a little, the rain drumming noisily on her coat. She wondered if Bridget's boyfriend was real. Lanny and Julia didn't seem to think so. But did eighteen-year-olds make up imaginary boyfriends? Weren't they too old for games like that?

Running footsteps splashed through the rain, heading straight for Emily. She looked up and quickly side stepped, narrowly missing a collision with a student in a yellow mackintosh.

"Sorry!" he called over his shoulder.

Emily watched him dash through the quad then disappear through a set of glass double doors. An idea came to her, and she quickly followed in his direction,

The cafeteria was full of students sitting in clusters on long white benches. They chattered noisily to each other, but it wasn't the usual carefree banter of young people, Emily noted. They were all talking about Wendy Wilson.

Emily's gaze flicked from table to table, searching each cohort of fresh faces for Bridget. She was not among them, but it was possible she had friends here. Friends who could shed light on where she had disappeared.

Glancing over at the kitchen staff, Emily made her way to the nearest table, where a group of young men and women sat with plates of pizza in front of them and their eyes glued to phone screens.

"Excuse me," she said, making them look

up. "Do you happen to know Bridget Jackson?"

They all stared at each other and shook their heads. Emily moved on to the next group, a gaggle of young men who were gathered around a tablet, laughing at a video compilation on YouTube. She cleared her throat and asked them the same question.

"I know who she is," a young man with tattoos on his neck and hands said. "She's the psycho bitch who killed that quiet girl."

Emily scowled at him. "You don't know that."

"Everyone knows that," he said, with a casual shrug, before returning his attention to the tablet screen.

Moving on, Emily crossed over to the next table. Two more groups down and she was none the wiser. She was wondering if this line of questioning was a waste of time when a horrified shriek split the air.

A shocked hush fell over the room as heads turned towards one of the centre tables. Emily twisted around. Three young women were staring at a phone screen, hands clamped over their mouths, their eyes round and wide.

"What is it?" someone yelled.

Emily stepped closer. Another cry rang out from the far end of the room, and a horrified female student jumped to her feet.

"It's Wendy Wilson's Facebook page!" she gasped, tears leaking down her face.

Every person in the cafeteria reached for a phone. Emily pulled hers from her pocket and quickly found Wendy's profile. What she saw made her stomach turn.

CHAPTER 17

Angela had been sitting at the kitchen table for an hour now, her laptop open and worry lines creasing her brow. She'd been busy, scrolling through Bridget's various social media profiles, then compiling a list of her sister's friends and sending private messages to them all, asking if they'd seen or heard from Bridget. Two hours had passed since Emily's departure, but so far Angela had heard nothing from her. In fact, she hadn't heard from anyone. Not from Trevor. Not from Bridget's friends. Not from Bridget. The silence was feeding Angela's anxiety, which now taunted her mind with terrible thoughts. Leaning back on the hard kitchen chair, she removed her glasses and rubbed her eyes. She hadn't eaten in hours, yet despite feeling empty, the idea of food made her want to vomit.

Perhaps Emily's right, she thought. Perhaps I really should call the police.

But something was preventing her from picking up the phone. A voice, whispering in her mind. Telling her that involving the police would only put Bridget at risk.

Why was that?

Because part of you thinks she may be involved, the voice whispered. Part of you wonders if she's responsible.

"No," Angela said aloud. It was a ridiculous thought. Bridget was her sister. The only blood relative she had left. Yes, she could be moody sometimes, and bad tempered, but she was never violent. She just didn't have it in her to kill someone. Did she?

Angela stared at the laptop screen, at her sister's many profile pictures. There was nothing malicious in Bridget's eyes. Maybe a little sadness. A little grief. But nothing cruel.

Next to the laptop, Angela's mobile phone began to ring. She snatched it up without looking at the screen.

"Bridget?"

"It's me."

"Oh. Trevor." The disappointment in her voice was quickly replaced by hope. "Did you find her?"

"Not yet. I've driven around the town centre, even around the outskirts, but nothing. You hear anything?"

"No. I'm going out of my mind with worry."

"She's probably gone home. She probably just wants to be left alone for a while."

"She would tell me if that's what she wanted. She wouldn't leave me worrying like this. Anyway, Emily's driven up there. I haven't heard from her either."

"Maybe she's chasing up a lead. Or she's with Bridget right now, talking things through."

"Emily would have called. I don't think Bridget's there. I think something terrible has happened."

"Babe . . ." Trevor was quiet for a moment,

the sounds of passing cars filling the silence. "I'm coming home. I'm not going to find her out here, and you sound like you need some company."

"No, you can't. You need to keep looking. She's out there somewhere, Trevor."

"I've been driving around for hours. Looking for Bridget in Taunton is like looking for a needle in a haystack. I seriously don't think she's here."

"Please, Trevor." Angela's throat grew tighter, making it hard to breathe. "Please keep driving around. We need to find her."

Trevor was silent again. Then he expelled a long, deep breath. "Okay, fine. Anything for you. But I honestly don't think Bridget's walking around in the rain."

The tears were coming again, filling her eyes and threatening to spill down her face.

"I'm sorry, Trevor. None of this should be happening. We're supposed to be on our honeymoon."

"Hey. You don't need to apologise. None of this is your fault. I'll keep driving, okay?

Who knows, maybe I'll even get lucky and find her."

Angela wiped her eyes again then slipped her glasses back on. "Thanks. I love you."

"Love you too."

Trevor hung up. The silence of the kitchen pressed down on Angela, crushing her lungs. She stared at the phone, resisted calling Bridget's number again. Suddenly, she wanted nothing more than her parents to be here, alive and taking control of things. Telling her not to worry and that Bridget was safe. That she would be home soon.

"Breathe," she whispered. "Just breathe."

She stared at the laptop screen. There were still more of Bridget's friends to contact. Someone, somewhere, had to have seen her in the past twenty-four hours. Which meant if Angela kept reaching out, and with both Emily and Trevor out there searching, Bridget would be found very soon.

What if she isn't? the voice whispered. What if you never see her again?

Ignoring it, she focused on the next friend on the list and began typing out a message.

A text alert pierced the quiet. Grabbing the phone, Angela swiped a thumb across the screen. The message was from an unknown number. Her first thought was that one of Bridget's friends had received her message and was texting a reply. But as she opened the message and read its contents, her heart began to race.

Look what your sister did . . .

There was a website link below the words. Angela hovered her thumb over it. She read the words again. The room fell away from her.

Look what your sister did . . .

What if she opened the link and it showed her something she didn't want to see? What if the voice whispering in the back of her mind was right?

The phone trembled in Angela's hand. Look what your sister did . . .

Angela held her breath and tapped the link. She stared at the phone screen as the link took her to a video on Wendy Wilson's

Facebook page. The video began to play. And Angela saw exactly what her sister had done.

Her eyes grew impossibly wide. A strangled gurgle lodged in her throat. Angela opened her mouth and let out a terrible, high-pitched shriek. She dropped the phone. Her knees buckled and she went down.

She sat in the middle of the kitchen floor, her face contorted into a grimace, the horrors of what she'd just seen and heard forever burned into her mind.

CHAPTER 18

Bridget sat at the back of a single decker bus as it chugged along a winding road, rain hitting the large windows. Countryside stretched out on both sides; waterlogged fields, hedgerows and copses of trees all filling her vision. There were only three other passengers on the bus. Two elderly women sat up front, deep in conversation, while a middle-aged, balding man sat halfway along on the right. None were paying her any attention. Good, she thought. If it was the closest she could get to invisible right now, it would have to do.

Ever since boarding the bus, the panic consuming her had started to recede. Now, she felt almost nothing, as if her insides were made of time and space. She had even stopped feeling guilty for not returning her sister's frantic, persistent calls.

The bus drove deeper into the countryside, passing small hamlets and clusters of cottages. This far out, the traffic was sparse, with just a few cars passing by on the other side of the road. Bridget thought about everything that had happened in the past few months. About how it had all come to fruition, and about how and when she had stopped considering herself a victim. Because she had played her role in the murder of Wendy Wilson to perfection. If only she could go back to the days before Cobb.

The gradient suddenly dipped, making Bridget lean forward as the road descended into a valley. Angela's face swam behind her eyes again. Somewhere deep down inside, she felt a twinge. Guilt, trying to push its way back to the surface. She pushed it down. The bus drove on, the road still descending. Then the landscape was flattening out for miles around. The rain grew heavier, lashing against the windows. Up ahead, on the right, the middle-aged man had taken out a bag of boiled sweets and was now sucking noisily, his lips smacking together on the sugary goodness.

Cobb. He had stolen into her life like a shadow under the door. He had pressed and prodded, kneaded her like dough and shaped her into something new. Something unrecognisable. How had he manipulated her so easily? Maybe it was the grief for her father still flowing through her body like underground caverns of water, invisible to the naked eye but nonetheless still present. Or maybe Cobb was just a highly skilled abuser. Either way, Bridget had no choice but to play his games. Because the consequences of not playing them were far, far worse.

She felt a twinge deep inside her again, but this time it was sharp and painful. Angela. She needed to contact her. To put her mind at ease.

Bridget pulled her phone from her jacket

pocket. Her thumb hovered over the screen. How did she explain what had happened? How did she tell the truth without making Angela hate her? How did she—

Bridget's phone vibrated and a push notification appeared at the top of the screen. It was quickly followed by a second. Then a third. Then a fourth. Then another. And another, until the phone was vibrating constantly in her hand.

Some of the numbness melted away. The notifications were all from Facebook. Which was strange. Yes, she had an account, everyone did, but no one her age used it regularly. It was for older people. Yet the notifications kept on coming. Twenty-five. Twenty-six. Twenty-seven. And now her numbness was receding like an ebbing tide, and waves of panic were rushing in.

What was happening?

Bridget glanced up at the other passengers, then back at her phone. Tapping the screen, she jumped on to Facebook. There were now forty-two notifications. Now forty-five. Bridget tapped the screen again.

The world flew away from her, leaving her flailing in darkness and gasping for air. She had never seen so much hate. So much vitriol.

And when she saw the reason for all the poisonous words, she realised with sickening clarity that Cobb had finally brought the game to an end.

--You murdering bitch!

--You fucking psycho!

--She was your friend. Look what you did to her!

--I've called the police. Rot in hell, bitch!

--Bitch!

--Bitch!

--Murdering whore!

On it went. On and on. Toxic rage from friends and classmates. From total strangers. They had all turned against her. All wishing her dead. And she deserved it.

Bile burned the back of Bridget's throat as she stared at the source of all the hate. At the top of Wendy Wilson's Facebook page was a video. The video. It had somehow been posted to Wendy's profile via Bridget's own account.

Before she could press pause, the video automatically began to play. And there she was. Wendy Wilson. Teetering on the edge of the Blackdown Hills, her back turned to the camera, as she took pictures of the breathtaking landscape.

"It's beautiful, isn't it?" she says. "We're so lucky to live here."

As she continues to take pictures, Rick Frost creeps up from behind. There's a rock the size of a fist curled in his hand. He comes to a stop three feet behind Wendy. He turns to the camera and winks. Even sticks out his tongue, like he's about to play a cheeky prank. Then his eyes go dark.

He raises the rock high above his head and smashes it down hard on the back of Wendy's skull. The noise of the impact is sickening, and loud enough to be caught on film.

Wendy drops her phone and staggers forward. She slides to a halt. One hand grips the back of her head, while the other paddles through the air, as she teeters on the edge of the hilltop

Rick steps back, the rock still swinging in his hands, except now it's slick with Wendy's blood.

Wendy makes a strange noise. Regaining her balance, she slowly turns around. Her eyes are glazed. She removes her blood-soaked hand from the back of her head and holds it up in front of her.

"What?" she says. Almost curiously. She tries again, but now the words are all scrambled, like an anagram.

She stares at Rick. At the camera. At the person filming. More unintelligible words come out. Blood runs down her face.

Then she speaks. Not Wendy. The young woman who's filming. Her voice is at once sickened and horrified and exhausted.

"What are you waiting for?" she says.

Wendy tries to say something too. It comes

out as a gurgle.

"Just do it!" the woman who's filming yells.

Rick swings the rock like he's pitching a baseball. He brings it down hard, smashing Wendy right between the eyes. And then she's gone, her body tumbling down the Blackdown Hills, flipping over and over, heading towards its final resting place. Rick stares at the rock, then tosses it into the distance as hard as he can. It sails through the air, high over the hills, before tumbling down again to disappear among the swathes of bracken.

Rick turns to the camera, a giddy expression lighting up his face. He bends over to pick up Wendy's phone.

"Did you get it?" He sounds almost proud of himself.

"I got it," the voice says. There's no pride there. No emotion whatsoever.

The camera cuts to black.

Bridget glanced up from the phone screen to see the other passengers staring at her. She was sobbing loudly, not caring who could hear. The truth was out now for everyone to see. Except it wasn't the whole truth. Not that it mattered now.

"Are you all right?" one of the elderly women called out.

But Bridget didn't hear her. She was going to be sick. She could feel the bile rising in the back of her throat, her stomach churning and heaving like a stormy ocean.

Her phone was vibrating again. She looked down. But it wasn't a notification. It was Angela calling. The timing could only mean one thing—her sister had seen the video.

How did she explain the truth to Angela? How did she get her to understand? Perhaps it was better not to answer at all. To lose her sister forever. But then she would only be adding to Angela's pain.

Bridget tapped the answer key with a trembling thumb. The first thing she heard was Angela's horrified sobbing, filled with shock and pain and disbelief.

"What did you do?" her sister wailed. "What did you do?"

Bridget tried to speak, found that she couldn't. She sucked in a breath and tried again. "I'm sorry! I'm so sorry. But it's not what it looks like."

"It's not what it looks like?" Angela repeated, and her sobs gave way to fury. "How could it not be what it fucking looks like? You filmed it, didn't you? That's you. Your voice. You helped kill Wendy!"

"No, I—" Fresh tears spilled down Bridget's face and splashed on her lap. Why was she still trying to deny it? "I'm sorry, Angie. I wish I could explain to you. But I can't."

Angela was crying again, her tears heavy with desperate grief. "Tell me there's been a mistake. Tell me you weren't involved."

"I can't. And I'm sorry." The pain was falling away again, along with the guilt, leaving only emptiness. It was better that way. To feel nothing. "I can't explain right now. But I know how to solve the problem. How to make it all go away. It will hurt for a while. Maybe a long while. Then everything will get better. You just have to be patient and ride through the pain."

"What are you talking about? Where are you? You're not making any sense."

"Don't cry," Bridget said, trying to sound soothing when all she felt was nothing. "It will be okay. Once you get over the hurt, it will all make sense."

The bus ploughed deeper into the countryside, the rain-drenched land, flat and wide, spreading out for miles.

"I love you," Bridget said. "I love you more than anything else. All I ever wanted was to keep you safe."

"Bridget, what—"

"I love you," Bridget said again. Then she hung up and pressed the standby button, switching the phone off. She returned to staring out the window, a strange calm slowly wrapping around her.

It was true. This would all be over soon. Because now Bridget knew how to make all the pain go away.

CHAPTER 19

Emily pulled up outside of Angela's house and jumped out of the car. She was still in shock, horrified and confused by what she had seen. Nothing made sense, which meant she was missing several of the facts. But right now, her main concern was Angela. She had tried calling as soon as the video had gone online, but Angela hadn't answered. Now, Emily raced up the garden path and knocked on the door. When there was no answer, she tried the handle and found the door was unlocked. Stepping inside, Emily called Angela's name.

Silence. She checked the living room, then

the dining room. Finally, she entered the kitchen.

Angela was sitting on the floor, her back resting against the sink unit, her legs splayed out in front of her like a child. Piles of broken crockery were scattered across the floor. She had been crying. Her face and eyes looked red and raw. Her glasses lay next to her on the tiles.

Emily picked her way between the broken shards and sat down next to Angela.

"You've seen it," she said. "You've watched the video."

Angela began to sob, her shoulders shaking up and down as tears coursed down her face. Emily wrapped an arm around her friend's shoulders, pulling her into an embrace and gently rubbing her back.

"I don't understand what's happening," Angela said. "Is this because of Dad dying? Did it make her lose her mind? Or was it me? Did I do something wrong? Did I break her somehow?"

Emily shook her head. "All you've ever

done is love her. Right now, we don't have all the facts. It looks bad. Really bad. But we don't know the full story, and none of what we do know makes sense. Why would Bridget post the video online like that? Why would she incriminate herself? Can we even be sure it was Bridget who filmed Wendy . . ."

Angela pulled back from Emily's embrace.

"It's her," she said through a clenched jaw. "That's Bridget's voice on the video. I recognised it instantly."

She collapsed again. Emily continued to rub her back.

"I just spoke to her, Em. She finally answered."

"What did she say?"

"Nothing. Just that she was sorry and that she was going to solve the problem. She said it would hurt for a while, but then it would all be over. What does that mean? Because I know what that sounds like to me."

"Did she say where she was?" Emily asked. "Were there any clues to where she might be?"

Angela's face went blank, her eyes glazing over.

"Angie? Did Bridget say where she was going?"

"No. There was an engine sound, like she was in a car or a bus or something. But that's it. I don't understand. She's not a violent person. She would never hurt anyone."

"Which is why we have to keep an open mind. There are some things I've learned. Things that don't make sense."

"Like what?"

"The man in the video. The one who . . . I think his name is Rick. Bridget's housemates said he'd been hanging around lately and that he was bad news, as in he'd tried to molest both of them. You know your sister better than anyone—why would she be friends with someone like that?"

Angela stared at her with wild eyes. "She wouldn't. She's helped campaign against domestic violence, for God's sake!"

"There's more," Emily said. "Did Bridget ever mention a boyfriend to you?"

"A boyfriend? No."

"Well, according to Bridget's housemates, she's been dating a man named Cobb. Although Lanny and Julia seem to think it's just an online thing and Bridget has never met him in real life."

More tears spilled down Angela's face. "Emily, what's going on? Why is this happening?"

"I don't know yet."

Getting to her feet, Emily found some kitchen roll, tore off a length and handed it to Angela. Her mind was racing, trying to piece the puzzle together, even though several pieces were still missing.

"Where's Trevor?"

Angela dabbed at her eyes and winced. "He's still out looking for Bridget."

"What about the list you were going to make? Of all the places your sister might go?"

Angela pointed at the kitchen table. Emily snatched up the notepaper and skimmed through it.

"There were only three places I could think

of," Angela said. "The first is Glastonbury Tor, where our parents' ashes are scattered. The second is Clevedon, a seaside town on the north coast. We used to go there a lot with Mum and Dad when we were kids. Bridget loved walking along the pier."

"And the third?" Emily stared at what looked like a home address.

"Our grandmother's cottage. She left it to us in her will. We don't go there very often, but we both have a key."

Emily folded the paper in half and slipped it inside her back pocket. "Come on, let me help you up."

She reached out a hand and pulled Angela to her feet, then fetched her a glass of water.

"Drink it down. All of it. Where do you keep your dustpan and brush?"

Angela nodded at the pantry door. As Emily hurriedly swept up the debris, Angela stood numbly by the sink, sipping water and staring into space.

"Em, we have to find her. She needs to explain what this is all about. Why she—"

Angela clamped her jaw shut, trying to stem the grief.

A loud buzzing resounded through the house. Both women turned their heads. Emily held up a hand, telling Angela to stay where she was, then hurried through the hallway and into the living room. Peering through the rain speckled window, she saw a uniformed police officer and a man in a grey suit. A detective. Which meant the police had seen the video, too.

The detective turned towards the living room window. Emily quickly stepped back. The minute that Angela answered the door, the search for Bridget would begin. And when the police caught up with her, she would have little chance to tell her side—because the video was all the police needed to charge both Rick and Bridget with murder. Unless . . .

The door buzzer rang again. A fist hammered on the door.

"Police!" a firm voice called out.

Emily crept back to the hall, where Angela now stood, eyes fixed on the front door.

"Em?" she whispered.

"I know. But you have to let them in. You need to talk to them and you need to be honest. Tell them everything you know, including that Bridget just called you. Don't hide anything from them or you'll only get yourself in trouble."

Angela's pale face turned towards Emily. "What about you? What are you going to do?"

"I'm going to get a head start on them. I'll try to find Bridget. Which of the three places is she most likely to go to?"

The police knocked on the door again, the hammering sounding like thunder.

"Glastonbury Tor's closest, but it's a public space," Angela said. "Clevedon is an hour's drive away. Our grandmother's house is on the Levels. That might be your best bet. It's the one place she could hide away."

Emily nodded. "Okay. I'll try to find her. See if I can get her to talk to me." She squeezed Angela's hand, turned to leave, then turned back. "Maybe don't mention your grandmother's house just yet. The shock made you forget all about it."

She smiled at Angela, squeezed her hand again, then she was heading down the hall and through the kitchen. As Angela opened the front door, Emily slipped out to the backyard. Following a path alongside the house, she reached the corner and heard the front door close. Emily peered out. The garden was empty. A police car was parked on the roadside, its passengers now inside Angela's home.

Emily hurried through the garden and out to the street. A minute later, she was in her car, heading north, away from Taunton, hoping that she could find Bridget before the police did.

CHAPTER 20

The country lane was narrow and winding, coiling like a snake. Bridget stayed close to its edge, her arm brushing the wet hedgerow as she walked. Above her the sky was a grey expanse. The rain stung her skin, but she was oblivious to it. She had stepped off the bus ten minutes ago, leaving civilisation behind. She hadn't seen a vehicle since, making her feel as if she were the only person in the world. It was a comforting feeling.

Leaving the road, Bridget turned onto an even narrower lane, just wide enough for a single car. The surface beneath her feet was uneven and cracked, her feet splashing in and out of rain-filled potholes.

There were three homes situated on the lane, each property evenly distributed and protected by tall hedgerows on her right. As she reached the gate of the first house, she stared down the cement drive and caught sight of a white brick building. Bridget held her breath and hunched her shoulders, making herself small as she hurried by. A minute later, she reached the middle house. She didn't know who lived there now. Its former owners, a kindly old couple who were retired farmers, had passed away last year, just two months after her father. Now, as she ducked past, she hoped that whoever had bought the place was not as neighbourly as its previous occupants.

Up ahead, the lane curved to the right, heading towards an enclosed yard surrounded by fields and a river. Just before the curve was a wooden field gate. She slid to a halt, the rain drumming on her plastic raincoat, and peered inside.

Her grandmother's house looked the

same, its impressive stonework and slate roof shimmering in the wet weather. But its garden had changed dramatically since Bridget's last visit. The wide stretch of lawn had been left to grow wild, blades of grass reaching at least a foot tall. Flower beds were choked with weeds, any surviving plants ruined by the constant onslaught of rain. A small orchard of apple trees stood to the right of the house, each branch bereft of leaves and fruit. Next to the orchard, a vegetable patch lay barren and swamped with bog water.

Bridget lifted the gate latch and pushed the gate open with both hands. She and Angela hadn't visited the house since their father's death last summer. It was the one place the three of them would come each year, spending a long weekend together tidying up the garden, playing board games, and taking long country walks. When her father had died, the annual tradition had died with him, and the house and garden had been left to rot.

Shutting the gate, Bridget stumbled along the narrow stone path that led to the front door. She fumbled with the key, let herself in, then locked the door behind her and slid the bolt across. She stood in the darkened foyer, listening to her shallow breaths and the gentle patter of rain on wood. She shut her eyes for a moment, relishing the shadows, pretending she didn't exist. Then she shouldered off her jacket, hung it on a coat hook to dry, and made her way to the kitchen.

It was cold in here. A fine layer of dust lay on the kitchen surfaces. Cobwebs hung from the low ceiling and in the tiny kitchen window. Bridget half smiled, picturing her diminutive grandmother hunched over the cooker, preparing Sunday roast dinners. An open doorway stood on the right and led to the living area. The light was dim in here too, the single window not big enough for the size of the room. A dining table was pushed up against the wall on one side with a dust cloth draped over it. On the other was a fireplace with a pyramid of seasoned logs stacked next to the hearth. Armchairs and a sofa took up the rest of the space, all draped in sheets.

They were like ghosts, Bridget thought. Ghosts of the past and the present, all meeting together. She removed each sheet, bundling them up and choking on the dust they had collected. She found the light switch and flicked it on. Pale yellow light illuminated the gloom.

Bridget stood in the centre of the room, rain still dripping from her hair, an icy chill seeping into her bones. Then she dumped the sheets on a chair and went upstairs for a hot shower.

———

An hour later, Bridget sat on the living room floor in front of a crackling log fire, watching the yellow flames dance and destroy. She had changed into some of the clothes she'd brought with her. Her right hand nursed a full glass of brandy, poured from the large, dusty bottle she'd found inside the cherry wood cabinet under the window. The brandy made her insides burn, obliterating all feelings.

Bridget emptied the glass and refilled it for a second, then third time, as she contemplated what Cobb had done to her, and what she had done to Wendy.

Thanks to the video, the whole world knew about it. Including Angela. But the irony was that no one knew about Cobb. So, Bridget was the monster. Lady Macbeth whispering in Rick Frost's ear. Angela would never understand Bridget's role in all of this. She would never understand why she had been compelled to do what she had done. And that meant Angela would never forgive her.

How could you forgive a murderer? Someone who had willingly taken the life of another?

But there was a reason behind it all. Bridget had done it for her sister. She had killed for Angela, and she couldn't even tell her why.

Lifting the glass to her lips, Bridget swallowed more brandy. Her stomach grumbled. There was no food in the house, and in her desperation to run, she hadn't thought to bring any. There was only brandy. So, she drained the glass and refilled it again.

There was no coming back from this. Wendy could not be brought back from the dead. The video could not be erased from the internet or from people's minds. Neither could the memories that plagued Bridget's mind. Oh, she could try to drown them with brandy, but they would still be there, haunting her dreams at night. They would still be there in the morning, tormenting her in the daylight. It was her punishment. No matter what happened— whether the police caught up with her or she kept on running—she had already been sentenced to a life of torment.

Glass still in hand, Bridget got to her feet and staggered over to the window, where she swayed from side to side, her vision swimming in alcohol. The rain was still falling, growing heavier as the daylight grew dimmer.

It was only a matter of time before the police found her. Then she would be put in handcuffs, put on trial and imprisoned for the rest of her life. Even if she was eventually released, there would be no hope for her. Her friends would be long gone. The one person that mattered to her in the world would not be able to look her in the eye without remembering what she had done. She would not be loved. And without love, in any shape or form, life had no meaning.

Which left Bridget with only one alternative.

She lifted the glass. swallowed its contents, and wiped her mouth with the back of her hand. Stumbling over to the table, she opened a side drawer and pulled out a notepad and a pen. Sitting down heavily, she removed two sheets of paper from the notepad and laid them out, side by side, on the table. Bridget shut her eyes, drew in a long, deep breath, and let it out again. She began to write.

CHAPTER 21

Emily drove along a winding road that sliced through the Somerset Levels, a strange and bewitching flat landscape unlike anywhere else in England. Thousands of years ago, the area had been underwater. Now it was made up of coastal plains, snaking rivers, and wetland that had been artificially drained, irrigated, and transformed into farmland. With an altitude just above sea level, it was also one of the lowest land masses in the United Kingdom, which didn't come without its problems.

In 2014, the Levels experienced one of the worst floods in recent memory. A decrease in river dredging to remove build ups of silt, and an increase in intensive farming, left the land less able to retain water and unable to cope with a succession of violent Atlantic storms, strong winds, and relentless rain. Rivers burst their banks. Water seeped up from the ground. Thousands of acres of farmland, hundreds of houses, and networks of roads were suddenly covered in water. Entire villages were cut off. Homes and businesses were destroyed. Millions of pounds worth of damage was done.

With much of the farmland underwater for three months, it had taken almost two years for the land to recover. Since the devastating flood, new measures had been introduced to prevent it from happening again, including the building of more water pumps, the reintroduction of river dredging, and the construction of tidal barriers. Even so, that didn't stop Emily from nervously eyeing the surrounding waterlogged fields as she drove through the pouring rain.

She had driven past Glastonbury Tor, the

first destination on Angela's list, where her parents' ashes had been scattered. But with the famous hill and its ancient tower exposed to the driving rain, there was no place for Bridget to hide. It was possible she was somewhere in the town of Glastonbury, but Emily suspected that Angela's instincts were right: Bridget would go somewhere she could not be found. If she didn't find Bridget at her grandmother's house, it would mean driving up to Clevedon. But with a population of twenty thousand and no idea where to start looking, Emily knew her chances of finding Bridget there were slim.

As she continued to drive, the rain hammering the windscreen, images of Wendy's murder assaulted her mind. She tried to push them out, but they were relentless in their demand to be seen. Poor Wendy, she thought. No doubt the video would be going viral at this very moment, despite efforts to have it taken down. She wondered if Wendy's family had seen the video. What an awful shock that would be. She hoped someone would stop them from seeing it, before it was too late.

As for the rest of the world, everyone would see the terrible violence that had ended Wendy Wilson's life. As for Bridget, the release of the video had condemned her to a life of living hell. Maybe she deserved it. Maybe she didn't. Until Emily had caught up with her and found out the truth, she needed to remain unbiased. But it was proving difficult.

A large hill had appeared on the horizon, dominating the flat landscape. Brent Knoll was four hundred and fifty feet tall, with an old stone monument at the top and a village nestled at its base. Emily drove through the village's main street, passing redbrick houses and cottages with thatched roofs. Leaving Brent Knoll behind, she took a right, turning off the road and onto a single lane track, following the instructions of her phone's map application. A minute later, she turned again, navigating the vehicle onto an even narrower lane, which was slick with rain and in dire need of resurfacing.

Easing her foot off the accelerator pedal, Emily rocked from side to side as the Audi's wheels rolled in and out of potholes. Angela's note said her grandmother's home was the last house on the right. With the noise the car was making, it would be impossible for Emily to make a quiet entrance. She drove past a house, then another, killing her speed, before finally pulling the vehicle over and switching off the engine. She sat for a moment, listening to the rain drumming on the car roof and fighting images of Wendy tumbling backwards into an infinite skyline. Then Emily pulled up the hood of her raincoat and stepped outside.

The lane was empty, the splash of rainfall the only sound. Keeping close to the hedgerow, she stalked forward, until she reached a wide gate. She peered over it, staring at the unkempt garden and the sturdy brick house standing in its centre. There were no lights on despite the gloom of the day. No smoke spiralling from the chimney. She stood for another minute, waiting and watching, before quietly opening the gate. She ducked inside and shut it behind her, then tiptoed towards the house. Reaching the front door, she tried the handle and found it locked. Maybe Bridget wasn't here after all. Or maybe she was hiding inside.

Dropping to a crouch, Emily flanked the house, moving beneath the windows, until she reached the corner. Straightening up again, she hurried through a small apple orchard, until she reached the next corner of the building. A large, stony yard sat at the back of the house, bordered by tall hedgerows. The yard was empty of vehicles, which meant if Bridget was here, she had made it on foot. Emily leaned out further. No one was around, so she stepped into the yard. Then frowned.

The back door of the house was open, letting the rain in. Moving towards it, she mounted the doorstep and peered inside.

"Hello?" she called. When no answer came, she crossed the threshold and found herself in a kitchen. A layer of dust covered the surfaces, which hadn't been disturbed. "Bridget? Are you here?"

Nothing. Only the rain hitting the flagstone floor. Emily advanced, stepping through an open doorway into the living area. There was a table on her right, and on the other side of the room, a fireplace. One that had been recently used. Blackened wood and mounds of ash sat lifelessly in the hearth, but the room was still warm.

Spying another door next to the table, Emily pulled it open and slipped inside a darkened hallway. Stairs were on her right, the foyer and front door on her left. Climbing the stairs, she reached the landing. Three doors lay before her. The first revealed an empty bathroom. The second, a cramped and musty bedroom with the curtains drawn. Behind the third door was the master bedroom. As Emily entered, she spied a closed carry case sitting on the bed. But still no Bridget.

Emily opened the case and peered inside. There were clean clothes that had been hastily folded, two mobile phones, both of which had been switched off, and a wallet. Fishing it out, she checked the contents: a small wad of banknotes, a zip pocket filled with loose coins, and a number of cards.

"Bridget," she whispered, pulling out a Quantock University student ID card. "Where did you go?"

Emily had searched every room of the house. Which meant Bridget had seen Emily coming and was now either hiding outside in the rain or she'd taken off. But without money, she wouldn't get far.

Emily replaced the ID card and returned the wallet. She peered at the two mobile phones. Her stomach fluttered as she returned downstairs to the living room. Where was Bridget? She gazed at the remnants of the fire. An empty glass sat on the carpet next to a half empty bottle of brandy. Emily turned a half-circle, stared at the table in the corner, where two sheets of notepaper lay folded neatly in half and side-by-side. She moved closer. The one on the left had Angela's name scrawled on top. The other read: To the parents of Wendy Wilson.

Emily stared at them, her heart racing, as a

cold wind blew in from the open back door and made the letters flap on the table. Slowly, she reached for the one addressed to Angela and unfolded it.

Angie,

By now you've seen the video. Everyone has. I'm so sorry. Please know that I love you. I can't explain my role in Wendy's death. But you need to know that I'm responsible. I played my part in her murder, and I'm sorry. All I can tell you is that I had no choice. That I was only trying to protect you. Now, the only way I can keep you safe is if I'm not around anymore. What I have to do will hurt you for a while. But eventually you'll forget me and your life will get better. You'll be safe at last.

I'm sorry from the bottom of my heart. That's all I can say. I wish I could go back to that day. Make it so none of this ever happened. But I can't. So there's only one way out now. One way to make it right. To even the balance.

Please forgive me.

Love always, your sister, Bridget.

A sliver of ice slipped down the back of Emily's neck. Blood rushed in her ears. Dropping the letter on the table, she hurried from the living room, through the kitchen, and outside to the backyard. The rain was coming down harder now, stinging her skin.

Where was Bridget? She couldn't have gone far.

Emily spun around, the smell of wet earth flooding her senses. Halfway along the hedgerow, she spotted a small wooden gate. Running towards it, she wrenched it open and darted through. She was on a swamped, muddy track, tall grass flanking both sides. She followed it along, half running, trying not to slip in the sludge.

The grass grew taller. Stinging nettles lashed at her limbs. A roaring sound reached her ears. The roar of running water.

The path came to an end, emerging on the

sodden bank of a wide river. The water was dangerously high, a thick brown soup, bubbling and frothing as it gushed along, slapping and splashing at the earth. The opposite bank was covered in more wild grass. Beyond it, was a thicket of pine trees. As Emily stepped forward, her foot kicked something on the ground. She looked down. It was a shoe, splattered with mud and lying on its side.

Emily stared at the churning river, watching it rush by as a sinking sensation pulled at her limbs.

"Oh God, no!" she gasped.

She turned her head to the right, looking down the length of the river, following its flow. But there were no signs of Bridget, in or out of the water. Was she too late?

Cold pierced Emily's heart. Her breath caught in her throat. Then she glanced to the left and her heart smashed against her rib cage.

Fifty feet along the bank, Bridget stood, teetering at the river's edge, staring down at its violent, muddy water. She hadn't seen Emily. Not yet.

Emily dropped the shoe. She darted forward, racing towards Bridget.

The flooded ground squelched beneath her feet, shooting earth and rainwater into the air. She drew nearer, closing the gap.

Bridget looked up and saw Emily hurtling towards her. She cried out, her face twisting in despair.

"Bridget, don't!" Emily screamed.

But Bridget was already turning around. In one swift movement, she flung herself at the river.

Emily launched forward. She slammed into Bridget in mid-air, wrapping her arms tightly around her. They fell, hitting the wet ground together, punching the air from their lungs.

They rolled once, twice, drenching their bodies in icy mud and water. Then they were still.

"It's okay." Emily wheezed, gasping for breath. "I've got you."

Bridget didn't fight or try to free herself.

Instead, she pulled her knees up to her chest and let out a terrible, grief-filled scream. They lay there together on the riverbank, dirty and freezing, the rain lashing down on them, as Bridget sobbed and Emily held her tight.

CHAPTER 22

Emily and Bridget sat on the carpet in front of a freshly built fire, both cradling glasses of brandy. They had stripped down to their underwear, hung up their wet clothes to dry, and wrapped themselves in thick, warm blankets. But despite the heat from the fire, the chill that gripped Emily's bones was refusing to let go. She stared at Bridget, who was still shivering, sending ripples through the brandy. She was terribly pale, her eyes sunken in their sockets.

"So," Emily said, gently. "You want to tell me what's going on?"

Bridget avoided her gaze. "I can't."

"The police are looking for you. If you tell me, perhaps I can help."

"No."

"They're going to lock you up, Bridget."

"Maybe they should. Maybe that's all I deserve."

Emily shifted on her haunches. "Maybe. Maybe not. But I know there's more to what happened to Wendy than what's in the video. People don't just plan to murder their best friends."

Bridget winced, shuddering visibly, as if reliving the terrible moments of that day.

"I saw the letter you wrote to Angela. You tried to kill yourself. Don't you think your sister deserves to know why?"

Tears ran down Bridget's face, the flames making them shimmer like gold. "You can't tell her I'm here."

"I have to. Otherwise she's just left thinking the worst."

"But I can't face her."

"All the same, you'll need to, sooner or later."

Bridget bowed her head and shut her eyes. "You should have let me jump in the river."

"I couldn't do that. What do you think that would have done to Angela? She deserves an explanation. She's your sister."

Bridget was unmoving, her eyes still shut, tears silently splashing on the carpet.

Emily rubbed her eyes and sipped her brandy. She was beginning to warm up now, the cold finally melting away. "If you don't want to talk, why don't I start? I'll tell you what I know so far, and you can fill in the gaps. How about that?"

Nothing. Not even the twitch of an eye.

"Well, let me see. I know that you and Wendy became friendly about a month ago. That over the past few weeks, you became inseparable, always sitting together in class and hanging out at your house. I know you've been spending time with someone called Rick, and that he's probably the psychopath you filmed murdering Wendy."

Bridget looked up, flames crackling in her eyes. But she remained silent.

"I also know you have a boyfriend," Emily said. "One you met online, and whom you've never met in person. Your housemates aren't entirely convinced he's real. But I think he is."

Bridget's face was a deep shade of red now, her mouth open and her eyes wide.

Emily shrugged. "I'm a private investigator. I'm good at finding things out. But the one thing I just can't fathom is why. Why did you kill Wendy? Why are you refusing to tell the truth, even now?"

"I told you. I can't."

"Which makes me think someone has a hold on you. That you're being threatened. So, who is it? Rick? Or this mysterious boyfriend with the unusual name? Cobb, isn't it?"

Bridget let out a shuddering sigh. "I can't tell you. If I do, Angela will suffer."

"Angela is already suffering. Maybe if you told her the truth, she'd be able to help you."

"You don't understand."

"Then help me. Tell me why you lured your best friend to the Blackdown Hills. Tell me why you filmed that monster bashing her head in with a rock."

"Stop!" Veins protruded from Bridget's forehead as she stared helplessly at Emily, who stared right back, the silence between them growing thick and heavy.

"The police are coming for you," Emily said. "It's only a matter of time. When they find you, it's over. They won't care about why you helped to kill Wendy. All they'll care about is the video you filmed, and your voice telling Rick to finish the job. But I care because you're Angela's sister. I care because it seems to me that you're possibly a victim in this too. Tell me what happened. Maybe I can figure out a way to help you, or at least find evidence to support you in court."

"I can't. He'll kill her. He'll kill my sister!"

Emily stared at Bridget. "Who?"

Bridget shook her head, more tears streaming down her face.

"Damn it, if someone is threatening Angela's life, I want to hear about it. Now!"

"Cobb!" Bridget choked, her shoulders collapsing. "It's Cobb."

"The boyfriend?"

Bridget didn't speak, only nodded as she sucked in shuddering breaths and let them out again. When she'd finally calmed enough to speak, she set the brandy glass on the carpet and stared into the crackling flames of the fire.

"You're right. Wendy and I weren't friends for long. Friends is the wrong word. It was all a lie. Just a part of the plan. His plan."

And so the story began. The start to Bridget's first semester at Quantock University had been overshadowed by the death of her father earlier that year. But she had thrown herself into her English lectures and seminars, and she had started to make new friends. A semblance of normality was returning to her life. Until along came Cobb.

"He was very nice at first," Bridget told Emily. "Charming. And cute. We got talking online, realised that we liked the same music, the same films, talked the same politics. At first, we stuck to instant chat through the dating site. Then I suggested meeting up in person, you know, going for coffee, or maybe a drink. But Cobb was reluctant. He said he'd been hurt before, and although he liked me very much, he wanted to take time to get to know me first."

"Did he live locally?" Emily asked.

"His dating profile said he was in Bridgwater. But now, I honestly don't know if that's true." Bridget paused, bitter memories making her jaw clench. "We continued chatting online, getting to know each other. Because Cobb was reluctant to meet face-to-face, I suggested video chat. But he said he was shy, which I thought was sweet at the time, and maybe a little odd. Then he asked for my home address, said he wanted to send me a gift. It arrived a few days later. It was an iPhone, the latest model.

"I thought it was too much. Not just the expense, but a little out of the ordinary, you know? But Cobb said he wanted to thank me, for being patient and for bringing light into his life. He told me he'd lost his Dad recently too.

Which surprised me because he hadn't mentioned it before. But we bonded. Then we began to talk on the phone, but only ever on the one he sent me. He said it was nice to know I was using it. He had a nice voice, smooth and calming, and we chatted for hours and hours."

Emily frowned. Everything she had heard so far sounded like classic grooming techniques. "What did you talk about?"

"Everything. Losing our parents. Politics and the state of the world. Literature. The arts. Cobb was kind and funny. He was always complimenting me. Making me feel good. I suppose I started to fall for him, which I know sounds silly because we'd never met. But he made me feel special. I wanted to meet in person and say thank you. I pressed him on it, but he still refused." Bridget leaned back a little and shook her head. "After a while, university got busy. I had more classwork and I was spending more time with new friends. Just talking to Cobb and never meeting up started to get a little boring. I mean, I'm eighteen. I'm supposed to be out having fun."

Emily smiled, but inside she was deeply troubled. "How old was Cobb?"

"He said he was twenty-three. But he sounded older than that. Anyway, I felt like we were growing apart. I mean, really, I guess I was losing interest and didn't have much time for him anymore. He didn't want to meet in person, so what else was I supposed to do? But Cobb started calling more and more. If I didn't pick up, he'd send me jealous text messages, accusing me of being out with other guys, and saying I didn't care about him anymore. Eventually, I got fed up. I told him that he needed to stop. We weren't anything more than friends, and we wouldn't even be that for much longer if he couldn't treat me with respect."

"How did he take it?"

"He called me a slut. He said he was surprised anyone would want to date me because I was a fat, ugly bitch. I got angry. I told him not to call me again. And you know, at that point, I was starting to believe the reason Cobb kept refusing to meet in person was because he wasn't who he claimed to be."

"What do you mean?" Emily asked.

"I mean like I was being catfished. You know, when someone creates a fake persona online and pretends to be someone else. Well, after I hung up, I thought that was the end of it. But Cobb kept calling. On the hour, every hour. And he sent text messages, saying I'd broken his heart and he was going to kill himself. I was stupid. I called him back because I was worried he actually might do it. But Cobb just acted normally, like he hadn't called me all those terrible names. I blocked his number and got on with my life. Then a few days later, the video came."

"It was of Angela. He'd followed her, filming her in the street, then through the windows of her house. A call came through from the same number that had sent the video. It was Cobb. I went nuts, told him I was calling the police. But he said, and I remember this clearly, 'If you go to the police, if you tell anyone, you'll find your sister strung up like a dog with her guts spilling out on the floor. And she will suffer. She will feel every cut, every twist of the knife. I know people,' he said. 'People who will kill her before you've even had time to pick up the phone and dial 999.' I believed him. The video was proof enough to take him seriously."

Emily swallowed, the acrid smell of burning wood reaching down her throat. "What happened next?"

"Cobb told me I belonged to him now, that I was his to control. I was terrified he was going to hurt Angela. I didn't know what to do. Cobb told me we were going to play a game, and that another player would show up at my house with instructions."

"Rick?"

Bridget nodded, her eyes like burning tar pits. "Rick Frost turned up the next day. I could tell right away that something was wrong with him. That he was dangerous. It was his eyes, I suppose. They were cruel. He said that Cobb wanted us to play a game called Smash and Grab. It involved breaking into someone's house and trashing it. I was terrified. But Rick, he was excited, like he wanted to play. I thought he and Cobb must have been friends. But Rick told me he'd met Cobb through an online gaming site, and that Cobb had promised him money to play real life games."

"Rick was taking part because he wanted to?" Emily said, troubled by everything she was hearing.

"I told you, there's something wrong with him. Anyway, Cobb had us break into houses. The first one was empty, whoever lived there had gone out. Rick smashed it up. I was too scared to do anything. Rick must have told Cobb because he called to say I was breaking the rules, and if I continued to do so, he would have Rick break Angela's legs. He sent us to another house. But this one wasn't empty. An old man lived there alone. We wore masks, so he couldn't identify us, but he stood there, terrified, while both me and Rick trashed his home. Then Rick turned on him. I tried to make him stop, but he was too strong. He pushed me over and beat the man. He enjoyed it. Hurting people, I mean."

Bridget paused to take a large drink of brandy, the glass trembling in her hand. "Things went quiet for a few days. I breathed a sigh of relief. But then Cobb called again. He said he'd thought of a new game. It was called Kill For Love. To play the game, he said I had to choose someone who was an easy target. Someone no one would miss. I asked him why. And he said, because when we love someone, we will do anything to protect them. And that if I loved Angela, then I would need to choose."

Bridget fell silent, avoiding Emily's horrified gaze, her complexion pale and sickly even in the glow of the fire. "He sent me another video. It was of Rick, filming himself as he followed Angela around a supermarket. Cobb said if I didn't choose someone, Rick would kill her. I'd already seen what he was capable of. I knew he'd do it without hesitation."

"So you chose Wendy." Emily felt sick. All the terrible details were quickly fitting together.

"That was the moment I should have gone to the police. But I was so scared, so under Cobb's control. I didn't want Angela to die." More tears sailed down to Bridget's chin, where they hung for a moment before falling to the floor. "Wendy was quiet. Painfully shy. She was desperate to make friends with someone. Anyone, really. No one ever seemed to notice her, like she was invisible. So, when I asked if I could sit next to her in class one day, it was as if she'd won the lottery.

"We started hanging out, just the two of us. Wendy was nice. Kind. She just wanted to be liked. But I hated every minute I spent with her because I knew exactly what Cobb was planning. I thought there had to be a way to get out of it. That if I played along, I could find a way to warn Wendy before it was too late. Then Rick showed up one day, while Wendy and I were going out to get ice cream. He was so mean to her. Teasing her and making her cry. And he laughed the whole time, like he was enjoying every minute. After he was gone, I apologised to Wendy. I should have told her then what was about to happen. But every time I tried, I thought about what Rick would do to my sister."

Bridget lowered her head in shame. "He kept sending me videos of Rick following Angie around. Even at the campus. I wanted to tell her. To ask for help. But she's all I have left. So I kept hanging out with Wendy, making her feel special, the same way Cobb had made me feel special, until she believed we were best friends. I kept trying to convince myself Cobb was only planning to humiliate Wendy. That it would all be over soon, and I could spend the rest of the year making it up to her. But deep down in my gut, I knew. I knew that I had to save Angela or Wendy. So I chose my sister.

"Cobb planned it all. He chose Durleigh Reservoir where Wendy and I would go for a walk. He had me take pictures of us together, and make sure that we were seen by other walkers. And then, at exactly three o'clock, Rick showed up in his car. Wendy was nervous, she wanted to go home. Rick apologised to her. Said that he was sorry for being mean to her when we went for ice cream. Wendy said nothing. She was too scared. Too weak. Rick said he'd drive us both home. So, we made sure no one else was around, then the three of us got into Rick's car. But instead of taking Wendy home, we drove out to the Blackdown Hills. Wendy didn't want to go. I told her we could take pictures. That the view would be amazing. And, well, you know the rest. The whole world knows."

Emily was silent, staring at Bridget with her mouth half open, a maelstrom of emotions churning inside her. Anger, horror, grief and confusion. But she said nothing, holding it all in so Bridget could finish her confession.

"After it was all over, I sent the video to Cobb, as proof we'd played his game. He was satisfied, told us that we should lay low for a while, and as long as I stuck to the story, I wouldn't be suspected. 'Girls don't murder each other,' he said. Except sometimes they do. So I waited. And then when they found

Wendy, I got scared. I tried calling Cobb, but suddenly his number didn't work. Even his old profile on the dating site was gone. I didn't know what to do, so today I went to see Rick. He got angry, warned me to stay away or he'd kill me. He must have told Cobb, because then Cobb called me. He was angry with me too. He told me it would all be over soon. That's when he uploaded the video. That was his plan all along, wasn't it? I realise that now. From day one. From that first flirtatious message on the dating site, it was all one big, fucked up game."

Bridget's shoulders slumped. She hung her head, spent and exhausted.

Emily remained silent, trying to make sense of her own thoughts. There was so much to process. In many ways, Bridget was as much a victim as Wendy. But in others, she was just as responsible for Wendy's murder as Rick Frost and Cobb. There had to have been opportunities to stop Cobb in his tracks. To save Wendy's life.

Bridget stared blankly at Emily. "What are you going to do?"

The truth was Emily didn't know. "I—I need time to think. But first I need to tell Angela you're safe." Panic rippled across Bridget's face. Emily held up a hand. "She has the right to know. We can't leave her sitting at home and thinking the worst."

"I wish I could take it all back," Bridget whispered. "I wish I'd never signed up to that stupid dating site."

Emily stared at her, pushing down her anger. "You should go upstairs and get some sleep. Now."

Getting up, she held out a hand. Bridget took it and Emily pulled her to her feet and led her upstairs. The carry case was still on the bed. Bridget stared at it, a little life returning to her eyes.

"The phone," she said, opening the case. "I still have it, along with all the text messages and voicemails Cobb ever sent me. You should read them. Then you'll understand the power he has."

Removing the phone, she switched it on and tapped the message icon. Bridget's expression suddenly numbed. She glanced up at Emily then back at the phone, her thumb swiping up and down the screen.

"What is it?" Emily asked.

But Bridget didn't answer at first. She tapped the screen repeatedly, her chest heaving up and down. "No. No. There has to be a mistake. Something's gone wrong."

"What?" Emily said, aware of her sharp tone.

"They're all gone. All the messages. They're not here anymore."

Emily leaned in, staring at the screen. The message folder was empty.

"You have to believe me!" Bridget cried. "I'm not making it up. They were all there. Every single one!"

"Maybe you deleted them by accident."

"No! I wouldn't do that. Oh God, where are they? How do I get them back?" She stared at Emily again, her face deathly white. "You do believe me, don't you? Cobb is real. He's real!"

Emily stared at her, feeling sick and conflicted. "Get some rest," she said. "I need to call your sister."

"But Cobb, he—"

"Lie down. Go to sleep. We'll talk about it in the morning."

She left Bridget standing in the middle of the bedroom, her mouth opening and closing, her eyes wide and pleading. Emily returned downstairs and stood for a moment, staring into the fire, at the flames licking the wood, still reeling from all she'd heard. Then, retrieving her phone from the table, she called Angela and told her that she'd found her sister.

CHAPTER 23

Blue light flickered over his face, making his already pale features gaunt and ghastly looking. His gaze flicked between the computer monitors in front of him, each one displaying a tale of horror. On one screen was a news feed filled with reports on the murder of Wendy Wilson. According to the latest update, Rick Frost had been identified by his former probation officer, and was now in police custody after being apprehended while boarding a train to London. Meanwhile, police were still searching for Bridget Jackson, who had uploaded the video of Wendy's murder and was believed to be the person who had filmed it.

Another screen showed Wendy Wilson's Facebook profile page. The social media giant had acted swiftly, pulling all traces of the video from its site. But not before others had copied it and uploaded it to other social media sites, or shared it with their friends. Wendy's murder was everywhere, and so were the names of her killers. It pleased him immensely.

His game with Rick and Bridget had been his most ambitious yet, and also his riskiest. But the current carnage had made it all worth it. Now he was curious about what would happen next. His fingers ran over the computer keyboard as his gaze shifted to another screen.

When Angela had clicked the video link he'd sent her of Wendy's murder, she had unknowingly downloaded spy software that now gave him access to her phone. It was like peering through a window. He could read every text message and email, could view all of her photographs, even the nude ones she'd taken for her husband's eyes only. And while he couldn't listen into her live calls, they were recorded and uploaded within moments of ending. He had enjoyed listening to Angela's phone call to Bridget earlier. The horror and disbelief in Angela's voice had made him smile. The guilt and desperation in Bridget's had made him hard. He had trained her well. Because even though Angela had begged, Bridget had refused to tell her the truth about Wendy's murder. She hadn't even mentioned his name or how he had manipulated her into doing such terrible things.

The only cause for concern now was the private investigator. Emily Swanson. She and Angela appeared to be friends, and from reading Angela's texts, it appeared the private eye was out searching for Bridget. She was a concern, yes. But only a mild one. Because he was clever. Far too intelligent to be outwitted by some PI. A female one, at that.

He leaned back on the chair and stretched out his arms. He'd been sitting here for hours now, watching the events unfold. He was already starting to feel boredom sink in. Once Bridget had been caught and charged, the game would well and truly be over. It would be time to play a new game. Usually, he would have someone lined up, ready to manipulate and mould, but this game with Bridget had been his most daring, taking up all his focus. It would be easy to find a new player. All he needed to do was find someone weak and vulnerable. Someone who was desperate to be loved. And once he had them, he would need to find someone who was unhinged and powered by greed. Someone like Rick Frost. Rick was dangerous, but he was also stupid. Anyone with an ounce of intelligence would have seen through the false promise of payment. Now, Rick would pay for his stupidity with his freedom. As for Bridget . . .

A series of electronic pips pulled his attention to a fourth screen, where a newly recorded call had appeared in his inbox. He clicked the computer mouse, removed the headphones that were wrapped around his neck and put them on. Voices filtered into his ears.

"Emily? Did you find her?" Angela sounded tired and frightened. Good, he thought. She deserved it.

"I'm with her now," the private investigator said. "She's safe."

"Thank God. Where are you?"

"At your grandmother's house. Good call, Angie."

"Okay, I'm on my way. Just don't let her leave."

"She's asleep upstairs. We're not going anywhere. Angie?"

"Yes?"

"Can you bring food? Some coffee too. There's nothing here."

"I'll grab something from the kitchen." Angela paused and he could almost hear her uncertainty in the silence. "Em? What did she tell you? About what happened . . ."

"She told me everything. But it's best you wait until you get here."

"That doesn't sound good."

"Drive safe," the private investigator said. "I'll see you soon."

The call ended. He tore off the headphones and dumped them on the desk.

"That fucking bitch!" he yelled.

How dare she defy him like that! She had been told to stay silent. She had been told what would happen if she talked. And now Bridget had told the private investigator everything. Nostrils flaring, he stared at the computer screens, eyes flicking from each one to the next and back again. The heat inside him grew stronger, making beads of sweat trickle from his forehead and the back of his neck.

No. He would not panic yet. So Bridget had told the private investigator about him. But without evidence to prove his existence, he was only a figment of her imagination. A made-up story. And if he was only a story, then Bridget would go to prison. He would still win the game.

But Bridget had disobeyed him. She had

broken his rules. That meant Angela had to die.

But now? Or later?

The private investigator could make things difficult. It was her job to find out the truth. To uncover mysteries and solve clues. He didn't know much about her yet, which meant she still presented a threat, no matter how minimal.

What if she had resources that could help her find him? That would prove he was real?

No. He'd been careful, erasing every trace and footprint, every path that could lead back to him.

He licked his lips and dug his fingernails into his knees.

Angela would have to wait. The sensible move was to lay low for a while and keep a very close eye on both the Jacksons and the PI. Tapping on the computer keyboard, he stared at a fifth screen, which displayed a satellite map of Taunton. He zoomed in, closing in on the town's outskirts. A circular white symbol blinked at him from its static position on a suburban street.

Why hadn't he known about the grandmother's house? He thought Bridget had told him everything. He swallowed, wincing at the bitter taste at the back of his throat. If he'd missed the grandmother's house, did that mean he'd missed other factors? Perhaps he was getting complacent. Uncertainty bred weakness. Uncertainty threatened control. He could afford neither.

Picking up a phone from the desk, he tapped at the keypad, then lifted the phone to his ear. The line connected and an anxious voice answered.

"Has she left the house?" he asked.

"Yes," the voice said. "She's getting into her car right now. She's pulling away."

"Then what are you still doing there? Get after her."

"But I've been here for hours and I need to go home. Why don't you just track her phone?"

"Why are you pretending you have a choice in this? You follow her now or you know what will happen."

Silence. Then the voice said, "Fine. I'm going."

"Good. Don't lose sight of her."

He hung up and stared at the satellite map on the computer screen. He watched the white symbol as it travelled to the end of Angela Jackson's road and headed right. It was true that he could track the GPS of Angela's phone and pinpoint exactly where she was going. But having her followed made him feel powerful. In control. And a GPS tracker couldn't commit violence if needed.

Satisfied for now, he turned his attention to another screen, brought up a fresh search page, and began finding out all he could about Emily Swanson.

CHAPTER 24

It was late, the countryside pitch black, as if all the stars had been snuffed out. Emily and Angela sat in the living room of the old stone house, dying embers desperately clinging on to life in the hearth. Upstairs, Bridget slept on.

Emily had told Angela the whole sorry tale —from Bridget meeting Cobb online, to her subsequent grooming and blackmail, and the inevitable, tragic murder of Wendy Wilson. Angela had sat silently and listened, tears streaming down her face, her complexion growing pallid and sickly. Now that Emily had finished, they both were silent and haunted.

Emily stared at the cold tea in her mug and her plate of uneaten sandwiches.

"What are you thinking?" she asked Angela, who blinked and rubbed her face.

"I don't know. I feel guilty, I suppose."

"For what?"

"For not protecting Bridget. For letting her down. I've been so wrapped up in wedding plans the past few months, I didn't even notice she was in trouble."

Emily gently squeezed her friend's hand. "You're not the one to blame here. Cobb is. He's clearly dangerous. A psychopath. He groomed Bridget. He exploited her vulnerability, used her grief over losing your dad. He made her feel special and important. And then he used you as a gun to her head. Cobb is to blame. Not you."

"I get that. I do. But Wendy is dead. Bridget helped murder her. She may not have picked up the rock, but she stood there, filming it, letting it happen. And she was the one who made friends with Wendy in the first place, just so they could . . ." Angela shook her head, over and over, as if she was having trouble believing it. "Why didn't she just tell me what was happening? I could have done something."

"Because she loves you. You're the only family she has left. People will go to brutal lengths to protect the ones they love. Even if it means doing terrible things they can never come back from. This Cobb had a hold on Bridget. He had someone following you around. Filming you. The threat of him killing you would have been real to Bridget. And we can sit here, and we can pick holes at the story, and we can wonder why she didn't go to the police or tell you in confidence, or try to find a way out. But at the same time, how can we possibly understand how trapped she must have felt? She must have believed she had no other choice than to do as Cobb told her." Emily leaned back, staring at Angela's tortured expression. "I'm not condoning what Bridget did, or excusing her actions. Far from it. I'm just trying to understand."

Angela sucked in a breath and reached for

the remnants of the brandy bottle. She removed the cap, poured the contents into a glass, then drained it in one gulp. "I can't believe he had me followed. I can't believe I didn't even notice."

She shuddered. They were quiet for a minute, listening to the sound of rain pattering on the window. It was oddly soothing.

"What do we do now?" Angela asked.

It was a question Emily had been asking herself for the past few hours. There were two options. Neither of which had a happy ending.

"We could talk to Bridget, convince her to go to the police and hand herself in. She could tell them about Cobb and about what he made her do. But without evidence or proof of his existence, I doubt they'll listen. She has the phone Cobb gave her, but it's been wiped clean."

"What are you saying? That Bridget made Cobb up?"

"No, not at all. I've been thinking about it— Cobb must have somehow deleted it all remotely."

"Can that even be done?"

"Sure, with the right technology and access. Maybe he's some sort of hacker. I mean, Bridget never met him in the flesh. He's run the whole operation hiding behind a screen, which is what makes it all so damn tricky. Without proof of Cobb's existence, I don't know how we can help Bridget. Even if Rick Frost corroborates her story, without evidence the police might see it as collusion. A story they've made up to protect themselves and to get a reduced sentence. The truth is, if Cobb is as clever as Bridget seems to think he is, the chances are that anything he's told her about himself is a lie. I'd be willing to bet even the profile picture he used on the dating site where they met is fake."

Angela stared into the bottom of the empty brandy glass. "What about the other option? The one where Bridget isn't found guilty of murder?"

Emily winced. "Option two is we keep Bridget hidden, to buy some time while I try to find out more about Cobb. I can use the resources I have at Braithwaite Investigations to try to prove he exists and track him down. But I don't like option two because it means breaking some serious laws. You don't just get a slap on the hand for harbouring a murder suspect."

Angela leaned back in her chair and stared up at the ceiling. "I don't like either of those options."

"All the same, they're the only options we have right now. Bridget is an adult. Perhaps the decision needs to be made by her."

"What do you think her chances are of getting out of this?"

"Honestly? Slim to none. With evidence to back up her story, maybe the courts will go easy on her. But I'm not a lawyer. And I hope you know a good one."

The reality of what would happen next, with either option, was fast sinking in. No matter which path they chose, Bridget would invariably end up in prison.

A blood-curdling scream rang out from upstairs, making Angela and Emily jolt in their seats. Angela jumped up and dashed towards the door, with Emily on her heels. She hung back as Angela entered the bedroom, where Bridget was now sitting up in bed, panting and heaving and drenched in sweat. Seeing Angela, she promptly collapsed into fits of tears.

"I'm sorry!" she wailed. "I'm sorry, I'm sorry, I'm sorry!"

Angela hesitated at the foot of the bed, her body pulling forward and pushing back. Then she went to her sister, throwing her arms around her. They both sobbed together, lost in each other's embrace.

Emily stood in the doorway, watching them, her heart feeling heavy in her chest. Then she quietly shut the door and left the sisters to grieve.

CHAPTER 25

Thunder rolled over the dark morning sky. Emily had slept badly in the cold single room upstairs, trying to switch off her mind while listening to the sobs and whispered chatter coming from the adjacent bedroom. It had taken Angela several attempts to convince Bridget to hand herself into the police. The alternative, that they harboured her until Emily found evidence of Cobb's existence, would likely end up with them all in prison. Then no one would be able to help Bridget. Now, the three of them were driving back to Taunton, Angela and Bridget in one car, Emily following behind in the Audi.

Emily had already checked the morning news bulletins to learn that Rick Frost had been apprehended and the police were still urgently searching for Bridget. She felt conflicted, as if she and Angela were escorting Bridget to her execution. But it was the right thing to do. As much as Bridget was a victim, she had played a role in the murder of an innocent young woman. It wasn't up to Emily to decide her fate, but she could help persuade the police to take Bridget's allegations seriously, which, in turn, might persuade a jury to err on the side of leniency.

Following Angela's vehicle through the busy morning traffic, Emily wondered what was being said between the sisters. Angela had been swinging between anger and horror at Bridget's actions, while Bridget was floating between acceptance and denial. Emily didn't envy either of them.

Reaching Taunton at a little after ten, they drove through the town centre, where shoppers were out in full force despite the wet day, and made their way to the police station on Belvedere Road. Angela parked in front of a terraced row of three-storey houses. Emily found a parking space further along, then walked over to Angela's car. Climbing into the back seat, she shut the door and felt the air clamp around her like a straitjacket. The Jackson sisters sat up front, silent and unmoving, eyes fixed on the windscreen. Emily peered through the passenger door window, staring across the road at the circular parking area in front of the police station, then up at the imposing red brickwork of the building.

"Are we ready?" she asked, forcing the words out. From her position in the back seat, she couldn't see the sisters' faces. Right now, she was glad for it.

In the driver's seat, Angela reached out and held her sister's hand. Bridget began to tremble and sob.

"They're not going to believe me!" she cried, her voice high-pitched and childlike. "I don't want to go to prison for the rest of my life. It's not my fault!"

She was sobbing loudly now, her chest heaving up and down, her breaths fast and shallow. Angela tried to soothe her as best as she could, but it wasn't working. She glanced over her shoulder into the back seat, silently begging for Emily's help. But Emily had nothing to offer. What could she say to offer them comfort? There was no getting out of this. No pardon for Bridget's actions, even though she was a victim too. An innocent young woman had been murdered. As much as Emily wanted to tell Angela that Bridget would be admonished for her crimes, she knew it would be a lie. And lying wasn't going to help anyone right now. So, instead of words, she could only reach out and squeeze her friend's shoulder.

Angela turned back to her sister.

"I can't tell you everything is going to be okay," she said. "I can't tell you how it will all turn out. But whatever happens, I'll be here, by your side, every step of the way. I'm going to call Marc Edelmann. Dad always said he was a great lawyer. And Emily is going to help prove that Cobb is real, so the police can go after him. Right, Em?"

Emily leaned forward and tried to speak, but the words were still stuck. She cleared her throat and tried again. "I'll find him. No matter what it takes."

Angela stroked Bridget's cheek and patted down her hair. "You see? We're all going to be looking out for you. Every step of the way."

Bridget nodded, then sobbed even louder.

"I'll go ahead and talk to whoever's in charge," Emily said. "I'll try to buy you a couple of minutes."

"I can't breathe!" Bridget cried. "Oh God, I can't breathe!"

Angela shot a hand towards Emily. Emily squeezed it tightly. Then she was opening the car door and stepping out onto the pavement. Thunder rumbled loudly overhead. The rain, which had eased a little during the last few hours, grew heavier. Emily walked towards the police station, feeling wretched and tearful, the pressure of proving Cobb's existence pressing down on her shoulders.

Crossing the parking area, she reached the entrance doors and glanced back at Angela's car, barely able to make out the shapes inside.

She pushed the doors open and entered the building. The waiting area was warm and airless, the plastic seats empty of people. Marching up to the front desk, she caught the attention of the station duty officer, produced her private investigator license, and asked to speak to the investigating detective in charge of Wendy Wilson's case.

The duty officer stared at her with an arched eyebrow. "May I ask why?"

Emily held her gaze. "Because I know where to find Bridget Jackson."

A minute later, Detective Sergeant Wyck, a tall man in his late forties, stepped into the waiting area and introduced himself to Emily. She showed him her credentials and repeated what she'd told the duty officer.

DS Wyck stared at her intensely, as if trying to decide whether to take her seriously. Deciding that he should, he nodded towards a door. "If you'd like to follow me, you can tell me what you know."

Emily held up a hand. "Before you arrest Bridget, you need to know that she's also been the victim of a crime. A man known as Cobb has spent months grooming and manipulating her, taking advantage of her vulnerabilities to gain control. Not only that, he had Bridget's sister, Angela, repeatedly followed and filmed, so he could use the footage as another form of control—do as he says, or Angela would be killed."

Reaching into her jacket pocket, Emily pulled out Cobb's phone, which she'd sealed inside a plastic bag. "He used this to communicate with Bridget. It's also the phone used to film Wendy Wilson's murder."

DS Wyck's eyes flashed as he stared at the phone.

"Don't get too excited," she told him. "Until last night the phone contained all sorts of incriminating evidence, including proof of Cobb's existence. But he was able to erase it remotely. It's empty now, but you should have your tech team take a good look. Maybe they can still pull something off it."

The detective sergeant snorted. "So, you're telling me the evidence against this . . . Cobb, was it? That it's just magically disappeared?"

"There's no such thing as magic, Detective. But there is such a thing as phone hacking."

She handed the plastic bag containing the phone to Wyck, who stared at it sceptically. "And where is Bridget Jackson now?"

Emily hesitated, staring into the detective's eyes. He wasn't taking her seriously. Yet.

"She's right outside, waiting with her sister across the street."

The change in Wyck's expression was dramatic. His shoulders tensed and his spine straightened. His free hand shot out in the direction of the duty officer and he snapped his fingers, barking instructions and names, demanding uniformed officers come to the waiting area right now. Then he started towards the entrance doors.

Emily stepped in his way.

"Let Bridget's sister bring her in," she said, quietly. "She's come here voluntarily."

Wyck stared at her, adrenaline making his pupils dilate.

"Please. She won't run. I promise."

DS Wyck blinked as he stared at the doors. "Fine. She has one minute to enter the building or I'm sending officers out there with handcuffs."

Emily thanked him and headed out the door. Hurrying across the parking area, she saw Angela stepping out from the car. She froze, staring in Emily's direction.

Emily gave a nod. Angela slowly walked around to the other side of the car and helped Bridget out. Together, the sisters crossed the road, Angela's arm wrapped protectively around Bridget's shoulders, Bridget deathly pale and clinging to her sister.

Emily watched them draw nearer, her heart weighing her down. She was vaguely aware of DS Wyck exiting the station and appearing at her side. Halfway across the road, Bridget's knees buckled and a cry escaped her throat.

Angela held her up, whispered in her ear, kissed her temple. Then they were on the move again, one foot unsteadily in front of the other, Bridget's horrified gaze fixed on the detective sergeant.

Two uniformed officers burst through the entrance doors, their bodies poised for action. On Wyck's signal, they hurried forward, grabbing Bridget by her arms and peeling her from Angela's embrace. Bridget wailed, like a child waking from a nightmare, as the officers frogmarched her towards the building. DS Wyck followed alongside, reading Bridget her rights. The doors swung shut and then Bridget was gone.

Emily and Angela were alone on the forecourt, rain chilling their skin. Angela stood motionless, her face twisted in a silent grimace. Emily stared at her, fighting back tears.

"You're doing the right thing," she said, knowing the words provided little comfort. "The alternative would have been much worse."

She reached a hand towards Angela, who backed away, almost tripping over herself.

"I should go inside. I'll call Marc Edelmann. He was an old friend of Dad's. I'll ask him to come down here as soon as he can."

"I'll call Trevor," Emily said. "I'll let him know what's happened. He should be here with you."

Angela said nothing, just stared at the police station doors as rain speckled her glasses.

Emily pulled out her phone.

"You should go," Angela said. "The quicker you find Cobb, the quicker we'll know where Bridget stands."

"Don't you think I should wait until Trevor—"

"No. I want you to go. I'll feel better knowing you're out there looking for him."

Emily stared at the phone, then back at Angela. "Okay. I'll need to head back to London. Back to the office. I'll call Trevor on the way. You sure you'll be all right?"

Angela laughed. Her eyes went dim.

"Angie," Emily said softly. "I promise you, I'll do everything I can to find Cobb."

"Good. That's good," Angela whispered. She walked towards the police station. Stopping outside the doors, she paused to remove her glasses and wipe the rain from the lenses with the edge of her sleeve. Then she disappeared inside.

Emily watched the doors swing shut, feeling lost and alone, and hoping they'd done the right thing. Turning her back on the police station, she sucked in a shuddering breath and headed back towards her car.

———

Four vehicles down from Emily's silver Audi, a man sat behind the wheel of a red BMW, watching as Bridget Jackson was grabbed by uniformed police officers and escorted into the police station. The figure watched Emily and Angela talk quietly, then saw Angela follow her sister inside. The private investigator stood there for a moment, looking lost and deflated.

Then she was on the move, hurrying towards her car. The man grabbed a mobile phone from the dashboard and dialled a number. A moment later, a familiar voice answered.

"The police have arrested the girl. Her sister's with her," the man said.

"What about the PI?"

The man paused, spying the silver Audi pulling away from the kerb. "She's on the move."

"Then follow her. And don't be stupid enough to get caught."

The man said nothing. The line went dead.

The private investigator was getting away, moving further down the street. Turning the key in the ignition, the man started the car, turned the wheel, and began to follow.

CHAPTER 26

Emily pushed open the smoked glass doors of Braithwaite Investigations and marched into the reception area, where Jerome sat behind the desk, eyes glued to a computer screen. He looked up, the usual smile in his eyes strangely missing.

"Hey," he said, as Emily approached. "I saw the news about the video. Are you okay?"

Reaching the desk, Emily stood for a minute, feeling lost and empty, the image of Bridget being dragged away by police officers playing on repeat in her mind. "Bridget is in custody. Angela is in pieces. They're relying on me to fix this mess. The trouble is, I'm not sure I can. Not in the way they want me to."

"So, she really did film Wendy's murder? I'm shocked."

Emily's shoulders tensed. "You didn't watch the video, did you? It's everywhere."

"God, no. I wouldn't, even if I could bring myself to, that girl deserves more respect than her murder being beamed across the world for everyone to see. Her parents must be devastated."

Emily felt a surge of relief. The images of Wendy's death were burned on her mind forever. She didn't want her friends to suffer the same fate. "There's more to the story than the press knows right now. Someone else is involved. Someone who forced Bridget to select Wendy as a victim then film her murder."

"You mean that Rick guy?"

"No. Rick Frost is a dangerous psychopath who was just waiting for an excuse, but someone else is pulling the strings. Before all this, Bridget was a sweet young woman who'd experienced personal loss, but was beginning to turn her life around. Now it's all gone to hell. She's been manipulated and coerced. Blackmailed and threatened, until she felt she had no choice but to play a role in Wendy Wilson's murder."

Jerome stared at the desk. "I'm sorry. Do you know who it is?"

"I only have a name. Cobb. But I have a feeling even that's not real. I don't think the police are interested either. Why would they be? They've got their murderers in custody, and there's no evidence Cobb even exists. Without it, Bridget doesn't stand a chance."

Emily shut her eyes for a moment, trying to pull her thoughts together. She felt Jerome reach over and gently squeeze her hand.

"Bridget and Angela, they're counting on you to prove this Cobb person exists?"

"Whoever he is, he's highly intelligent and knows how to cover his tracks. He hid behind a false name and a fake profile. He was able to remotely delete incriminating files from a mobile phone, which means he has access to hacking software and knows how to use it. In fact, he's operated so smoothly that I'm willing to bet this isn't his first time." Emily chewed the inside of her mouth as her mind raced. "Who here's good with tech?"

Across the room, a door opened and a tall, broad-shouldered man in his mid-thirties stepped out.

"Sorry, what?" Jerome said, turning around.

"I need someone who knows their way around a computer. Software programming, that kind of thing. You know, Geek 101 stuff."

Jerome didn't reply. Instead, he hurriedly tidied the papers littering his desk, then swung around on his chair as the man approached. Their eyes met and they smiled at each other. Emily muttered under her breath.

"Hey, Lee," Jerome said. "Are you any good with computers?"

"Computers?" the man repeated, his voice deep and rich. "Well, I can log on and off. I can even click a mouse and type on the keyboard. Need some help with yours?"

Lee Woodruff was a fellow private investigator working for Erica Braithwaite. A former homicide detective who'd retired early due to injury in the field, he not only had years of investigative work on Emily, but Erica had tempted him away from another agency, with a promise of interesting cases and a substantial salary. He exuded confidence and, except for a slight limp, was in great shape. When Emily had first joined Braithwaite Investigations, she had felt utterly intimidated by him. But Lee was friendly and keen to help, treating Emily as an equal regardless of her lack of experience. In short, he was one of the good guys.

"Emily needs a tech nerd to help with a case," Jerome said.

"It's not a case." Emily lowered her voice as she glanced at Erica Braithwaite's office door. "Not an official one. You know anything about hacking?"

Lee arched an eyebrow. "I have a friend who works in the cybercrime unit for the London Met. He may be able to help if he has the time. Which, to be honest, he probably doesn't. Are we talking online fraud?"

"It's more complicated than that. I need to find someone who doesn't want to be found. A possible hacker."

Lee scratched the stubble on his square jaw, his eyes momentarily darting towards Jerome. "In that case, I know someone else. A contact I've used a few times in sensitive cases. They're a total tech geek and a little temperamental. Probably don't get enough sunlight." He smiled at Jerome, who smiled back. Emily cleared her throat. "If you need someone found, my contact will find them. They don't work for free, so you'd have to pay for their services. And there's a caveat."

"Which is?"

"Some of their techniques aren't exactly legal."

"In what way?"

"To catch a hacker, you have to play them at their own game."

Emily chewed her lip. She'd already avoided breaking the law today by persuading

Bridget to hand herself in. But technically speaking, by outsourcing the work to Lee Woodruff's contact, she wouldn't be the one breaking the law.

"Fine," she said. "How do I contact them?"

"You don't. Hackers can be a little paranoid. Give me your number and I'll set it up. They'll call you."

Emily grabbed a notepad from Jerome's desk and wrote down her phone number. "Thanks. I owe you. You'll tell them it's urgent?"

The private investigator nodded, slipped the notepaper inside his shirt pocket and tapped it protectively. "I'll tell them. Now I'm off. I have a hot date with a microwave meal and Celebrity Master Chef. Don't judge me." He smiled at Emily, then at Jerome, who beamed up at him.

"Just so you know, 'microwave meal' and 'Master Chef' don't go together in the same sentence."

Laughing, Lee waved a hand and exited through the smoked glass doors.

"Will you please just ask him out already?" Emily said. "It's getting embarrassing."

"I have no idea what you're talking about. And what about you? Are you still avoiding Carter?"

Emily felt her neck muscles tense. "In case you hadn't noticed, I've been busy. Besides, I'm heading there now."

"Don't look too excited about it. Wait a minute, you still haven't made a decision, have you? Don't you think you should—"

Emily held up a hand. "When you finally pluck up the courage to ask Lee Woodruff out on a date, then I'll gladly listen to any meaningful relationship advice you have. Until then, you want a lift to the tube station?"

"Sure," Jerome said, shutting down the computer for the day. "If it doesn't stop raining soon, we're all going to drown."

CHAPTER 27

It was already dark by the time Emily arrived at Carter's house in West Hampstead and let herself in with her key. Carter was in the kitchen, where tantalising food smells hung in the air. He glanced up while stirring the contents of a bubbling pan and smiled. It wasn't the blinding, pleased to see her smile that Emily had grown used to.

"What's cookin' good lookin'?" she chirped, slinging her bag over the back of a chair. Usually, she would slink up behind him and wrap her arms around his waist. But now, she held back.

"Irish stew. Should be ready in fifteen

minutes." Carter stared at her for a moment longer, the smile now gone.

"So . . . how are you?"

"Fine. You?"

"Fine."

"I just saw the evening news. Bridget's been arrested?"

Emily stared at her feet, which seemed to be nailed to the floor. "She gave herself up to the police. I found her yesterday. Stopped her from jumping into a river."

Carter turned around again. "You were in Somerset?"

"Angela called. It was an emergency."

"Well, that explains why you didn't return any of my messages."

Emily narrowed her eyes, staring at the back of his head. "Like I said, it was an emergency. And that's beside the point—did you miss the part where I said Bridget tried to kill herself?"

Carter was quiet, stirring the pot. "Is she okay now?"

"Not really. She's done the right thing,

though. If she'd kept running, she would have only made it worse for herself."

"So, she's guilty?"

"It's more complicated than that. I'm looking into it. Trying to help."

Moving away from the stove, Carter pulled two wine glasses from a cupboard and filled them with red wine. He held one out for Emily to take. "In an official capacity?"

"No, as a friend," she said, taking the glass. "A friend who also happens to be a private investigator."

"I see. Well, I hope you're staying safe."

The frustrations of the day were simmering beneath Emily's skin. Carter wasn't helping. She glared at the floor tiles then back at him.

"Could you lay the table?" he asked, avoiding her probing gaze.

But Emily just stood there, frozen to the spot, feeling the weight of the room pressing down on her. "I'm sorry I haven't called. It's been a stressful twenty-four hours."

"I was starting to worry you were avoiding

me. I've barely seen you since we came back from the wedding."

"I've been busy."

"Too busy to answer my question?" Carter smiled again, but this time it had sharp edges. He stood for a moment, the silence growing thorns. Then he glanced at the empty dinner table. "I guess I'll lay it myself."

Emily watched him pull cutlery from a drawer and return to the table, slowly laying out each piece. It was hot in here. She pulled at the neck of her sweater. "Look, I'm sorry. Okay? I can't do this right now. I'm tired and I've had a really bad day. I don't need you putting pressure on me."

"No one's pressuring you, and I'm sorry you've had a bad day. But you can't just disappear and leave me to worry like that. It's not fair, especially with the risks that come with your job."

"So, you're telling me what I can and can't do now?"

Carter muttered under his breath. "No, I'm not. I'm just wondering why we can't have an adult conversation about us moving in together."

"An adult conversation?" Emily glared at him, her mouth dropping open. "Are you kidding me?"

"That came out wrong. All I'm trying to say is—"

"Oh, can we please not? I'm tired and I don't have the energy to talk about this right now."

Carter ran his hands through his hair and stared at the floor. "Well, maybe I need to. Maybe you avoiding me for days has put me on edge."

Emily gulped her wine. The room grew even hotter.

"Look," Carter said. "If you don't want to move in with me, I'd rather you just came out and said it."

"Okay, fine! I don't want to move in with you. Does that make you happy?"

She caught her breath, shocked by her own words. Carter flinched, like he'd been slapped. The only sound was the stew bubbling in the pan.

"I'm sorry," Emily said, quieter now. "I'm not ready, and I don't want to move in with you just because I feel like I should, only for things to fall apart six months down the line."

Carter stared at her, saying nothing, looking like a wounded puppy. Which did nothing to appease Emily's guilt.

"I love you, Carter. Living together, it's a big move. And it's one I'm not ready to make. Not yet. It doesn't mean I love you less. It doesn't mean our relationship isn't good enough or that I want it to end. But I've made terrible mistakes in the past. Mistakes I'll have to live with for the rest of my life. I don't want to make a terrible mistake with you. That's why I'm asking you to wait. If you can."

The words dried up in her throat. Now she waited, the air in the room growing thick and heavy. But Carter remained silent, his shoulders slumping, a look of utter defeat in his eyes.

"Say something," Emily whispered.

She wanted to go to him. To wrap her arms around his neck and press her lips against his. But she just stood, feeling wretched and miserable, worried for Bridget Jackson, and guilty for ruining what could have been a joyous occasion. But it was the joy she feared the most. It was fragile and precious and volatile. The only way she knew how to protect it, for now, was to keep it out of her reach.

Finally, Carter looked up. He opened his mouth. Closed it again.

Then he said, "Dinner's ready."

CHAPTER 28

The next morning, Emily made her way through the streets of Shoreditch, a fashionable area of East London that was close to the business district of Liverpool Street and populated by trendy bars and restaurants, artisan coffee shops, and pop-up clothing stores filled with edgy labels. She had visited here a few times before, under grave circumstances. Now, she weaved between the arty young pedestrians, before leaving the traffic-choked high street to enter a narrow alley, where small boutiques were open for business and rain glanced off the cobblestones. She passed Bramfords Diner, where, just a few years ago, she'd met a receptionist named Rosa, who'd helped Emily expose a shocking medical crime and unknowingly set her on the path to becoming a private eye. The glass store front was now painted white, and a large sign pinned to the door announced that Bramfords Diner was closed for business.

Leaving the alley, Emily turned onto Curtain Road. Halfway down the street, she turned again, entering a large courtyard, where ivy climbed the walls of a five-storey Victorian warehouse that had been converted into studio apartments. Reaching the steel blue entrance door, she pressed the top buzzer and peered up at the security camera blinking down at her. A moment later, an irritated voice growled through the intercom.

"Yeah? What do you want?"

"It's Emily Swanson. We talked earlier?"

"Top floor. First door on the right."

A loud buzzer filled Emily's ears as the

electronic door unlocked. Pulling it open, she stepped into an empty foyer with blue floor tiles and graffiti on the walls. An old service lift was at the far end, which she rode to the top floor as instructed. As she stepped out, a knot of anxiety twisted her stomach. Ignoring it, she pressed the buzzer next to the apartment door, then waited as heavy sounding door locks were pulled back. The door opened a few inches, a chain lock pulling tight. A young woman of average height and a mess of dark hair peered through the gap, glaring at Emily.

"You alone?" she grunted.

"Yes."

The young woman tilted her head, staring beyond Emily at the corridor behind. Satisfied, she shut the door to remove the chain lock, then opened it again. Now that Emily could see her fully, she was startled to find the woman was barely out of her teens. If she even was out of her teens. She stared up at Emily, a shock of dyed black hair sticking out at crazy angles. She wore skinny black jeans, a heavy metal band t-shirt that Emily didn't recognise, and a pair of rainbow coloured slippers on her feet.

The women stood for a moment longer, sizing each other up. Emily said, "Thanks for agreeing to see me. Lee told me you're—"

The young woman threw the door open wide and stepped aside. When Emily didn't move, she shrugged her shoulders. "Are you waiting for a written invitation?"

Emily raised her eyebrows and stepped inside. The studio apartment was huge, covering at least half of the warehouse floor, and it was bright and airy. Framed modern art filled the whitewashed brick walls. Large rugs covered the original floorboards. In the right-hand corner, two leather sofas and a huge flat screen television dominated the space, along with an intimidating sound system that looked as if it cost more than Emily's annual salary. On the left was an open plan kitchen, with shiny mod cons and an industrial-sized range cooker. Emily turned a half circle. In the third corner was an L-shaped desk filled with computers, laptops, and other gadgets she didn't recognise. Several chrome table fans were dispersed among the hardware, humming noisily. A mass of leads and wires sprouted from the equipment, all neatly taped together and free of knots.

Behind her, the young woman shut the door and slammed three large deadbolt locks home. She stared at Emily. "What were you expecting? A poky room and closed curtains? Let me guess, you were imagining me to be some sweaty, middle-aged blimp with thinning hair too?"

Emily opened her mouth but didn't know what to say.

"It's important to get daylight and exercise," the young woman said, thrusting a hand on her hip. "No one wants to end up a hunchback. And why should I work my butt off to live in squalor? No thank you."

She shrugged, her gaze never leaving Emily's.

"What should I call you?" Emily asked, her gaze moving down to the young woman's rainbow coloured slippers.

"My name would be a good start. It's Carla. What do you need from me?"

"Well, Carla. It's nice to meet you."

Carla yawned, stared at the empty space on her wrist.

"Okay . . ." Emily said. Still standing, she told Carla the story of Bridget Jackson, about how she had met Cobb online, and how that fateful meeting eventually led to the brutal murder of Wendy Wilson.

"The girl in that video?" Carla said. "I watched that. It was nasty."

Emily continued, telling her about the mobile phone Cobb had sent Bridget, and how the contents had been deleted remotely. "So, there's no trace of him. Nothing to prove he exists. Cobb's out there somewhere, while Bridget is in police custody and Wendy Wilson is in a morgue. He's very good at covering his tracks and he's clearly very good at getting people to do terrible things. We need to stop him before he hurts someone else. I need your help to find him online. I think that's the only way to get to him, and frankly, it's beyond my reach."

Carla chewed the inside of her mouth. She went into the kitchen space and removed a can of Coke from the fridge, offering it to Emily, who shook her head. Popping the tab, Carla leaned against the fridge and swallowed half the can.

"It would be easy enough to access a mobile phone remotely," she said, her brow creasing. "I mean, you'd need the right tools and you'd need to know what you're doing. But it's not rocket science anymore. You ever get a bogus text message from your bank saying your account has been compromised and to tap the following link to log in?"

Emily nodded. "Sure, but everyone knows not to tap the link or you get a virus."

"Not necessarily. Sometimes those links contain little hacking programs. The minute you click on it, it's like opening a door to scammers and saying, 'Here, have complete control of my phone.' Suddenly the perpetrator can read your text messages and access your pictures and videos. Look what happened to all those celebrities a while back, getting their nudes stolen and posted online." Carla wrinkled her face. "So, this guy you're looking for—Knobb, wasn't it?"

"Cobb."

"Whatever. He's either a hacker or he's working with one. No doubt about it. What do you have on him?"

"Not much. A couple of phone numbers. One for the phone he sent to Bridget. The other is the number he used to call and text her. But it's been disconnected now."

"That's it?"

"Well, there's the dating website Bridget met him on, but he's deleted his profile already."

Carla swallowed more Coke. "It's not exactly much to go on. I could try to trace the numbers, see where they lead to. You have the phone he gave your friend?"

"The police have it," Emily said, now regretting that she'd handed it over. "What about the dating site? Can't you hack into it, pull his deleted profile and trace him from that?"

Carla snorted. "You've been watching too many movies. But it's not entirely impossible."

"So you could help me?"

Finishing the Coke, Carla crushed the can and tossed it into a recycling bin. "It'll cost you five hundred. Half now. Half on completion."

Emily stared at her. "Five hundred?"

"Take it or leave it."

"What if you can't find anything?"

"Time is money, woman."

Five hundred pounds was more than Emily had been expecting, and she would be paying for Carla's services out of her own pocket. But picturing Bridget's terrified face as she was dragged into the police station, she remembered how distraught Angela had looked, standing lost and hopeless in the rain. Emily slowly nodded. If there was one thing she couldn't stand, it was misogynistic pricks who enjoyed hurting women.

"I want Cobb behind bars before he hurts

anyone else," she said. "Lee Woodruff says you're good, so I'll take him at his word."

Carla shrugged off the compliment and scratched her cheek. "I take cash or card. Don't even think about coming at me with a chequebook."

CHAPTER 29

Evening came. Back at The Holmeswood, Emily sat at the table in her living room, picking at her dinner and stewing over the terrible events of the last few days. She hoped Carla would be able to trace Cobb, even if the young and tempestuous hacker had complained the phone numbers weren't much to go on. Until they found him, Cobb was just a figment of Bridget's imagination, and Emily could understand why the police might think that. She wondered how Bridget was coping, locked up in a police cell, undergoing hours of scrutiny in an airless interview room. Her terrified face haunted Emily. So did Wendy

Wilson's crumpled form, tumbling backwards into open space, the light dying in her eyes.

As for her own personal troubles, Emily had barely given a moment's thought to last night's fight with Carter. The guilt was still present though. Now, she wondered if their relationship would survive her decision. Carter had barely spoken to her through dinner. Emily had returned home after deciding it would be better for them to have space and let the decision sink in. She hadn't heard from Carter since. She hadn't contacted him either.

Nursing a mug of herbal tea, she got up and moved to the centre window, which stretched from floor to ceiling, and stared at the city below. Her eyelids grew heavy. Her shoulders drooped. Sleep called to her, but she couldn't rest. Not yet.

Angela answered after one ring, her voice cracking with anguish and desperation.

"What is it?" Emily asked, sensing something had changed.

"They're charging Bridget with murder," she sobbed. "They don't care if she wasn't the one who picked up the rock. They don't care if she was groomed and blackmailed. They're saying she helped plan it and that filming it proves her guilt. That she's just as sick as Rick Frost."

"I'm so sorry." But the news was unsurprising to Emily. She had consulted her law books and learned that, unlike America, there were no degrees of murder in the British justice system. Murder was murder, plain and simple, regardless of the nuances of individual cases.

"But it's not the worst part," Angela continued. "Because Marc Edelmann said Bridget's going to plead guilty."

"But she can't! If she does, it's over for her."

"I know that. You know that. But Marc says she's adamant. She says it's the least she deserves."

Emily paced the room. She had not expected this. But now, she supposed it made sense. Yesterday, Bridget had tried to end her life and Emily had stopped her. The next best thing was to plead guilty.

"We have to find a way to change Bridget's mind," she said. "What about Cobb's phone? Do you know if the police are looking into it?"

"Marc is trying to find out if it's been sent to digital forensics, but he's doubtful the police are going to chase it up. There's no evidence that Cobb exists. Right now, he's just a story that Bridget and Rick have cooked up. You know, it wasn't their fault, they were made to do it. The police aren't buying it for a second. And it won't matter, not if she's going to plead guilty." Angela caught her breath, choking on her sobs. "What about you? Did you find anything?"

"Nothing concrete, but I'm working on it, and now I have some technical help. Hopefully, it will lead to something." Emily paced the living room floor, fighting off exhaustion. "I'm worried about you, Angie. Cobb threatened you. If the police don't think he's real, that leaves you vulnerable. Maybe we should move you to a safe place."

"I'm fine. Besides, Trevor isn't letting me out of his sight. I just wish I could see Bridget so I can try to change her mind. Marc's been the only one allowed in with her right now. She'll go before the magistrates court first thing on Monday to enter a plea. If she pleads guilty, she'll be sent straight to remand to await sentencing at Crown Court. Even if she doesn't, Marc says the chance of her getting bail is slim to none. But either way, Bridget's not going to cope with prison. I know her. She'll lose her mind. Or try to kill herself again."

Biting down on her lip, Emily pressed the phone tightly to her ear. She wished she could tell Angela that she was close to finding Cobb, that he would soon be in police custody. But giving Angela false hope would be cruel. Lies and deception were what had trapped Bridget Jackson in a deadly corner. Lies and deception were what led to Wendy Wilson's brutal murder. And Cobb had covered his tracks so well, the chance of finding him was slim.

"Listen to me," Emily said. "I'll be working night and day to track this bastard down. If we can prove he's real, then maybe she'll change her mind about pleading guilty. And if we can prove he blackmailed Bridget into committing a crime, then maybe it will persuade the courts to go easy on her."

"Do you think it would keep her out of prison? That they'd see her as a victim too?"

The truth was the prosecution would want to know why Bridget hadn't told the police about Cobb, despite his threats to have Angela killed. There would have been opportunities, they'd say, to put an end to his plans. Emily had even wondered it herself. But now, listening to Angela's quiet sobs, she wondered what she would have done in Bridget's position. What if Cobb had threatened Carter or Jerome? She found she couldn't answer.

"You need to stay strong, okay? Bridget needs you right now. Maybe even more than she needs Marc Edelmann. But you also need to stay safe. Cobb is still out there, and we don't know if he'll act upon his threats now that Bridget has told the police everything. Are you sure there's nowhere else you can stay?"

"No. I need to be here with Trevor. It's where I feel the safest. But Emily?"

"Yes?"

"Promise me you'll do your best to find that bastard? Even if Bridget goes to prison, knowing that he's been caught, that he can't hurt anyone else—maybe it will give her the strength she needs to keep going."

Emily hesitated. "I promise to do my best. Hang in there. I'll be in touch soon."

She said goodbye and hung up. Her throat was dry. Her heart ached. Tiredness pulled at her limbs, calling her to bed like a Siren. But Emily knew she wouldn't sleep, not while Angela and Bridget were depending on her.

Making a pot of coffee, she sat at the dining table and opened her laptop. She spent the next hour trawling through news articles and blog posts, reading story after story about catfishing cases. Although the stories were troubling, she found nothing as extreme as what had been done to Bridget Jackson.

Narrowing the search down to women within the United Kingdom, she scanned through troubling tales of romantic scams on dating websites, where fake profiles had been created and amorous intentions feigned. Once the scammers had gained the victims' confidence and trust, they moved swiftly, clearing out bank accounts and maxing credit cards.

Another hour passed by. Emily made more coffee. Outside, the night turned from olive green to blue-black. She narrowed her search again, this time scouring the community forums of Reddit and Quora, where users posted questions and stories on every conceivable topic imaginable, including the deplorable act of catfishing. Ninety-two minutes later, Emily stumbled upon a story that made her skin tingle. One that sounded unnervingly similar to what had been done to Bridget.

CHAPTER 30

Jenna Laurent was twenty years old and lived with her mother in a two-bedroom house in Tooting Bec, South London. She was tall and filled with nervous energy, hiding her slim frame beneath an oversized hoodie and loose jeans. As Emily sat in her living room, nursing a cup of coffee and mourning the hours of sleep she'd lost, Jenna perched on the edge of an armchair, her right knee jigging up and down.

"So you met him online?" Emily asked, interrupting the quiet that had settled between them.

Jenna nodded, avoiding her visitor's gaze.

"I don't even know why I went on that dating site," she said, her voice quiet and unsure of itself. "I mean, I wasn't expecting to meet anyone. It was more curiosity than anything else. To see if anyone would be interested. She paused, glancing at Emily, returning her gaze to the carpet. "It was his username that appealed to me, I suppose. 'Shyboy Eighty-eight.' I thought maybe he would be like me. Socially anxious and not very good with people. Plus, his profile picture was . . . well, he was cute." She blushed, bowing her head.

"And you got talking?"

"Just messaging online at first. It turned out we liked the same things. The same films. The same music. The same politics. It seemed almost too good to be true. Which, obviously, it was. Anyway, we connected. Brian kept saying he was shy and didn't want to talk on camera, which I thought was strange, seeing as he was an investment banker; I always imagine people like that are super confident. But it was okay with me because I'm not great with that kind of thing. Brian asked for my phone number instead, so we could talk for real. I gave it to him. He would call and we'd talk for hours. Mum works night shifts at the hospital, so I'm here by myself a lot."

"Are you at college?" Emily asked.

Jenna flinched, like she'd been stung. "I was, for a while. I'm taking time out right now. Figuring out what I want to do with my life."

Emily nodded, waiting for her to continue.

"Brian was really nice to me. I liked him and he made me laugh. He was the first person I'd met in a long time who I thought really understood me. He knew what it was like to live with depression and anxiety. How it can make you hide away from the world or feel scared of everything. I don't have many friends. I don't like going to bars or clubs. I don't know why, it's just how I am. Brian was the same. He said he found it difficult to make friends too, but he was glad he'd found a friend in me."

Emily frowned, troubled by what she was hearing. Cobb's vulnerabilities and interests had been almost identical to Bridget's own. Now Jenna and Brian's. He's a researcher, Emily thought. Mimicking what he sees as his victims' weaknesses so that he can make a connection. So they would lower their defences and let him in.

"Did you ever meet 'Brian' in person?" she asked.

Jenna shook her head again. "We were supposed to. One day he asked if I'd like to finally meet up. He said he lived just outside of London, but now that we knew each other well, he'd happily travel in to meet for dinner. I was nervous, but I agreed. I even ordered a new outfit. We were going to meet at an Italian restaurant in Soho. I didn't feel comfortable about going somewhere so crowded, but seeing as he was making the effort to travel in, I thought it was the least I could do. And sometimes it's good to test your own boundaries, isn't it? But Brian said it would be okay, that we could be uncomfortable together. So, I got on the train and arrived at the restaurant just before seven. And I waited.

And when he didn't show up after a while, I tried calling him. And when he still didn't turn up or answer the phone, when I couldn't stand everyone in the restaurant staring at me any longer, I went home."

Jenna laughed, but there was no joy in her voice. "Can you believe I was actually worried about him? I thought something bad had happened. The next day, I tried calling him again. He answered, all casual and cool, like a completely different person. He said he'd forgotten about our date and that was it. No apology. He didn't even sound like he cared. Naturally, I got upset. I surprised myself because I told him so too. But Brian got angry. He told me I should count my blessings that he showed any interest in me at all. Because, God knows, no one else would. Then he laughed, like the past two months had been one big joke to him."

"I'm sorry," Emily said, watching the young woman's eyes flash with anger. "No one deserves to be treated like that."

"Yeah, well. He made me cry on the phone.

I was so confused by the change in him, I kept wondering what I'd done wrong. But I had enough self-respect to tell him not to call me again. But he didn't listen. He kept on phoning. At first, it was once a day, and I ignored it. But soon, it was on the hour, every hour, with horrible, nasty text messages in between.

"I blocked his number. Thought it was all over and done with. But a few days later, he started calling again, from a different number. He caught me unawares. I picked up the first time and he just screamed at me, hurling abuse down the phone. Calling me a slut and a fucking whore, screaming that no one turned their back on him. I blocked him again. But he just kept calling from different numbers."

"I'm sorry," Emily said. "What did you do?"

"I changed my mobile phone number. No more calls from Brian." Jenna looked up, finally meeting Emily's gaze. Her hair parted to reveal dark, angry eyes. "A week later I got an email containing a video file. It was of my mum. He'd followed her to the hospital, where she works as a nurse. Then on the tube and around the shops. The email said that if I continued to ignore him, he would have my mum killed."

Emily straightened up. It had to be him. Cobb. Whoever he was, the similarities were too great to ignore.

"I called my mum and we went straight to the police. But when I tried to show them the video, it was gone. Deleted. I tried showing them all the abusive text messages, but they were gone too, along with his dating profile and any trace of him. I don't know how he did it. But it was like Brian never existed. Like I'd imagined it all in my head. I didn't hear from him again. Nothing happened to my mum. Without evidence, the police couldn't do anything. And that was it."

Drained of energy, Jenna let out a heavy sigh. "The only proof I have left that I wasn't losing my mind is Brian's photo from the dating site. I printed it out and kept it, back when I thought he was a nice guy."

Emily leaned forward. "Do you still have it?"

Jenna got up and left the room, returning moments later with the picture. The image was of a brown-eyed young man in his mid-twenties, good-looking, if not extraordinary.

"It's probably fake," Jenna said, hiding behind her hair again.

With Jenna's permission, Emily snapped a picture of the image with her phone.

"Have you heard about the murder of Wendy Wilson?" she asked Jenna, who nodded.

"The girl from Somerset. I heard about the video. Everyone's sharing it online. I didn't watch it though. It's sick, getting a thrill from watching something like that."

"I think the person who catfished you is the same person who orchestrated Wendy's murder."

Jenna's eyes flew open as she drew in a shocked breath.

"Bridget Jackson, the young woman who filmed the video—this man threatened her sister's life in the same way he threatened your mother's. He forced her to take part in Wendy's death."

"My God," Jenna gasped, her hand pressed to her cheek. "That could have been me."

Emily leaned forward again, deadly serious. "I'm going to catch him," she said. "I'm going to make sure he doesn't do this to anyone else. You could help, by speaking to Bridget Jackson's defence lawyer and telling him your story. It won't change what that psychopath did to you, but you could help put him behind bars."

Jenna clenched her jaw and her eyes narrowed, all traces of the nervous young woman Emily had met twenty minutes ago now gone. Slowly, she nodded.

"Good," Emily said, getting to her feet. "I'll arrange for Mr Edelmann to contact you."

Jenna showed her to the front door. Emily thanked her and turned to leave.

"Do you think I'm stupid?" Jenna asked her. "For falling for his lies."

Emily smiled, but only for a moment. "This man, whoever he is, he's very good at what he does. You were clever enough to get away from him. But now that he's forced someone to commit murder, there's no telling what he might do next. Which is why we need to find him and stop him."

Saying goodbye to Jenna, Emily crossed the suburban street, heading towards her car. Her mind raced along with her heart. As she'd suspected, Bridget was not Cobb's first victim. Perhaps with Jenna, he'd been just starting out, feeling his way around and testing how far he could go. Getting the police involved had scared him off. But somewhere between Jenna and Bridget, he'd grown cockier.

Taking out her phone, Emily tapped out a text message to Angela: I'm sending you a picture. Have Edelmann show it to Bridget and see if Cobb used the same one. Ask her if he used the name: Shyboy88. I found another one of his victims. She's willing to talk.

She sent the text message, along with the picture, then crossed the road back to her car.

Emily drove away, heading to Grosvenor Square and Braithwaite Investigations.

Moments later, a red BMW with blacked out windows rumbled to life and began following Emily at a discreet distance.

CHAPTER 31

Now back in her office, Emily connected her phone to the desktop computer, then transferred the photograph that Jenna had taken from Cobb's dating profile. Bringing up a web browser, she clicked on Google Images, uploaded the picture, and clicked the search button. She scanned the results, picking through images of similar looking men in similar poses. She sat up. Halfway down the screen, she found two identical copies of the photograph. The first had been pulled from LinkedIn, the professional networking and career development website. Emily clicked the link, which took her to a profile page.

The man in the photograph was named Duncan Scott. According to his LinkedIn profile, Scott was an investment banker who had worked for some of the country's biggest banks. Strangely, his employment record had not been updated in over a year. Bookmarking the profile, Emily clicked on the second link from the image search results and found out why.

According to the news story, Duncan Scott had been twenty-six years old at the time of his death. In January of last year, he had been struck down by a drunk driver in West London, along with his fiancée, Tara Bloomfield, twenty-seven. The couple had been walking home from a friend's birthday drinks at a local bar, when a car veered off the road and onto the pavement. Scott was killed instantly. Bloomfield died from her injuries a day later.

Cobb had stolen a dead man's life for his fake dating profile, which, in Emily's eyes, made him even more depraved. But she could see why. Duncan Scott had been young and handsome, with solid career prospects and financial stability. He was an attractive package. All Cobb had to do was fill in the charming personality.

Emily leaned back, spotting the case file for a new insurance fraud job that was sitting on her desk. She rolled her eyes. Her friend desperately needed help. A psychopath was still out there, preying on vulnerable young women. Meanwhile, Emily was expected to be chasing after some chancer with a pretend frozen shoulder. But until Carla got back to her, or Bridget had been shown the picture, there was nothing more she could do. Picking up the file, she slumped against the back of her chair and began reading through the case notes.

Her phone chimed on the desk, announcing a text message. It was from Carter. A moan escaped her, followed by a guilty sigh. Swiping her thumb across the screen, she cast a cautious eye over the text message: Thinking about you.

Emily relaxed her shoulders. Maybe he wasn't as mad with her as she'd anticipated.

There was a link at the bottom, which she tapped. An animated GIF popped up, showing a cute bear hugging a heart.

Emily smiled. She didn't even know that Carter knew how to send GIFs. He was always claiming to be the world's worst technophobe. He didn't even have a Facebook profile. Shrugging, she replied, sending him an animated firework that exploded into hearts. She winced. When had she become so gooey?

Her phone chimed again. But this time it wasn't Carter. It was a text message sent from an unknown number. Curious, Emily opened it.

--Hello, Emily Swanson.

She stared at the words. Her stomach fluttered. The hairs on the back of her neck tingled.

--Hello, Emily Swanson.

Who had texted her from a masked number? But deep down, in the darkest recesses of her mind, she already knew.

Her thumb hovered over the screen. It wavered for a moment, twitching back and forth. Emily tapped out a message: Who is this?

She pressed send. The reply came back twenty seconds later: Don't pretend. You know who this is.

"Shit." Her heart was racing now, her blood pounding in her ears.

She replied: Cobb?

How had he found out about her? More to the point, how did he know her number?

Her phone chimed again.

I want you to mind your own business. This isn't your game. Stop trying to play.

A knock on the door made Emily jump in her seat. Jerome leaned into her office and waved a hand. "Hey, you want to knock off early and get some lunch? I'm starving."

Emily stared at him then back at the phone.

"Em? What is it?"

"He's been watching me," she said, staring at the words.

"Who has? What are you talking about?"

But Emily wasn't listening. Her eyes were

fixed on the screen. On Cobb's words: This isn't your game. Stop trying to play.

"Are you going to tell me what's going on?" he said. "Or are you going to make me stand here and gape like an idiot?"

Emily got up and hurried over to the window. Below, the greens of Grosvenor Square had been painted in a wash of wet gloom. Parked cars lined the road, bumper to bumper. Emily stared at each one, trying to peer inside.

"Trouble, that's what," she said. "Trouble with a capital 'T'."

CHAPTER 32

Emily pressed the buzzer beside the old red door and stared up at the camera above her head. The rain was coming down hard, slapping against the cobblestone courtyard. Her journey had been fraught with paranoia, with Emily constantly checking the rear-view mirror. She had parked several streets away and glanced over her shoulder every minute or so, as she completed the journey on foot. Cobb's text messages had rattled her, which made her angry as well as scared.

The intercom crackled and a voice filled with rattlesnakes blared from the speaker. "What the hell are you doing here? You don't just show up unannounced. It's against the rules."

"I'm sorry," Emily said. "And normally I wouldn't, but it's urgent. I found another one of Cobb's victims, a young woman whose life he tried to ruin last year."

"So, what do you want from me? A medal? You don't come here unless I tell you to."

"Please, Carla. He contacted me. Somehow he found out my number and now he's making threats. I need your help."

The intercom was silent for a long time, until a buzzer sounded and the door unlocked.

As Emily exited the lift upstairs, she saw Carla standing in her apartment doorway, hands thrust on hips, her face pulled into a sneer.

"I'm only letting you in to stop your whining," she said, stepping aside. "I bet you're one of those people who think it's cool to just pick up the phone and call unannounced for a chat too."

Emily grimaced. "God, no."

She quickly told Carla about meeting with

Jenna Laurent, the photograph of the dead investment banker, and the text messages from Cobb.

"He sent them from an unknown number," she said, showing her the messages.

"You know your phone is, like, five models out of date, right? Anyway, looks like he used a number masking service. Anyone can do it. You just visit one of the websites, enter the number you want to send a message to, type in the text, press send, and boom! It's a stalker's delight. And that shit is legal."

"Can you hack into it? Trace it back to Cobb's number?"

Carla snorted. "That's the whole point of those services. You can't trace them."

Emily pushed wet hair from her face and tucked it behind her ear. "What about the number I gave you? The one Cobb used to call Bridget?"

"I was going to call you this afternoon, but since you rudely intruded on my day off. . .To be honest, I didn't find anything. This guy is clever, and he knows his stuff. The number he used is out of service. The last person it was registered to was an eighty-three-year-old grandmother of three from Scotland. As far as I can tell, most eighty-three-year-old grandmothers don't know how to turn on a computer, never mind spoof a caller ID. Especially ones who are dead."

"Spoof a caller ID?"

"I thought you were a private investigator. Shouldn't you be up to date with these things?" Carla rolled her eyes. "Caller ID spoofing is when you hide your number from the person you're calling by making a different number appear on the phone screen. It's easy to do these days. You can even download an app. Because, again, this shit is legal in this country, so long as you're using it for privacy reasons and not to rip people off. Which means your friendly neighbourhood pervert could call you right now and make it look like it's your boyfriend or girlfriend or whatever. Or a scammer could make the name of your bank appear in the Caller ID, then try to trick you into giving away your security codes, along with all your money. The list goes on . . ."

Emily stared at her, mouth half open. "But Bridget called Cobb on that number several times. She talked to him. How is that even possible?"

"Call forwarding. You do know what that is, right?"

"Like when you miss a call and it's forwarded to your voicemail to leave a message. Or you set up your house phone so that any calls are automatically redirected to your mobile phone."

"Very good," Carla said, slow clapping. "So, Bridget calls what she believes is Cobb's number, when, in actual fact, it's dead Scottish lady's number. From there, the call is redirected—or forwarded—to Cobb's real number. Meanwhile, Bridget is none the wiser."

"But dead Scottish lady's number has been disconnected," Emily said. "Bridget tried calling it after Cobb disappeared. So how did he set up call forwarding on a disconnected number?"

"Because disconnected phone numbers aren't really dead. They go into quarantine for several months before being recycled and reissued to new customers. My guess is that our friend is hacking quarantined numbers and using them for call forwarding purposes. Once those numbers come out of quarantine for reuse, he switches to another quarantined number. And in Bridget's case, once she's served her purpose, he simply deactivates the call forwarding and she's left calling a dead number." Carla shrugged a shoulder. "I'm telling you, this guy is clever. He knows his stuff and he's meticulous. Which makes him a tricky character to catch."

"You almost sound impressed," Emily said.

"That's because I am."

What did she do now? If Carla couldn't track Cobb down with all her computer hardware, how was Emily going to?

"What if I could somehow get Cobb to call

me? Could you trace his number back to him?"

Carla laughed, shaking her head as she opened the fridge and pulled out a large can of energy drink.

"You know those things will kill you, don't you?" Emily said, irritated.

"Not if this conversation kills me first. And in answer to your question, maybe. If he's using the call-forwarding method, it's possible I could trace its trajectory back to him, maybe even track his geolocation. I'd need to download a piece of software to your phone and you would need to activate it when he called."

"So that's a yes?"

"It's a maybe. And it will cost you."

"Or you could keep the money I already gave you for not doing much at all, and we'll call it quits."

"I told you, woman. Time is money. Even if it doesn't get you results."

"And how long did that take you? All of two minutes?"

Snorting, Carla took another swig from the can then snapped her fingers at Emily. "Just give me your piece of junk phone."

Emily unlocked it and handed it over.

"You do realise you'll be handing over full access to me. There better be nothing gross that's going to make me puke." Carla crossed the room and sat down at her desk of computers and tech gear. Connecting Emily's phone to a port, she ran her fingers over a computer keyboard, and Emily's phone screen appeared on one of the monitors.

"You're not going to read all my text messages, are you?" Emily asked, standing over her shoulder.

"I'd rather watch paint dry." She glanced up as Emily leaned in closer. "You ever hear of personal space?"

Emily stepped back, wondering how Lee Woodruff managed to deal with Carla without hitting his head against a wall. But then Carla was leaning forward and whistling.

"Well, well. What do we have here?".

"What is it?" Emily asked, staring at the screen.

"Looks like someone's already hacked into your phone. There's a piece of spy software installed here. The kind that lets you read text messages, call logs, you name it." She looked up at Emily. "Didn't we have a conversation the last time we talked about not clicking anonymous links?"

"But I haven't," Emily said. "The only link I've clicked recently is one that my boyf—"

She caught her breath, remembering what Carla had told her a few minutes ago about text message masking.

"You have a boyfriend?" Carla said. "That surprises me."

It was Cobb. Of course it was. Pretending to be Carter. Getting her to click a link to download the spyware to her phone, giving him a window into her investigation. Emily shivered. It meant Cobb knew who Carter was. Just how closely had he been watching her?

"I'll get rid of it," Carla said, dragging the mouse pointer across the screen.

Emily shot out a hand and gripped the hacker's shoulder.

"Um, don't touch me. Like, ever."

"Sorry," Emily said. "But don't delete it. Leave it there."

"So you want a deranged nutjob watching your every move? Okay . . ."

An idea was forming in Emily's mind. A stupid and dangerous idea. But one that could work.

"Yes," she said. "As a matter of fact, I do."

CHAPTER 33

Pale blue light washed over Emily's face as she sat in the darkness of her living room, her mobile phone clutched in both hands. Cobb's words stared up at her, taunting her: I want you to mind your own business. This isn't your game. Stop trying to play.

She thought about how easy it had been for Cobb to install spy software on her phone by pretending to be Carter. It made her wonder just how secure anyone was online. Because it seemed if someone wanted to infiltrate your life or steal personal information, and they knew how to do it, it was theirs for the taking. And if Cobb had been able to install software on her phone in a matter of seconds, who else had he done it to?

She stared at his words on the phone screen, hearing Carla's warning in her mind. Time was running out. Bridget's first hearing was tomorrow and she was going to plead guilty. Her case would be passed on to the Crown Court for sentencing, and then she would go to prison. Her life would be over. Meanwhile, Cobb was free to torment and manipulate and control whomever he pleased.

Her thumb hovered over the screen, twitching as her heart argued with her brain. The last thing she wanted to do was endanger her friends and loved ones. She already knew Cobb was powerful, that he not only hid behind computer screens but behind the violence of others, controlling and manipulating them to do his will. If she goaded him, if she tried to draw him out, there was no way of knowing what he might do to retaliate.

Emily tapped the screen, bringing up the keyboard. She hit the back button again and expelled a heavy sigh.

Suddenly the screen lit up and the phone vibrated in her hand, making her gasp. It was Angela.

"How are you doing?" Emily asked.

"Hanging in there. I have some good news. If you can call anything good news right now."

"The photo?"

"You were right. Edelmann showed it to Bridget and she says it's the same picture Cobb used on his dating profile. The same username too. Shyboy88."

"Really? That's great." Cobb had messed up. Anyone else would have been cautious enough to use a different picture and username to ensure their crimes couldn't be traced. But for Cobb, this was a display of sheer arrogance. A sociopathic belief that he was too clever to be caught. That he was unstoppable.

"There's more," Angela said. "Edelmann's convinced Bridget not to enter a plea tomorrow. He says that's allowed with more serious cases. Whether she pleads guilty or not guilty, the case will go to Crown Court, but this way, she'll get a fair trial. And it will buy more time to gather evidence."

Emily bit down on her lip. A lot more time, she thought. Because from what she knew, it took at least a year for a murder case to go to trial at Crown Court. Sometimes more, depending on the complexity of the case, not to mention the number of cases already waiting to go to trial. Marc Edelmann would have already discussed this with Bridget, but Emily wondered if anyone had discussed it with Angela.

"That's good news," she said, clearing her throat. "Maybe that will give Bridget the hope she needs to stay strong."

"Can you do something with this? I mean, now that she's confirmed Cobb used the same picture."

Emily paused, conscious there was a possible third, silent partaker in the conversation. "Let's just say, I have a feeling we'll be catching up to Cobb sooner than he thinks."

"You found something?" Angela's voice

was filled with hope, making Emily shift uncomfortably on the sofa. But this was an opportunity she couldn't miss.

"Cobb thinks he's clever," she said calmly. "But he's a coward. He hides behind computer screens and fake pictures, too scared to step out and show anyone who he really is. But I might have found a way to stop him in his tracks. I'm going to drive down tomorrow. If you can arrange it with Edelmann, I'll meet you both at his office after the hearing. I'll tell you about it then."

"Em, I can't ask you to keep driving down here. I've taken up so much of your time already. Why don't you just tell me now and I'll pass it on to Edelmann or get him to call you."

"No. Believe me, what I need to tell you is best done face to face."

"Okay. If you think so."

Emily could hear the worry in Angela's voice, as if what Emily was planning was something terrible. "Chin up, Angie. The closer we get to Cobb, the greater chance we have to help Bridget. Talk to Edelmann and arrange a time. I'll see you tomorrow afternoon."

They said their goodbyes and Emily hung up. Her heart raced as she wondered if Cobb had been listening in. But then guilt pressed down on her shoulders. Was she giving Angela false hope? Because right now, she wasn't any closer to identifying Cobb than she had been before speaking to Jenna Laurent. But Bridget's change of heart had flooded Emily's veins with determination.

Opening Cobb's text messages, she read through them again: This isn't your game. Stop trying to play.

Emily tapped out a message: I have a game of my own. It's called Catch the Snake. I'm coming for you . . .

She pressed send and held her breath. Setting the phone down on the coffee table, she waited and watched. But as the seconds ticked by, as the phone remained silent, anxiety fluttered in her stomach.

Five minutes passed with no reply. And now doubt filled Emily's insides, making her question if she'd done the right thing. Because goading Cobb, playing him at his own game, could go one of two ways. Either it would draw him out into the open and force him to make a mistake. Or he would lash out, striking Emily where it would hurt her most.

CHAPTER 34

Monday morning came, wet and cement-like, no different to any other day that had passed in the last two weeks. Except today was the day of Bridget's initial hearing at Taunton Magistrates Court. At first glance, there was nothing imposing about the building, Bridget thought, as she was escorted towards the doors. Situated on St John's Road, a narrow residential street with two storey homes lining one side, it was yet another redbrick building on Taunton's urban landscape, easily mistaken for an office block or a leisure centre. In fact, with its two pointed roofs, it had an almost church-like appearance. Bridget didn't know what she'd been expecting. Something Gothic and imposing maybe. If it weren't for the towering police officers flanking her, or what she knew was waiting for her inside, she could almost believe she was here for something mundane like a job interview.

She looked up, suddenly realising she was no longer outside but inside a cramped waiting area, where she sat on a plastic chair next to Marc Edelmann, while the officers stood by the door, her cuffed hands resting on her knees. This had kept happening over the past two days—one minute she was conscious, aware of the world around her, the next, unknown periods of time had passed. Morning had slipped into afternoon, afternoon into evening. It was as if her mind were shutting down like a mobile phone drained of its battery life, and only sleep could recharge her. Not that she felt refreshed. Far from it. Sleeping on the thin blue mattress in that claustrophobic, sterile police cell, its only other furnishings a toilet and sink, was a far cry from her comfortable double bed at home. But she didn't deserve sleep, she told herself. Not for what she had done.

Marc Edelmann was talking to her, going over what would happen inside the courtroom yet again. He was a short man in his late fifties, with broad shoulders and thinning salt and pepper hair. His eyes were piercing blue and seemed to penetrate her skull. He was a kind man, she thought, with a great deal of empathy. Edelmann and her father had been childhood friends, and he had visited the family home on a few occasions. Bridget had always thought of criminal defence lawyers as cold and corrupt. Her fifteen-year-old self had told Edelmann too. "Why would you defend a criminal when it's the victim who's been hurt?" she'd asked him. Edelmann had smiled softly and replied, "Because sometimes criminals needed help too. Sometimes their story isn't so black and white."

It didn't look good for Bridget, Edelmann

had said back at the police station. It would be nearly impossible to convince a jury that she was a victim who deserved to be set free, but he was going to try his best. Bridget wasn't sure she agreed with him. A few days ago, she'd tried to end her life. But now it didn't seem like a fitting punishment to make up for the one she'd stolen. Rotting away in a prison cell, spending every minute of every day reliving the horror in Wendy's eyes as Rick Frost brought the rock down—that was more appropriate.

Bridget blinked. Edelmann's voice filtered into her ears. He was reiterating that today's hearing would be brief; no more than a matter of administration for the magistrates to transfer her case to Crown Court. Today she would only be asked to confirm her name and address, and to enter a plea. Inside Bridget's mind, a word screamed, over and over: Guilty! Guilty! Guilty! But Edelmann had convinced her to not enter a plea at all, which meant the case would go to trial. It would take a long time. Time in which he didn't fancy her chances of getting bail. She was being charged with murder. Suspected murderers didn't get to roam the streets while they awaited trial.

He would try to argue in her favour, perhaps suggest house arrest with strict bail terms. After all, the crime had been committed under duress, making Bridget a victim herself. She heaved her shoulders, wishing Edelmann would stop using that word. Victim. There was only one victim, and that was Wendy.

But if letting the case go to trial meant buying more time, then not entering a plea was what she would do. Because buying more time would allow Emily Swanson to track down Cobb. If Bridget was going to go down for Wendy's murder, along with that psycho Rick Frost, it was only fair that Cobb did too. Because if Bridget had never met Cobb online, she wouldn't be sitting here right now, guarded by police officers, her fate in the hands of people she'd yet to meet. More importantly, Wendy wouldn't be lying in a morgue, cold and dead, her body sliced open and sewn back together again with crude stitching. Wendy's parents wouldn't be in a state of grief and shock, their lives ripped apart, never to be repaired. Angela's wedding wouldn't have been ruined, and her eyes wouldn't fill with horror and repulsion every time she looked at her little sister.

Cobb. He deserved to be sitting here, trussed in handcuffs, next to Bridget. He deserved to be dead, his body blue and slowly decomposing inside the cold chamber where Wendy currently lay.

A woman had entered the room and was saying something. Bridget stared at her, watching her lips move up and down. But it was as if she were under the ocean, her ears flooded with water. She felt Edelmann gently squeeze her elbow. A police officer came over and removed Bridget's handcuffs. Then she was on her feet, being escorted towards the courtroom, where Edelmann had said reporters would be waiting inside. Where she knew Angela would be waiting, even though she'd begged Edelmann to make her stay away.

The doors were coming into view. Bridget felt her body pull away from them. Hands gripped her arms, and then there was nothing she could do but keep moving forward.

CHAPTER 35

The atmosphere in Marc Edelmann's office was heavy and sombre, the air thick and clammy. Rain drummed against the windows as the day turned dark. The lawyer sat at his large desk, brow pulled down over his eyes, hands clasped together and resting on his stomach. Angela and Emily sat together on the other side. Angela's face was very pale, the rims of her eyes red and sore-looking. Emily glanced at her, deeply worried about her friend, then at Edelmann, who seemed lost in thought, processing the day's events.

The initial hearing had not gone well. Bridget had been refused bail, despite

Edelmann's argument that Bridget had no prior convictions and that she too was a victim of crime. Now Bridget was on her way to HMP Eastwood Park, a mixed category prison for women that held both remand and sentenced prisoners. Serving Wales and the south-west of England, the prison was in South Gloucestershire. It was only an hour's drive from Taunton, but the short distance provided little comfort for Angela, who'd not even had a chance to say goodbye to her sister.

She looked up, fighting back fresh tears. "You should have seen her face. She looked so lost. Like a ghost. How is she going to last five minutes in prison, let alone months?"

"I'm so sorry," Emily said, squeezing Angela's hand. "Hopefully you can visit her soon."

"What if she tries to . . . I mean, there's a chance, isn't there? Just a few days ago, you had to stop her from jumping in the river."

Across the desk, Marc Edelmann cleared his throat and tucked his hands beneath his chin.

"It's early days, Angela," he said, "and I can't promise it's going to get easier. But right now, you need time to let it all sink in."

"Time?" Angela smiled bitterly. "If we don't find Cobb, time will be all Bridget has left. Time to rot in a prison cell. Time to think of all the ways she could have saved Wendy, or reached out for help. Until she eventually goes insane. That's what I worry about the most. That bastard has taken everything from her except her mind. But now he's going to take that too."

"So let's talk about that bastard," Edelmann said, staring at Emily now. "Because without him, Bridget doesn't stand a chance in hell. We need to convince a jury that she had no choice but to comply with Cobb's plan. That she was subjected to months of grooming and manipulation, then blackmail and threats to murder Angela. We need to make the jury believe that if Bridget refused to go along with Cobb's plan, that if she tried to warn Wendy or to go to the police, that Angela would have been murdered in Wendy's place.

To do that, we need concrete evidence. Right now, we have nothing. Just Bridget's statement."

"And Rick Frost's statement," Angela said, dabbing her eyes with a tissue. "He backed her story up."

"Forget Rick Frost. He's a dangerous thug with priors for assault, and that video will ensure he goes to prison for life. No, what we need is for Cobb to be identified and apprehended. But even that's not enough."

"Then what is?"

"Irrefutable proof that Cobb masterminded Wendy Wilson's murder, and that he blackmailed Bridget by making credible threats to your life."

"What about Jenna Laurent?" Emily offered. "She's willing to testify about what Cobb did to her. That's something, isn't it?"

"Yes, it is, and I've already spoken to Ms Laurent this afternoon. But one piece of circumstantial evidence does not prove a case alone, especially when it's not tied directly to Wendy Wilson's murder." Edelmann removed his hands from beneath his chin and linked his fingers behind the back of his head. "Angela says you have a way of catching Cobb. Of drawing him out into the open."

Emily's gaze moved from the lawyer to Angela, who was staring at her hopefully. "Cobb made contact with me. He sent text messages, warning me to stop investigating. I have an associate, highly skilled in technology. She discovered that Cobb has downloaded and installed spy software on my phone. It's still there, and I assume he's still listening to my phone calls and reading my messages. I've been deliberately goading him, feeding him exaggerated information, making him think I'm close to catching him. My associate believes that if he calls, she can trace him. She says hackers are not as untouchable as they think. It's all about reversing their trail and following it right back to them, if you know how."

Edelmann was staring at her now, his sharp eyes unblinking. "And what makes you think you can get Cobb to call you?"

"Because he's a psychopath. Psychopaths like to win at all costs."

"Psychopaths will also destroy anyone who gets in their way," the lawyer said. "It sounds like a very dangerous game to play."

"Men like Cobb think they are above the law. They think nothing of wrecking people's lives. It's a game to them. Entertainment. Cobb isn't going to stop. The fact Bridget's been charged with murder is only going to fuel his confidence and make him go even further next time. And there will be a next time."

"I don't like it," Angela said, looking up with wide eyes. "Yes, Cobb thinks he's above the law. So let the law bring him down."

"The police don't even believe he exists. We can't wait for them to examine that phone and in all likelihood find nothing there. Cobb is out there right now, laughing at what he's done to your sister. He probably even has his next victim lined up." Emily shook her head. "I've encountered people like Cobb before. They think they're gods, and that us mere mortals are toys to be played with then thrown away. He needs to be stopped."

"But at what cost? My sister has already been charged with murder. There has to be a safer way to draw him out."

"There isn't. Cobb has made direct contact with me. He wouldn't risk exposing himself like that unless he felt threatened, which means he probably hasn't been challenged before. He'll be watching me closely, trying to anticipate my next move. He won't be feeling completely in control. And when men like Cobb don't feel in control, they make mistakes. Mistakes that can be traced back to them. Mistakes that will get them caught."

Angela fell silent and stared at her hands. The rain continued to spatter on the windows, a soothing sound despite the tension.

"Cybercrime isn't my strongest area," Edelmann said. "But I know that it's continually on the rise, and police hi-tech teams are under constant pressure, with an ever-growing waiting list of evidence needing to be analysed. Even if you're wrong about Cobb somehow wiping Bridget's phone clean, by the time the police get around to it, precious time will have been wasted." He leaned forward, his eyes fixed on Emily's. "I don't know you. I don't know anything about your investigative work. My professional opinion is that your plan is reckless and half-baked. But I've known Angela since she was a little girl. She's a good judge of character. And Braithwaite Investigations has a fine reputation, so I can only trust that you're just as reputable."

Emily stared back at him. "I take my work very seriously, especially when friends are involved."

"I'm glad to hear it. The last thing Bridget needs right now is for someone to jeopardise her chances. I don't need to tell you that the press will be watching this case very closely, not to mention Wendy Wilson's grieving family. And it goes without saying that any evidence, no matter how incriminating or exonerating, should at least have the perception of being legally obtained. I assume you and your 'associate' know what I mean?"

Edelmann smiled wryly and arched an eyebrow.

"Of course," Emily said, keeping her expression neutral.

Angela let out a faltering sigh. "What if it works? Say Emily manages to find Cobb and prove he's responsible. Do you think Bridget will go free?"

For the first time since meeting Edelmann, Emily saw his eyes soften and sadness creep in.

"That will depend on the judge and the jury, not to mention the strength of the evidence and the case I present to them. I don't want to get your hopes up, Angie. The best we may have to hope for is a change in the charge to manslaughter, or a reduced sentence. If we can at least prove that she was under duress, Bridget could be out of prison by the time she turns thirty. At least then she would have an opportunity to rebuild her life. Unlike Wendy."

Quiet fell over the room. Emily stole a glance at Angela, saw her friend crumble in on herself, felt all her hurt and pain rush out like a silent scream. She thought about the danger she was putting herself in. She had come close to death before, on more than one occasion. Perhaps that was why she felt unafraid now. Cobb could destroy her and yet she felt strangely calm. She didn't know if that was a good thing or a bad thing. Maybe it was both.

CHAPTER 36

The day was already growing dark as Emily drove Angela home. Rush hour in Taunton was nothing compared to the chaos of London, and the traffic was already thinning out, each road growing steadily quieter as the car headed for the suburbs. Its passengers were subdued, the squeak of the windscreen wipers and the drum of the rain the only sounds. Visibility was already poor and it would only get worse with nightfall.

As she drove, Emily stole little glances at her friend. She yearned so much to take Angela's pain away that it made her chest ache. Empathy had to be one of the more positive aspects of the human condition. The ability to stand in someone else's shoes, to be aware of how they're feeling, to show compassion, it kept humanity from disintegrating. But Emily sometimes wondered if she had too much empathy. Was it normal to carry around other people's pain as if it were her own? Sometimes it felt as if she were sucking poison from a snake bite, but instead of spitting it out she was swallowing it down, the venom pooling inside her stomach. Sometimes she wondered if having too much empathy would be the death of her. But having too much had to be better than having none at all. She was sure that where Cobb's heart should be, there was a vast, gaping hole.

Emily shifted her eyes from the road to the passenger seat. "Are you okay?"

Angela heaved her shoulders and let out a heavy sigh.

"Sorry, stupid question."

Soon, the Audi turned onto Angela's street, where soft, yellow light filtered through living room windows and parked cars lined both sides of the street. Finding an empty space, Emily pulled over, but kept the engine running. Angela's home was three houses along to the right. The windows were lit up on both floors.

"I don't like this," Angela said, shaking her head. "I don't like that you're putting yourself in danger to catch Cobb. And yet, at the same time, I want nothing more than for you to catch him. For him to pay for what he's done to Bridget. To Wendy." She glanced over at Emily with sad, glistening eyes. "I don't want you to get hurt."

Emily reached over and rubbed her friend's shoulder. "I won't. I'll be careful. But you know this needs to be done."

"I suppose it does." Angela turned away again, staring up at her house. "What if Cobb is someone that we know?"

"I thought about that," Emily said, following Angela's gaze. "But I don't think he is. Bridget would have recognised his voice for one thing. And look at Jenna Laurent. She lives in London, has never been to Somerset, and her encounter with Cobb was over a year ago. I looked for a connection between her and Bridget, but there's nothing.

"I honestly believe that meeting Cobb was simply bad luck on their part. But for him, it was by design. He uses dating websites to pick out young women he believes are vulnerable, then he goes to work on them. He's a coward hiding behind a computer screen. And unfortunately, that means he could be anywhere in the country. Maybe even in a different country entirely. That's why I need to get his interest and draw him out. If I don't, he'll disappear and move on to someone else. He may even have his eye on someone already."

"What if that someone is you?" Angela lowered her head. "I just wish there was another way. I wish I could afford to hire you officially. At least then you'd be getting paid for putting yourself in danger."

"I don't need to be paid. You're my friend, Angie. I don't like to see my friends in trouble."

"But still . . ."

"Go on, go home. Spend some time with

Trevor. Let him take care of you for a little while. I'll call you tomorrow."

"You should stay. It'll be late by the time you get back to London. You'll burn yourself out."

"You both need to spend some time alone. And there's an insurance fraud case that's been sitting on my desk for two days now. I'm supposed to be working my way back into Erica Braithwaite's good graces. That's not going to happen if I don't toe the line."

"Whenever have you toed the line?"

"What can I say? It's not my strongest point."

They both smiled then.

"You sure I can't tempt you?" Angela said. "This rain is only getting worse."

"I'll be fine."

Unbuckling her seatbelt, Angela stared at Emily in the growing shadows, then leaned over and wrapped her arms around her neck. "Thank you. For everything."

Emily watched her hurry through the rain towards her house and disappear inside. She sat for a long moment, staring into space, until her gaze wandered down to her mobile phone that was sitting inside the cup holder. Tiredness crept in from the edges of her mind. She thought about Carter. They still hadn't spoken to each other. She hadn't even checked in with him, despite Cobb's text message stunt. Carter was clearly hurting. Maybe even questioning if Emily cared about him at all. The truth was that Emily hadn't given Carter much thought these past few days, her mind laser focused on catching Cobb and bringing him to justice.

Why couldn't she be normal? Any other person would have said yes to Carter without blinking an eye. But she couldn't help who she was, or what she'd been through. She couldn't help that the thought of moving in with Carter was more terrifying than deliberately making herself the target of a dangerous maniac.

She reached for the phone, then drew her hand back. To call Carter now would only invite distraction. And it would put him in danger, she thought, reminding herself that

Cobb was still able to listen in. Tomorrow, once she was done with the fraud case, she would drop by the workshop to triage their relationship and see if it could be healed. Or maybe she would wait until this was all over. Until she knew Cobb couldn't hurt anyone else.

Pulling away from the roadside, Emily got driving again, heading through the rain and the falling darkness.

CHAPTER 37

With Taunton shrinking in the rear-view mirror and the rain battering the car, Emily was starting to regret turning down Angela's offer. Both the A38 and M5 motorway were somewhere up ahead, but now the line of traffic in front of her was slowing to a halt.

"Great," Emily muttered, tiredness making her irritable. "What now?"

She squinted through the windscreen, watching brake lights glow like demonic eyes in the dark. The wipers continued to squeak, losing their fight against the heavy rain. Now, vehicles up ahead of her were making U-turns into the opposite lane and heading back the way they came. The car in front of Emily did the same, clearing her field of vision.

Two vehicles, one lying on its side, the other on its crushed roof, were blocking the glass-covered road ahead. Ambulances and fire engines were parked close by, while police cars created barriers on both sides, preventing further accidents. Paramedics in hi-vis jackets were stretchering a body towards one of the ambulances. Firefighters crowded around the upturned car, orange sparks flying through the rain as they attempted to cut off the driver door.

Emily stared in horror, her anxieties momentarily forgotten. A police officer strode towards her, shouting something as he lifted a finger in the air and made a circular motion, telling her to turn around. She did as she was told, making a U-turn into the opposite lane. Perhaps she would be staying at Angela's after all. Or a hotel. But if she stayed here overnight, it would mean another day of not working on the case. Another day of the client growing impatient and Erica Braithwaite losing faith.

Emily was desperate to get off the insurance fraud grind. If she didn't deliver that case tomorrow, she'd likely be stuck there forever. Unless . . .

She grabbed her phone and opened Google Maps. Keeping one eye on the road, she searched for an alternative route. If she headed to the A358, she could drive through the Quantock Hills then join the M5 at Bridgwater. It would add another forty minutes to her journey, maybe a little more thanks to the weather conditions, but she'd still arrive home in time to get six hours sleep.

Her mind made up, she dropped her phone back inside the cup holder and started following the newfound route back to London.

————

Thirty minutes later, she was driving through the deep countryside of the Quantock Hills. It was completely dark now, with no light pollution to help guide her way. The road was narrow with sharp corners, growing steeper at every turn. Rain lashed the car windows and streamed beneath the wheels, transforming the tarmac into an amusement park water slide. Emily clenched her teeth as she drove, ignoring the voice in her head that was repeatedly telling her to turn around and drive back to Angela's. But it was too late now.

The road seemed to narrow even further, twisting and coiling like a snake. Emily checked the rear-view mirror, saw a pair of headlights in the distance behind her. At least she wasn't alone out here. The road suddenly flattened out. In daylight, the view would have been breathtaking, but now all Emily saw was heavy darkness and endless, driving rain.

Her gaze flicked to the phone screen and the GPS map. A few more miles and she'd be back in civilisation. A few more hours and she'd be back in London, amid all its chaos and noise. It was strange to feel glad about that; the countryside had been her home for most of her life. Yet, out here, in the darkness, she felt ill at ease. Like a stranger.

The road began to descend again, sharply

now, forcing Emily to press down on the brake pedal. She lurched forward. The road flattened out once more, then twisted to the right, tall hedgerows flanking her on both sides.

Someone was calling her, the phone's ring tone blasting through the car speakers. The road twisted to the left. As Emily glanced at the phone screen, the rear wheels slipped in the rain and the vehicle began to skid. Gasping, she lifted her feet from the pedals and steered into the skid. Somehow, she managed to gain control. The phone was still ringing. Her heart was still thumping in her chest. Slowing her speed, Emily reached a hand towards the Bluetooth device clipped to the sun visor and pressed the answer button.

"Hello? This is Emily," she said, aware of the tremble in her voice.

"Hello, Emily."

The voice rumbled through the car speakers, strange and inhuman, as if it were coming from a machine. Despite the warm air blasting from the heaters, Emily felt an icy chill.

"Cobb," she said.

"The one and only. You've been a busy girl. Poking your nose into things that are none of your business. Even though I told you to stop."

The road turned again. Emily's eyes shot towards the phone screen. She needed to type in the code that would activate Carla's tracing software. Her fingers reached out. But then the road turned yet again, needing both hands on the wheel.

A flash of light lit up the interior of the car. Emily glanced at the rear-view mirror and saw headlights drawing closer. Easing her foot off the accelerator, she slowed down to let the other driver pass. The vehicle slowed down with her, staying close behind.

Cobb's strange, synthesised voice filled the car interior. "Emily, Emily. Are you ignoring me? Because I don't like to be ignored."

"I'm kind of busy right now." Emily's fingers gripped the wheel tightly, turning the tips white. Behind her, the other vehicle nudged even closer.

She needed to pull over. To activate the tracking software before Cobb could hang up.

But the way the other driver was behaving, pulling over right now seemed like a bad idea.

Emily lunged for the phone. With her eyes darting between the screen and the road, she quickly brought up the keypad and typed in the three-digit code that Carla had given her, then pressed the hash key.

The road dropped sharply, making Emily yelp. Tossing the phone into the cup holder, she returned her hand to the wheel. The car lurched to the right and clipped the hedge. Emily spun the wheel, correcting her course. Behind her, the driver slowed down and pulled back to a safe distance.

"Em-i-ly," Cobb sang. "If you don't talk to me, I'm going to get angry."

"Too bad," she said. "But yes, for your information, I've been very busy. I told you, I'm going to find you. And every step I take is one step closer to putting you behind bars, where you belong."

The car engine growled as the hill continued its descent. The other vehicle had dropped back even further now. But Emily was pressing down on the accelerator pedal even though she knew she should be easing up. The car gathered speed.

"Aren't you a brave little girl?" Cobb said, the unnatural voice hissing in Emily's ears. "I hate it when people don't do what I tell them. It's disrespectful. It makes me want to lash out."

"Well, boohoo. We don't always get what we want. Throwing a tantrum isn't going to change that. You've destroyed lives. Poor Wendy Wilson is lying dead in a morgue, her head bashed in because you thought it would be fun. I'm not going to let you hurt anyone else."

The road was descending further, tall trees growing up on both sides, their canopies masked by darkness. Rain lashed down relentlessly, the windscreen wipers struggling to clear a path.

"I always get what I want," Cobb said, his voice sharp and angry. "Always. That little bitch Bridget is on her way to prison. Just like that idiot Frost. As for poor, pathetic, little

Jenna Laurent—if you think you can use her against me, you're living inside a dream."

"You can't hurt Jenna," Emily said. "You failed to break her the first time around. What makes you think you can break her now? Even if you did know where to find her."

Cobb laughed. "I know exactly where Jenna is. I never stopped tracking her."

Blood rushed in Emily's ears. Her foot squeezed down, making the car speed even faster. "You're lying."

"Am I? You know, Jenna was such a troubled girl, long before I met her. It's such a shame that she'll decide to end it all tonight. And to think, she would never have been driven to it if you hadn't come barging into her life, dragging up all those terrible memories, making her weak, fragile mind finally snap."

"I don't believe you. You're bluffing."

"I suppose her mother will find out soon enough. You, on the other hand. . . Driving through the countryside in a rainstorm at night, it's terrible the kind of accidents that are just waiting to happen."

Emily's eyes shot to the rear-view mirror. Her breath caught in her throat.

"Goodbye, Emily Swanson," Cobb said. "I don't expect to hear from you again. Which means I win. And you lose."

The phone line went dead. Emily leaned forward, keeping her eyes fixed on the road, which bucked and twisted beneath the wheels, as trees closed in on both sides. Now, the other vehicle that had dropped behind flashed its headlights. It sped up, the roar of its engine drowning out the rain, as it hurtled towards Emily at full speed.

CHAPTER 38

Jenna Laurent sat on the living room sofa, with her feet up and her mobile phone balanced on her knees as she swiped through social media photographs of her ex-college friends. The TV was on with the volume down low, the canned laughter of a sitcom filling the silence. Thick, full length curtains were pulled across the windows, shutting out the night, while two table lamps illuminated the room in a dim yellow wash. She was finding it difficult to concentrate on anything. The lawyer, Marc Edelmann, had called earlier today. Jenna had told him the same story she'd told Emily Swanson just a couple of days ago. Marc Edelmann had a pleasant voice and sounded very caring. He'd told Jenna he was sorry for what had been done to her, and that he would very much like her help to put Brian or whatever that sicko's real name was, behind bars. Jenna had agreed to help, but now she was having second thoughts.

All those terrible memories were coming back, floating to the surface of her mind like drowned corpses. She thought she had buried them, that she had finally started to move on with her life. But it seemed the past had sunk its claws into her flesh and was refusing to let go. Maybe helping the lawyer was a way to finally free herself. Especially if it meant Brian would be sent to prison, where he'd be unable to hurt anyone else again. If only she didn't have to feel so afraid. If only those terrible memories would stop replaying in her mind. If only—

Out in the hall, the landline phone began to ring, making Jenna jump out of her skin. She checked the clock on the mantelpiece. 9 p.m.

The usual time her mother phoned from her night shift at the hospital.

Leaving her mobile balanced on the arm of the sofa, she got to her feet and padded out to the hall. Normally, when the nine o'clock call came, she would roll her eyes. She was almost twenty years old, an adult who didn't need her mum checking up on her. But tonight, the ringing phone made her feel more at ease. Besides, Jenna knew why her mum had to call every time she was left alone. It was because of what she did last year.

The hallway lights were on. Jenna glanced at the locked front door, then up at the staircase, where she'd also left the landing lights on. The phone continued to ring, making the small side table it sat on vibrate. Snatching up the cordless receiver, she turned to peer at the darkness seeping through the smoked glass of the kitchen door.

"Hi Mum," she said. "You on your break?"

"Yep. It's busy tonight." It was the exact same start to their nightly conversation. But tonight, there was an edge in her mother's voice. "Are you okay? I really didn't want to leave you alone."

Now Jenna did roll her eyes. "I'm fine."

"You've locked all the windows and doors?"

"Yes."

"Are you sure?"

"Yes. Seriously, will you stop worrying?"

"I can't help it. Ever since that private detective showed up the other day and dragged everything up again. . . How did she find you?"

"I don't know. Because she's good at her job, I suppose. But I'm glad she did. I spoke to that lawyer this afternoon. Mr Edelmann. I've agreed to help him."

Jenna cocked her head. Her mother had fallen silent, which was usually a sign she wasn't happy.

"Why would you do that? I thought we'd agreed to put this all behind us."

Here we go, Jenna thought, puffing out her cheeks. "Because he's still out there somewhere, and he's hurt more people. You heard about that girl in Somerset. About what she did to her friend. That was him."

"And what about the terrible things he did to you? We had to move house because of him. I had to change jobs. We had to start over. I don't think it's a good idea to be dredging it all up again."

"That psycho needs to go to prison," Jenna said, feeling irritated now. "Mr Edelmann says my testimony could help make that happen. Don't you think he deserves to rot in a cell?"

"Of course, I do, but—"

"I think it would be good for me to know that he was locked up. I'd feel safe again. I could get my life back. I could return to college and make new friends who don't think I'm a head case."

"Jenna," her mother said softly.

"What? It's true, isn't it? They all think I'm crazy."

"Your friends didn't understand what you were going through, that's all."

"Mum, they thought I was lying. That I

made it all up. And when I tried to ki—"

Jenna's voice caught in her throat as tears welled in her eyes. Perhaps her mum was right. Perhaps it wasn't a good idea to be digging up the past, after all. Not if it was going to make her feel like this all over again.

"I'll see if I can change my shifts," her mother said. "I know they wouldn't let me before, but maybe if I said it was temporary, at least until this is all over."

"Honestly, Mum, there's no need to worry."

"It's my job to worry. Especially after everything you've been through. I don't like this. I think you should call that lawyer tomorrow and tell him you've changed your mind."

"I'm not going to do that."

"Jenna, please! If it's true what these people are telling you, that he got this girl to kill her friend, then there's no telling what he's capable of. What if he finds out you're helping to catch him?"

"He won't."

"What if you get sick again? What if you try to—"

Jenna rubbed the back of her neck, feeling the muscles bunch together at the base.

"I won't," she said, shaking her head. "Okay? And I hear what you're saying. But he can't be allowed to walk free after what he's done. If there's a chance to catch him, then I want to help. Don't I at least deserve that?"

Her mother was quiet again. Jenna stood, listening to the ticks and creaks of the house.

"Fine, but I'm not happy about it. I'll try to get off my shift early. In the meantime, do me a favour and check all the locks again. And keep your phone with you. The slightest sign of anything strange, you call the police. You hear me?"

"There won't be any—"

"I'm not even kidding! The slightest sign. Understand?"

"Yes, Mum."

"I love you, sweet thing."

"I love you too. See you in the morning."

Jenna hung up and replaced the receiver in

its cradle. She heaved out a sigh as she strolled up to the front door and rattled the handle. Satisfied it was locked, she returned to the living room and pulled back a curtain. The road was dark and quiet, orbs of streetlight illuminating the rain. She checked the locks, shut the curtain, then moved on to the dining room. Finally, she entered the kitchen and turned on the light.

Jenna froze.

Her eyes grew wide and confused as she stared at the darkness seeping in through the open back door. A breeze blew in, making the curtains dance from side to side.

She had shut that door. Locked it with the key. So, why was it open?

Jenna tried to move. To close the door and lock it again. But her feet were paralysed. So were her eyes, as they stared at the rectangle of darkness. What did she do?

She tried to think, but her thoughts kept getting swept beneath waves of panic.

She should leave. Get out of the house and

call the police. But her mobile phone was sitting on the arm of the living room sofa.

What if someone was out there, hiding in the dark? What if the open door was a trick? A way to lure her outside and into their arms? Because if someone was inside the house, wouldn't they have shut the door to make sure she couldn't leave?

Jenna stared at the darkness and shivered. Maybe you made a mistake, she thought. Maybe you didn't close the door properly when you took out the rubbish earlier. Maybe you forgot to lock it.

No. She could remember shutting the door and the satisfying click of the key turning in the lock.

Sliding a foot back, then another, Jenna spun around and hurried back to the hall, her hand already reaching for the house phone. She slid to a halt.

The phone cradle was empty.

She stared at the space where the receiver should have been, her heart thumping so hard now that it made her chest hurt. She clutched her hand to her throat, felt the room spinning around her.

Sliding her feet to the right, Jenna peered through the open living room door. No one was in there. The TV was still playing quietly to itself. Her mobile phone was still resting on the arm of the sofa.

She lunged forward, diving into the room and snatching her phone up. She ran back to the hall and towards the front door.

She reached for the key. But it was gone.

Jenna stared down at the empty keyhole then up at the wooden key rack hanging on the wall.

"Where is it?"

She slapped at her pockets. She turned a full circle, checking the floor.

Her body was trembling now, her blood icy cold.

It's okay, her mind whispered. You have your mobile. All you need to do now is get out of the house.

Spinning on her heels, she rushed forward into the kitchen.

The back door, which had been wide open just moments ago, was now shut.

She was losing her mind. All these memories returning to haunt her again were making her unstable. Just like her mother had said.

"No," she whispered. "I'm not crazy."

Which only left one alternative. She was not alone in the house.

Tears blurring her vision, Jenna lifted her phone in a trembling hand and unlocked the screen. She brought up the keypad then dialled 999. She was about to hit the call button, when a breath, hot and heavy, tickled the back of her neck.

Slowly, Jenna turned around. She opened her mouth to scream. A powerful hand clamped over her lips, silencing her.

"Hello," a familiar voice said. "Have you missed me?"

CHAPTER 39

The roar of the car engine filled Emily's ears as the vehicle came dangerously close to her rear bumper. She slammed her foot down hard on the accelerator pedal. The Audi surged forward then down, as the road descended in a steep curve. The rain battered the windscreen and hammered the roof. Emily's heart was stuck in her throat. A drum pounded loudly in her ears.

Her eyes shot to her mobile phone in the cup holder then back to the road. She needed to warn Jenna. But now the other car was bearing down on her again.

The road continued to dip, plunging

downward into darkness. Shadowy trees whipped by on both sides. The other vehicle was inches behind, its headlights dazzling her vision.

Emily floored the accelerator pedal, hurtling downhill.

Voice activation. Why hadn't she thought of it before? Her fingers gripping the wheel, Emily cleared her throat.

"Call Jenna Laurent," she shouted over the din of the engine.

"I'm sorry, I don't understand," the cheery automated voice of her mobile phone replied. "Please say it again."

Emily growled. "Call Jenn—"

The car behind clipped her rear bumper. The Audi shunted forward, then sideways, veering towards the trees. Emily shrieked and spun the wheel, trying to gain control. The Audi slid to the opposite side of the road, then back to the middle. The other driver was getting dangerously close again. Flooring the accelerator pedal, Emily pulled away from him.

She was going too fast. The descent of the

road was too sharp. The weather, too treacherous. If she didn't slow down, she was going to die. But in a matter of minutes she would reach the motorway, where there would be the safety of other drivers. And right now, her pursuer was giving her little choice.

Emily sped on, the gap between her and the other driver increasing. But as the road continued to drop, her eyes grew wide as she saw what lay ahead.

This wasn't a hill. It was a valley. A large pool of rainwater had gathered at the bottom. Lying across it, blocking the road, was a fallen tree.

Emily screamed and slammed on the brakes. The car began to spin. And then the world shattered around her.

The side of the Audi smacked into the tree trunk with an ear-splitting crunch. Emily's neck was wrenched sideways as the windscreen exploded.

The driver's airbag flew up from the wheel, inflating in an instant, It smacked her hard in the face, slamming her back against the head rest. Her vision flashed red, yellow, white. Glass flew around her and rain poured in.

The other driver slammed on his brakes, filling the air with high-pitched screeches and the scorch of burning rubber. The vehicle slid towards Emily, inching closer and closer. Then nothing. Only the sound of falling rain and howling wind.

Dazed, Emily opened her eyes. She moaned as she tried to sit forward, then cried out as a jolt of pain shot up her neck.

Out on the road, the other car had come to a standstill just ten feet away. Now, the driver door opened and a man stepped out. A beam of light cut through the darkness as he pointed a torch at the wrecked Audi.

"Get up," Emily told herself. "Get up now."

Pushing the airbag from her body. She tried the driver door and realised it was pinned against the tree. Ignoring the pain in her neck, she pulled one leg up, then the other, and hauled herself out of the driver's seat. Somehow, her phone was still sitting in the cup holder. She snatched it up and slipped it inside her pocket, before clambering into the back seat.

Her assailant was walking towards the car, torchlight bouncing off the wreck. Emily made herself still as her thoughts struggled to catch up with her body. Did she run? Or did she fight?

The man was bending down, peering into the front of the car. Now, he was trying the handle of the front passenger door. But the impact of the collision had bent the frame.

Adrenaline shot through Emily's body as the driver sidestepped towards the back of the car. Bright light shone in her face. The man reached for the door handle and pulled.

Bringing up her knees, Emily kicked out. Her feet hit the door and it flew outward, slamming into the man and knocking him sideways. He hit the water with a loud splash. The torch flew from his hand, sending arcs of light spinning through the air, before plummeting into the pool, where the bulb shattered and plunged the road into darkness.

Emily clambered out of the car, icy water

rising halfway up her shins. She stood there for a moment, rain lashing her skin, pain shooting up her neck as she stared at the man. He was on his hands and knees, coughing up swallowed water, his face still painted in shadows. Now he was getting to his feet.

Emily ran, heading for the trees. She entered the woodland, the ground slick and sodden beneath her feet. Branches and thorny scrub pulled at her clothes.

She could hear the man behind her, his boots thundering across the tarmac as he gave chase. She ran on, kicking up chunks of wet earth, air burning like acid in her lungs. Suddenly the ground vanished beneath her feet and she was falling.

She hit the slope hard, knocking the air from her body as she tumbled and flipped, rolling downward, until she landed in a heap of limbs, face down on the swampy forest floor.

Pushing up on her hands, Emily sucked in a breath and flipped over onto her back. She lay rigid, trying to silence her gasping lungs, every inch of her body aching. She heard the falling rain as it slapped against tree branches and wet earth. But she heard no more footsteps. And just as the cold sank its teeth into her flesh, she heard the growl of a car engine.

Emily held her breath and willed her beating heart to slow. The engine grew louder, angrier. Then it was on the move, rising, fading. Growing quieter, until it was only Emily and the rain and the darkness of the forest.

Frozen and shivering, she staggered to her feet. Her neck complained bitterly as she crawled up the muddy bank on her hands and knees, then limped through the trees. She emerged from the forest like a nightmarish beast, her body caked from head to toe in mud, her clothes drenched and filthy.

The man and his car were gone. The Audi was bent and smashed, partly submerged in water, and fused with the fallen tree. Emily hobbled towards it, wading through the growing pool and climbing into the back seat. Her phone was ringing in her pocket. Emily pulled it out, dropped it on the seat, then picked it up again. She stared at the caller ID: Unknown Number.

"No joy," Carla huffed in her ear. "That clever shit is bouncing from one number to another, and I can't get a fix on how he's doing it. I need some time to think, and I need him to call again." She paused. "Emily? Are you there?"

Emily hung up and let the phone fall into her lap. She rubbed her frozen hands together, as she tried to quell the wave of anger and despair that was quickly rising inside her. With her fingers feeling more limber, she scooped up the phone again, swiped the screen, and dialled 999 for the emergency services.

CHAPTER 40

Morning sunshine filtered through parting grey clouds. The rain had finally ceased, giving the county some much earned respite. Emily had spent the night at Musgrove Park Hospital in Taunton. She had been x-rayed and examined, and while she was found to have no broken bones, the impact of the car hitting the tree had left her with whiplash and bruising. She had been given strong painkillers and kept in overnight to monitor for signs of concussion. Her body spent and her brain exhausted, she had collapsed into a deep sleep, until a nurse had woken her.

Now, she sat on a busy ward, with a

curtain pulled around for privacy. Detective Sergeant Wyck and a nameless uniformed police officer sat on plastic chairs next to the bed. Emily had just spent the last twenty minutes recounting the near fatal events of last night, followed by everything she had learned so far during her investigation into the man known as Cobb. She had left out any mention of Carla. Emily had an idea the young hacker's methods lay outside the law, and because she had failed to trace Cobb, there seemed little point in risking both her anonymity and her freedom.

Tired from talking and irritated by DS Wyck's sceptical expression and constant glancing at the wall clock, Emily leaned back on the pillows and tried to ignore the discomfort in her neck.

"That's quite a tale," Wyck said, flashing a look at the uniformed officer next to him, who was busy writing down everything Emily had told them. "I'm assuming you have evidence to back up your story?"

Emily shut her eyes for a moment. "That's

what I'm trying to tell you. There's been digital evidence every step of the way, but Cobb is some sort of computer genius and has managed to delete every trace that leads back to him."

"Sounds a little sci-fi to me."

"Well then, perhaps you should spend a week with your nearest cybercrime unit to learn exactly what modern day hackers are capable of."

DS Wyck's face turned pink as Emily glared at him.

"This car that was chasing you through the Quantock Hills—in the middle of a rainstorm with minimal visibility—you're absolutely sure it wasn't a road accident?"

"I'm sure. Maybe you should have forensics check what's left of my car. He rammed into me. You might find paint samples."

"A license plate number would be better. Or any kind of description of the vehicle at all."

"I was in the middle of a rainstorm with

poor visibility, like you just said. Besides, he had his headlights on full beam."

They stared at each other, while the uniformed officer shifted on the chair.

"What about Jenna Laurent?" Emily asked. "I've tried calling her five times. She's not answering her phone. Is anyone checking on her?"

"How can you be sure the same person who harassed this Jenna Laurent is the same person who allegedly manipulated Bridget Jackson into murdering her friend?"

"I already told you that. There are too many similarities. He used the same photograph and the same username on two separate dating profiles. Why is it so hard for you to believe, Detective Sergeant?"

"It's not that I don't believe you," Wyck said, checking the clock again. "But so far, the only evidence I have is a video of Wendy Wilson's murder, which puts the weapon in Rick Frost's hand and Bridget Jackson at the scene."

Emily shook her head and instantly

regretted it as white-hot pain shot up to her skull. "What about the phone Cobb sent to Bridget? Did forensics even look at it yet?"

"As a matter of fact, they did. The only evidence they found was the deleted video file, proving it was filmed on Bridget's phone. There was nothing else, Emily. It was clean." The detective sergeant sighed and linked his hands together on his knees. "I appreciate that you're trying to do everything you can to help Bridget. But the truth is that without a single shred of proof that Cobb exists, what can we do? Bridget has already been charged. All the evidence points to her and Frost. It's for the courts to decide now."

"And meanwhile that monster is still out there, playing his games. Hurting people. Killing them."

"I'm sorry, but it's out of my hands. I shouldn't even be here today." DS Wyck let out an exasperated sigh and got to his feet. "I'll have someone check on Jenna Laurent. But the best thing you can do right now is go back to London and rest that neck of yours.

You're lucky you didn't die last night." He stared down at the police officer. "PC Pearce here will finish taking your statement. I wish you well, Emily. And if you do find proof that this mysterious Cobb exists, then absolutely get in touch. But I'm afraid you're being sucked in by Bridget Jackson's lies. Look after that neck. Shouldn't you be wearing a brace or something?"

Pulling back the curtain, he gave Emily one last look, nodded to PC Pearce, then was gone.

Emily stared at the curtain as it drifted shut, her nails digging painfully into her palms. PC Pearce cleared his throat.

"What?" Emily snapped. "You literally sat there while I told you the whole story. You seriously need me to go over it again?"

PC Pearce swallowed nervously.

———

Two hours later, Emily had been officially discharged from the hospital's care and was free to go. Angela met her in one of the waiting areas. Dark shadows ringed her eyes and she was still terribly pale. But somehow she looked even worse. She stared at the bruising to the right of Emily's eye.

"Are you okay?" she asked, hands clasping and unclasping.

"A few aches and pains. My neck feels like the worst crick in the world. But they've given me painkillers."

"No neck brace?"

"They don't use them anymore. Something about delayed recovery time." Emily studied Angela's taut expression and felt a fluttering inside her chest. "What is it?"

Angela's brow crumpled and her eyes filled with tears.

"What?" Emily pressed.

"I just got off the phone with Marc Edelmann. It seems that, well, Jenna Laurent killed herself last night."

All the air flew from the room. The bright florescent strip lights grew more intense.

"Her mother found her early this morning

when she got home from a night shift," Angela said, her fingers twisting in knots. "Jenna cut her wrists in the bath. She bled to death."

Emily pressed a hand to her throat and winced at the pain. "It was Cobb. He did this."

A wave of guilt came crashing down on her. The room began to spin, patients and hospital staff becoming blurred streaks of blues, greens, and browns.

"Em?" Angela stepped towards her. "You don't look so good."

Poor Jenna, Emily thought. She had only wanted to help. To bring Cobb to justice. And Emily had led him right to her.

"Emily? Maybe you should sit down. I'll find a nurse."

"Don't. I'm fine," Emily muttered. She closed her eyes. Opened them again. The room ceased to spin. The lights returned to normal. "Let's get out of here."

"Do you want me to call Carter? Get him to pick you up from my place? Maybe you should stay the night, get some more rest."

Carter. Right now, Emily wanted nothing

more than to feel his arms around her. But they hadn't spoken in days. How would he react when he saw her all bruised and banged up, or when he learned that she'd almost died last night?

"No," Emily whispered. "I think I'll get the train. Can you drive me to the station?"

She shut her eyes again, a headache pulsing at her temples. Jenna Laurent's sad, pretty face haunted her from the shadows.

"That sounds like a bad idea, Emily. What if you get sick? And what about Cobb? You shouldn't be alone right now. This is getting too dangerous. You're not supposed to be getting hurt."

Emily said nothing as she stared into space. The other patients waiting to be seen all melted away. Angela melted away too, leaving behind an empty white space. Emily stood, face to face, with Jenna Laurent, the young woman's lifeless eyes piercing Emily's soul.

"Take me to the station," she said. "Please. I just want to go home."

CHAPTER 41

Ignoring Angela's repeated protests, Emily took the next train from Taunton to London Paddington. She sat in the train carriage, feeling shell-shocked and distant, the pain in her neck only allowing her to stare ahead at the back of the next row of seats. The two-hour journey seemed to pass in seconds, her mind a haze of troubled thoughts.

Jerome was waiting for her on the busy concourse. He frowned as he stared at her bruised face and stiff gait.

"I'd hug you," he said. "But I don't want to hurt you."

Lee Woodruff was parked outside. He lifted

a hand as they approached. Jerome opened the back door and waited for Emily to awkwardly get in, then he shut the door and climbed into the front passenger seat. He smiled at Lee, who raised a questioning eyebrow and turned to stare at Emily.

"Looks like someone had a rough night," he said. Jerome shook his head and gave him a warning look, while Emily said nothing.

As Lee manoeuvred through busy London streets, heading towards The Holmeswood, Emily sat in the back seat, silent and only half aware of her surroundings. Jerome chatted to Lee, trying to keep the mood light, but every now and then he would shoot nervous glances at the rear-view mirror, watching Emily.

"Is Carter meeting you at yours?" he asked, when the small talk had dried up.

Emily shrugged, then winced in pain.

"He does know what happened, doesn't he?"

"I don't want to talk about it."

Jerome twisted around in his seat. "You

haven't told him? When was the last time you both talked?"

The traffic slowed to a halt as traffic lights changed to red.

"Em?" Jerome leaned further towards the back seat. "Did you hear what I said? When was the last time—"

"I said I don't want to talk about it!" Emily clamped her jaw shut, shocked by her acidic tone.

Jerome shrugged his shoulders and muttered inaudible words under his breath.

"I'm sorry," Emily said. "It's been a long twenty-four hours."

The truth was that, right now, she didn't feel like she deserved Jerome's concern. Or Carter's. Or anyone else's. Jenna Laurent was dead. If Emily hadn't sought her out, she would still be alive.

Jerome was staring out the passenger window, watching the throngs of pedestrians. It was getting dark already, but the rain was holding off for now. The lights changed back to green and the traffic got moving again.

Behind the wheel, Lee Woodruff cleared his throat and glanced at Emily's reflection in the rear-view mirror.

"If you need a few days, I can take care of that insurance fraud case that's still sitting on your desk. I'll speak to Erica too, let her know that you've been in an accident and need to rest. I'm sure she'll understand."

"Thanks," Emily said, avoiding his gaze. "But I'm fine."

Lee glanced at her again. Next to him, Jerome shook his head.

"So, is that it for Bridget?" Lee asked. "What happens now?"

It was a good question. One Emily couldn't answer. Cobb had managed to eradicate every shred of evidence that proved his existence. He'd erased every trace, every path that led back to him. Including Jenna Laurent. How could Emily ever hope to catch him when he was always five steps ahead?

Her throat was dry. She swallowed, sending a bolt of pain down her neck and into her shoulder.

"Honestly," she said. "I don't know."

"Maybe you should sleep on it," Lee said.

Jerome twisted around in his seat again, his eyes softening. "If you can sleep with that neck of yours. You want me to stay over?"

Emily offered him a sad smile. "I think I need to be alone for a little while. But thank you. To both of you. I know I don't always ask for help when I need it. I know I don't always appear grateful. But I appreciate your concern."

Jerome was still staring at her, a deep crease etched into his brow. "What if he comes after you again?"

"That's a good point," Lee said. "Maybe you should take Jerome up on his offer."

Emily's eyes darkened. "If he wants to come for me, I say let him. Maybe it's the only way I'll catch him."

She leaned back against the seat. Her neck felt too big for her body. Her head hurt. She was beyond exhausted. If Cobb decided to try again, she would be in no state to defend herself.

She pulled out her phone and swiped the screen. Cobb could still listen to her calls and read her text messages. He could still access her phone's geolocation, which meant he knew exactly where she was right now. But Carla had installed an app of her own creation. One that would erase Cobb's spy software with just two taps of the screen.

Emily activated Carla's app, deleting Cobb from her phone. Yet she didn't feel free of him. She could still hear him in her mind, taunting her: I win. You lose.

She wondered if he was right.

CHAPTER 42

It was late. Emily sat cross-legged on her bed, a table lamp casting shadows across the room. She should have been asleep, but the pain in her neck was keeping her awake. So was her mind, which would not stop churning. Last night's car chase through the Quantock Hills haunted her. She had almost died. Again. Now, she felt lucky to be alive. Unlike Jenna Laurent, whose death would be ruled a suicide, even though Emily knew different. Unlike Wendy Wilson, who had been sweet and harmless, and whose brutal murder would be immortalised thanks to the power of the world wide web. Bridget was not dead, but her life was over. Angela's had been ruined by proxy. Yet Cobb was still a free man.

He had won. Jenna, Wendy, Bridget—their loss had been for nothing.

Emily squeezed her eyes shut and focused on the pain racking her body. It calmed her. Reminded her she was still alive. And while she was still alive, there was still a chance.

Getting to her feet, she hobbled to the bathroom, where she swallowed more painkillers. In the living room, she sat down at the dining table, grabbed a notebook and turned to a clean page.

She could not let Cobb win. But she could let him think that he had. For now.

Picking up a pen, she began to map out everything that she knew so far, beginning with the murder of Wendy Wilson and ending with the murder—not suicide—of Jenna Laurent. When she was done, she sat back and stared at her untidy scrawl, reading and rereading, processing the words, trying to make sense of it all. The more she stared at the notebook, the more her mind circled back to the same two questions.

Why had Cobb used the same photograph of Duncan Scott, the dead investment banker, to lure both Jenna and Bridget? And why had he used the same username ShyBoy88 on two different dating profiles?

Was it carelessness? Emily didn't think so. Everything about the way Cobb operated was meticulously planned and executed. He took great pains to cover his tracks, masking text messages, relaying phone calls, deleting every trace of his digital footprint, so that even Carla, a skilled hacker, couldn't find him. He'd also used two different names to catfish the young women. To Bridget, he was Cobb. To Jenna, he was Brian.

Perhaps it was arrogance. A deliberate act of recklessness to confirm his belief that he couldn't be caught. Until Emily had come along. But that wasn't the reason either, she was sure of it. Could it be the simple fact that the combination of Duncan Scott's good looks and the vulnerability of ShyBoy88 had worked so successfully with Jenna that Cobb thought it would work on Bridget? Possibly. But even that seemed clumsy.

Picking up her phone, Emily opened up the pictures folder and found the dead man's photograph. Why Duncan Scott? Had Cobb simply Googled 'handsome dead guys' and Duncan's picture had been the first in the results?

Unlikely.

For someone like Cobb, who was so deliberate and exact in everything he did, such a random selection would be grossly out of character.

Emily leaned in closer, staring at the dead man's picture. Was Duncan Scott the link that connected everything together?

Grabbing her laptop, she brought up the search results she'd previously saved and read through them again. Duncan Scott was an investment banker. He and his fiancée Tara Bloomfield had been killed by a hit-and-run, and the driver had never been caught.

Was there a connection between their deaths and what was happening now?

Starting a new Google search, she typed in: 'Duncan Scott + ShyBoy88'. Nothing of relevance stood out in the search results. Emily's gaze flicked to her notes then back to the laptop.

Clearing the search box, she tried again, this time typing: Duncan Scott + Cobb. But there was still nothing.

Growing frustrated, Emily leaned back and rubbed her tired eyes. The painkillers had started to kick in, making her drowsy.

Perhaps she was wrong. Perhaps Cobb really had chosen Duncan Scott's picture at random. She stared at the screen. Her eyes flew open.

Of course! Why hadn't she seen it before?

Returning to Google, she typed: Duncan Scott & Brian Cobb.

The results flashed up on the screen. Emily sat up, adrenaline making her body tremble. Five minutes later, she had found her connection.

CHAPTER 43

Wilson Peck was a tall and imposing man in his early forties, who lived just a three-minute walk from the South Bank and the flowing water of the River Thames. Emily had taken the underground to get there. All the pushing and shoving through crowded platforms and carriages had only succeeded in worsening her neck pain. Now, she sat on a leather backed chair in Wilson Peck's study. Bookshelves covered each wall from floor to ceiling, filled with reference manuals and theory books. Peck sat behind a sturdy oak desk, thinning hair brushed over his scalp and a pair of thick framed glasses magnifying his dark brown eyes.

"Can I get you a hot drink?" he asked, staring at Emily with his head slightly cocked.

"No, thank you." She changed position on the chair, her neck stiff and unmovable. Peck's analytical gaze wasn't helping.

He pointed his index finger at her bruised temple. "What happened there?"

"Car accident."

"Oh dear. I wish you a quick recovery."

"Thanks. Perhaps we could talk about Brian Cobb? It's a matter of urgency."

"Of course. What would you like to know?"

"Everything you can tell me."

"Well, let's see," Wilson began, drumming his fingers against his chin. "Brian Cobb was one of the most gifted computer science students I've ever had the pleasure of teaching. He had an incredible mind, mathematical in nature and unclouded by human conditioning such as doubt or fear of failure. In fact, Brian seemed more aligned with the computers he worked with than his classmates. Which, of course, meant he had very few friends. Outwardly, he didn't seem to crave friendship. He presented as withdrawn and painfully shy, to the point I wondered if he was, shall I say, different from most people. But when it came to computers, he was an incredibly gifted developer, light years ahead of the other students. I knew within the first month of teaching him that he had a very special talent. I'll even admit, I found his talents intimidating."

Wilson Peck smiled, staring at Emily's bruising again. "Are you sure I can't get you a coffee? Or perhaps some painkillers?"

"I'm fine," Emily said. Which wasn't true. She felt as if invisible hands were wrapped around her throat, throttling her. "Please go on."

"Of course. Brian excelled in class. In fact, he was so successful that by the time he'd reached his final year, I felt like I was the one failing. I had nothing new to teach him, to the point he seemed utterly bored. So, to entertain himself, he founded his own company. Now, I was expecting great things from Brian. I imagined him using his extraordinary skills for the greater good in vital fields such as healthcare or education. But no. Mr Cobb decided his interests lay in video game development. It was disappointing.

"Nevertheless, one of his few friends, a business studies major called Duncan Scott, offered to fund seventy-five percent of the venture, while remaining a silent partner. Duncan was from a wealthy family with influential connections. I was always perplexed by their friendship. Where Brian was intensely shy, sometimes barely able to speak above a whisper, Duncan was confident, outgoing, and full of charm. I don't know if he actually liked Brian or if he recognised there was money to be made by investing in his talents. Either way, ShyBoy Games was born.

Emily leaned forward. "ShyBoy Games?"

"An apt name, I suppose." Peck's gaze drifted down to his desk, where a pile of untidy papers sat in a filing tray. Removing them, he began to shuffle and tidy the stack while continuing to talk. "The company did well, developing simple games for mobile phones and making money from advertising spaces. Brian had a knack for creating games that were highly addictive, and therefore highly popular. By the time he'd graduated, ShyBoy Games had grown into a solid money maker and expanded into developing games for the likes of PlayStation and Xbox. Thanks to Cobb's talents, his games were wildly popular and the company was a huge financial success. Until problems started to arise."

"What kind of problems?"

"Although Duncan had initially agreed to remain a silent partner with majority ownership, and was busy with his own blossoming career as an investment banker, he was troubled by the person Brian had become. As I mentioned, Brian was great with computers, but not so great with people. It seemed the success of ShyBoy Games had given his ego a significant boost. Instead of the withdrawn young man lacking in confidence, he became arrogant and greedy.

Staff members began to complain about the way he treated them. They were expected to work long hours to meet impossible deadlines, often without extra pay. Anyone who dared speak up was quickly replaced.

"When Duncan found out, the arguments began. It was a power struggle more than anything, about who was in charge and who had the final say. Duncan owned seventy-five percent of the company, while Brian insisted he did one hundred percent of the work. They were constantly at loggerheads. But the trouble between them grew even more serious over a woman."

Emily rolled her eyes. Men. Why did they always have to fight with their penises?

"Tara Bloomfield joined the ever-expanding company as a human resources manager, six months before its demise. She and Duncan were already an item and very much in love. To be perfectly honest, I believe Duncan had Tara installed at the company with the sole purpose of keeping a watchful eye over Brian. The trouble was, Brian quickly fell in love with Tara.

He'd always seemed secretly jealous of Duncan. His good looks and intimidating confidence meant he always got what he wanted, while Brian always lingered in the background. Anyway, Tara started to complain that Brian was making her feel uncomfortable. He was always staring at her, and always managed to be close by.

"One night, she caught him following her around a supermarket near her home. He denied it, of course. Said it was a coincidence, even though he lived on the other side of the city. Duncan confronted Brian, who, in turn, accused Tara of trying to sabotage their friendship. Duncan didn't want to hear it and threatened Brian. For a while, it all went quiet. But then Tara gradually became convinced that someone was accessing her phone. She would find opened emails that she had yet to read. Text messages that had been deleted. I think you can guess who she suspected.

"It was the final straw for Duncan. By then, he and Brian were fighting constantly. Duncan announced he wanted to sell the company and make a killing. Brian refused, but as the majority owner Duncan pulled rank. A few days later, when walking home from a friend's party, Duncan and Tara were mowed down by a speeding driver and tragically killed. As you know, the driver was never found."

Wilson leaned back, the pile of papers now impeccably neat and aligned. He stared at Emily, his expression grave. "It was a tragedy. But with Duncan dead, a stipulation in their original agreement meant that Brian was now the sole owner of ShyBoy Games. And just like Duncan had wanted to, he sold the company and made a small fortune. If you ask me, Brian didn't do it for the money. I think he sold it as a final, cruel jibe. "

Emily's mind was racing. It all fits, she thought. Brian Cobb's ingenious computer skills. His obsessive nature. His hunger for power and control. Even the name of the company. ShyBoy Games. ShyBoy88. It was him. And he'd been arrogant enough to leave deliberate clues that had been sitting there all along. Like it was all one big game.

She leaned forward, returning Wilson Peck's gaze. "How do you know all of this?"

"Because the night after Duncan and Tara were killed, Brian came to see me," Peck said. "We'd always had a good relationship. He lacked a father figure in his private life. So, at university, I became his mentor. After he graduated, we stayed in touch from time to time. And even though I was disappointed he'd chosen not to use his skills for the greater good, I continued to follow his career with pride. That night, he showed up at my house in a state of deep panic. He told me everything, confessing that he had been in love with Tara, and that he'd always admired Duncan, wanting to be just like him. But Duncan's rejection had hurt Brian beyond reproach."

"He confessed to killing them?"

"I asked him outright if he'd been the one behind the wheel. But Brian simply smiled." Peck expelled a deep breath. "That smile stays with me. It was cold and empty, devoid of feeling."

"Mr Peck," Emily said, her pulse thumping in her ears. "Where can I find Cobb now?"

"At home, I imagine. That night, he made me feel as if I were a priest in a confessional box. Once I'd served my purpose, he left and I haven't seen him again. The last I heard, he'd become a recluse and runs a new software development company from his house." He leaned forward, his expression grave. "You told me on the phone that he's responsible for the murders of two people. What if it's four?"

"Then I say it's likely we have a serial killer on our hands. So, if you know where Brian Cobb lives, now would be a good time to tell me."

"A serial killer?" Wilson Peck had turned very pale. "What if he finds out I told you? What if he comes after me?"

"He won't. Not when he's behind bars." Emily stared at him, her eyes imploring. "Please. A young woman's future depends on me catching him."

Peck rubbed his jaw and let out a trembling breath. "Very well. But you didn't come here today. And you certainly didn't get his address from me."

———

As Emily limped her way back towards the tube station, excitement thrummed in her veins. Pulling her phone from her jacket, she called Braithwaite Investigations. Jerome answered cheerily, but when he learned it was Emily calling, he dropped his voice to a hush.

"Where are you? I thought you said you were coming into the office, even though you should be at home resting. Which I hope you are, even though it sounds like you're in the street right now. Anyway, Erica is asking questions. She's wondering why that fraud case is still sitting on your desk. She looks pissed off and I'm running out of excuses." He paused for breath. "How's that neck of yours?"

"It's fine," Emily said, ignoring the prying stares of passers-by. "And forget about Erica for a second. Is Lee in the office?"

"Yes, he is. You want him to take on that case? You know, like he offered yesterday?"

"No. I need his help with something else. Can you put me through?"

"Sure, but what about the case?"

"I'll get to it."

"And Erica?"

"I don't know. Tell her I'm running late. Use that brain of yours."

"Someone's in a bad mood."

"Sorry. It's this damn neck. So . . . Lee?"

Jerome cleared his throat. "Yes, madam. One moment, please."

Emily hissed as she stumbled over a broken paving stone and a jolt of pain shot through her neck.

Lee Woodruff's deep, velvety voice filled her ear. As Emily sucked in a breath and began to talk, she suddenly realised that Cobb was not going to win this game after all.

She was.

CHAPTER 44

Brian Cobb sat at his computer station in a large white room with no other furniture. The window blinds were closed and the lights were on, despite it being mid-afternoon. He stared at the multitude of computer monitors before him, the glare from the screens making his pasty white skin even more sickly looking. He had been awake since 4 a.m. He rarely slept these days, his mind always running on full power, processing information, chewing and crunching data, just like his precious computers. He'd been sitting in front of them for hours now, only getting up to grab an energy drink and junk food from the fridge, or to use the toilet. His back ached and his shoulders were knotted. At twenty-six years old, he should have been in better shape, but what he lacked in physical strength, he made up for in mental prowess and financial wealth. And money could buy just about anything these days, including a better body.

He leaned back on the chair, stretching out his arms then cracking his knuckles, his eyes shifting from screen to screen. He smiled. One screen displayed the private email account of a top politician. Another showed the substantial funds in his offshore bank account. Another displayed a text message thread from a mobile phone that he'd been monitoring for a while now. One that belonged to someone who had become a serious thorn in his side. A thorn that would soon be plucked out.

Cobb twisted his neck to the left, then to the right, attempting to ease the tightness in his joints. He had never imagined partaking in a life of crime—much less a life of cybercrime. But it had been so easy. His degree in computer science had provided him a basic foundation, but it was the hours he'd spent locked away in his dormitory room, hunched over his old laptop and accessing the dark web, that had been his true schooling.

He'd started small, hacking the social media accounts of his fellow students, then moving on to his university lecturers. It was frightening how easy it had been. But not as frightening as the amount of private information people kept on their phones and computers with little to no protection.

The stealing had come later, after dear, dead Duncan Scott had started throwing his weight around. At first, it had been an outlet for his frustrations; siphoning small amounts of money from other businesses gave him a thrill and a sense of control that Duncan had tried to take from him. But it was a temporary fix. So, Cobb began stealing more than money. Passwords, confidential documents, intimate photographs: they were all his to take. It was shocking what other people got up to when they thought no one else was looking. But even that grew boring after a while. Just like the success of ShyBoy Games, it was all too easy and oh, so tiresome.

Then Duncan had installed that whore Tara into the company. She was like a virus, infecting his psyche. Corrupting all his defences. He didn't know if it was love he was experiencing or a need to control. All he knew was that Tara was a distraction, one that Duncan had introduced to help keep Cobb in his place. Which meant Tara was a problem that needed to be solved. Just like Duncan. It had never been about money; by the time Duncan tried to sell the company, Cobb had amassed a stolen fortune that could have easily bought him out with cash to spare. No, it was about power. It always had been.

People took one look at Cobb's feeble physical form and saw him as weak. But in cyberspace, he was a god. All-powerful and all-knowing. Unstoppable. Or so he had thought.

He leaned forward, narrowing his eyes as he stared at the monitor displaying the hacked mobile phone. It had taken just one person to threaten everything he'd amassed. A single, weak-minded person who thought they could put him in his place, just like Duncan Scott had tried to. But a person, like any other problem, could be erased. It was simply a question of assessment and simulation, of testing their weak spots then attacking swiftly and without remorse. If Brian Cobb was good at one thing, it was making problems disappear. Problems like Duncan Scott. Problems like Tara Bloomfield. And now, problems like—

A loud buzzing resounded through the house, making Cobb jump in his seat. His eyes shot towards a small monitor, where a camera feed showed the front porch of his house. A tall, handsome man dressed in a navy blue suit smiled at him. He held himself confidently, his posture oozing authority.

Cobb stared at him. The only visitors he received these days were delivery drivers. There was the occasional salesperson or Jehovah's Witness, all of whom he ignored.

But someone in a sharp suit with an air of authority? What were they doing here?

Perhaps it was best to ignore him. Cobb turned away from the monitor, shifting his focus to the software code he was currently writing. The buzzer sounded again. Now the man was smiling and waving at the camera. Cobb huffed. That was the thing about problems. They didn't go away until you dealt with them.

Tapping an icon on the screen, he activated the intercom speaker.

"What do you want?" he snapped.

The man's smile grew even wider. "Good afternoon. This is Detective Constable Crane with the London Metropolitan Police. Could you come to your front door? I'd like to ask you a few questions."

Cobb froze. A detective? He shot a glance over his shoulder, then stared at the computer screens in front of him, all filled with illegally accessed accounts.

Was this it? Had he finally been caught?

Surely not. He'd been too clever,

eradicating every single pathway back to him. Unless. . .

He stared at the grainy black-and-white image of the man. His heart thumped in his ears. "What's this about? I'm extremely busy."

"Not busy enough to help with enquiries regarding a missing child, I hope," the detective constable said, his voice deep and authoritarian. "Please, come to the door. It won't take long."

"I don't know anything about a missing child."

"All the same, if I could talk to you face to face. It's just a couple of routine questions. Then I can tick you off the list."

Cobb's breathing was getting faster, his chest heaving up and down. "What list? You mean a suspect list?"

He stared at the monitors. Was it time to pull the plug? To erase everything he'd built up?

The alternative was to go to the door and answer the detective's questions, so that he would leave as soon as possible. Cobb had nothing to do with the missing child, but judging by the detective's expression, he was already arousing suspicion.

"Fine," he sighed. "Wait there."

He tapped the keyboard and all the screens went blank. He got up, stretched his spine, and left the room.

The hallway was painted pristine white, with polished cherry wood floorboards. There were no paintings on the walls, only a single hanging mirror. Cobb checked his ghostly appearance and quickly brushed his hair into a side parting. Patting out the creases from his clothes, he moved to the front door and pulled back each of the five locks that kept it secure. This left the flimsy chain lock. He wondered if he should leave it in place, but decided he would only appear more conspicuous. Instead, he opened the door just wide enough to fit his face through and squinted in the daylight.

Detective Constable Crane was tall and powerfully built, towering over Cobb's spindly frame. Up close, his smile was charming and confident. Just like Duncan Scott's had once been.

"Brian Cobb?" Crane said.

Cobb tried to slow his breathing. "That's right. Like I told you, I don't know anything about a missing child. Is it someone local?"

The detective nodded. "Missing since last night. We're conducting a routine search, going door to door in the hope one of the neighbours may have seen them."

"Well, I didn't."

"But I haven't described them yet."

"You don't need to. I haven't left the house."

"Not even looked out the window?"

Cobb glared at the man, anger brewing in his chest. Who did this arrogant piece of shit think he was? Cobb did not like to be questioned.

"Not even once," he said, and went to close the door.

Detective Constable Crane held out a hand. Cobb glared at him.

"Do you have any external buildings on

your property that a child could easily access? A garden shed perhaps? Or a greenhouse?"

"No, I do not. Now, if you don't mind."

"As a matter of fact, I do mind. Could I take a quick look? At your garden, I mean. Just to be sure."

"I already told you there's nothing like that here."

"All the same, it would really help the investigation if I could take just a quick peek."

"I said there's nothing in my garden. Please leave."

He went to close the door again. Detective Constable Crane shot out a hand and gripped the door jamb. "Sorry, just to be perfectly clear. You're refusing to help in the search for a missing child? That doesn't seem a little, I don't know, off to you?"

Cobb stared at him. His insides were heating up, the anger threatening to erupt. He pushed it back down. Something was wrong. This wasn't how police detectives behaved. At least, not on routine calls. And didn't they need a warrant to go searching people's properties?

He stared at Crane, who was smiling smugly at him. Something had changed in his expression. It was his eyes. They had turned cold and dangerous.

Something was definitely wrong.

"Fine," Cobb said. "But first I would like to see your ID."

Detective Constable Crane's smile grew wider. "Of course. You can never be too careful, can you? Especially these days, when it's so easy to steal someone else's identity."

He winked as he reached inside his coat pocket and produced a wallet. He flipped it open and held it up for Cobb to see.

Cobb leaned in closer, his eyes still adjusting to the daylight. The world flew away from him, then sprang back, as his heart smashed against his chest.

It wasn't a police badge that he was staring at. It was a private investigator license. And the man's name wasn't Crane. It was Lee Woodruff.

Cobb stared up at the man's face, whose smile split open into a toothy grin.

"Surprise!" he said, then threw his shoulder into the door.

Cobb staggered backwards, arms spinning like windmills, feet tripping over themselves. As Lee stepped over the threshold, Cobb managed to regain his balance. Turning on his heels, he dashed through the hallway and wrenched open the far door.

He flew into the kitchen, a shiny, soulless space filled with expensive mod cons that were rarely used, and slammed the door shut behind him. Then he was racing across the flagstone floor, towards the back door.

He had no idea where he was going or what he was doing; his fight or flight instinct had taken over, and it had very much decided to run.

Lee Woodruff had reached the kitchen door, his towering shape casting a shadow on the smoked glass. Cobb pulled at the locks on the back door, then wrenched it open. He slid to halt and looked up.

A woman was blocking his path. He recognised her instantly and a flash of fury shot through his veins.

"You bitch!" he hissed.

Emily drew back a fist and delivered a vicious right hook to his jaw. Cobb went down like a sack of rocks.

Emily leaned over him, one hand clutching her neck.

"That was for Jenna Laurent and Wendy Wilson," she said. "And for wrecking my car."

Another face swam into Cobb's vision.

Lee Woodruff smiled smugly and said, "Game over."

CHAPTER 45

Night came. Emily had spent the last two hours in an interview room at Charing Cross police station, relaying everything she knew about Brian Cobb and his crimes. Now, the physical damage she had incurred, including an additional fistful of bruised knuckles, was taking its toll. As she signed out at the reception desk and dragged her stiff, aching body through the waiting area, all she could think about was going home. Cobb was in a holding cell and his computers had been seized. He was responsible for murdering four people and would spend the rest of his life in prison. Emily had been the one to catch him. But instead of feeling pride, unease tugged at her senses. She just hoped digital forensics would find all the proof they needed to ensure Cobb never walked free again.

Reaching the glass exit doors, Emily stared at the street outside. Despite the late hour, central London was still teeming with people and traffic. A wave of exhaustion threatened to topple her, so she sat down on one of the plastic blue chairs in the waiting area and took a minute to recover. She really needed to go home. But first, she needed to make a phone call.

As Emily tiredly relayed the good news, the anguish in Angela's voice was replaced with renewed hope.

"Thank God!" she cried in Emily's ear. "What did you find on his computers?"

"I only managed a quick peek before the police turned up and took them away," Emily said. "Cobb was a busy man. He's been stealing money from all sorts of places and depositing funds into what looks like an offshore account. He's also been enjoying a spot of blackmail, as well as hacking into the phones and computers of people in high places, then selling sensitive information to the highest bidder. I guess the world of cybercrime is more exciting than a games company could ever be."

"And Bridget?" Angela asked.

"I didn't see anything. Not yet. But the police will be sifting through his hard drives with a fine-tooth comb. It's only a matter of time before they find the evidence to prove what he did to Bridget and Jenna. He's killed before, you know. He murdered his former business partner, Duncan Scott, and Scott's fiancée, Tara. Made it look like a hit and run. The police have seized his car along with his computers. Hopefully, they can link him to their deaths too.

"And to running you off the road."

"Maybe. But Jenna was murdered at the same time I was attacked, which means Cobb has someone else like Rick Frost doing his dirty work. Hopefully the police will find out who it is soon enough." Emily rubbed her tired eyes. "Cobb is going away for a long, long time. He won't be able to hurt anyone else. As for Bridget, let's hang in there and see what the police find. But this is good, Angie. It could really help with the trial."

Angela breathed into Emily's ear. "I hope so. Bridget isn't doing well. I spoke to her yesterday on the phone. She sounded so tired, like she's ready to give up. I can start visiting her in a few days. I just wish I could go now."

"Maybe seeing your face will help. Maybe knowing that Cobb's been arrested will help too."

The pain in Emily's neck was becoming unbearable. She rubbed it and winced as her bruised knuckles complained.

"I should let you get home," Angela said. "I just want you to know how grateful we are for your help. I'm just sorry you got hurt in the process."

"It's nothing that won't heal. Narrowly

escaping death seems to be part of the job description these days."

"Maybe you should go back to teaching."

"Or maybe I should take up self-defence."

They said their goodbyes and Emily hung up. Her sleepy gaze returned to the glass doors. If she didn't leave now, she would never make it home. But there was one more call she had to make.

"Hi," she said softly, as Carter picked up.

"Hey."

Well, he was still speaking to her. That was something, at least.

"How are you doing? Sorry I haven't called. It's been a hectic few days."

"I'm fine. And I figured."

Okay, so he was still talking to her, but not exactly on good terms. Which was understandable.

"Listen, I'm sorry," Emily said. "For hurting your feelings. For not being able to give you the answer you wanted. I guess I still suck at relationships."

Carter was quiet, the silence making her shift on the chair.

"I was wondering if I could come over tomorrow after work. Maybe we could talk about it some more. Try to figure things out."

Carter blew out a heavy breath. "Em, are you okay? You sound, I don't know, like you're in pain."

"I'm okay. A little worse for wear. But it's all good. I'm safe."

"I'm glad to hear it. I've been worrying."

"I know. Sorry. So, tomorrow?"

"Sure. Are you staying for dinner?"

"Depends on what you're cooking," Emily said with a smile.

Carter paused again. "Are you sure you're all right?"

"I am now," she said. "I love you and I'll see you tomorrow."

"I love you too."

Emily hung up. She knew she had a lot of making up to do, and she still didn't feel ready to move in together, but Carter was still talking to her. Small steps, she thought. Now, exhaustion was taking hold of her body, threatening to pull her back down. Ordering a cab, she pushed through the doors and stepped into the cold night air. Twenty minutes later, she was fast asleep on top of her bed, too tired to even take off her shoes.

CHAPTER 46

Emily arrived at Braithwaite Investigations just before nine. She had slept deeply through the night, until two hours ago, when the pain from her neck had woken her with a cry. Swallowing more painkillers, she had downed three mugs of coffee, then braved the tube to get to work. Now, she eyed the empty reception desk, before shifting her gaze across the room to Erica Braithwaite's office door. It was deathly quiet, like a morgue.

Sliding one foot in front of the other, Emily slowly made her way towards her office. She should have been at home, recovering from her injuries, but the insurance fraud case still sitting on her desk wasn't going to solve itself, and she would happily brave the pain if it meant avoiding the fiery wrath of Erica Braithwaite.

Where was Jerome? He was usually on time for work, which for him started thirty minutes ago. Emily glanced at his empty chair as she stole towards her office. She had just wrapped her fingers around the door handle when a voice startled her.

"Oh, Emily. There you are," Erica Braithwaite said, leaning out of her office door. "I was forgetting what your face looked like."

Her heart sinking into her stomach, Emily turned stiffly. Erica's arched eyebrows suddenly drooped.

"However, I don't remember it looking like that," she said. "I heard about the car accident. How are you now?"

"I've been better," Emily said.

"Yes, I imagine you have. But I understand the company car fared much worse. Thank goodness for insurance." Erica crossed the room and examined Emily's bruised temple.

"What were you doing in Somerset? Because I know it couldn't have been anything to do with your current case. You know, the one that still appears to be unsolved."

Emily stared at the floor. "A friend was in trouble. It was an emergency. And I'm sorry about the car. I got caught in the middle of a storm, and you know those country roads can be murder."

"Yes, well, cars can be replaced. In fact, there's a replacement parked outside for you. The keys are on your desk, along with some forms for you to sign." She stared at Emily with a hawk-like intensity. "Cars are not the only thing that can be replaced, Emily."

"I know. And I'm sorry. It's been a difficult week, but I'm here now and the insurance job is top of my list."

"I'm glad to hear it. Because I'd hate to lose a client. Or an investigator. Especially one that's been doing so well lately."

Emily squirmed, feeling like a naughty schoolgirl called into the head teacher's office. It wasn't the first time Erica had made her feel this way. She had a feeling it certainly wouldn't be the last.

"Well, I shan't keep you," Erica said. "By the way, have you any idea where Mr Miller might be?"

Emily had been about to ask Erica the same question, but remembering how many times Jerome had covered for her, she instead cleared her throat. "He texted me earlier. Something about a broken down train?"

"I see." She raised a sharp eyebrow at Emily, before turning on her heel. "Oh, someone called for you. Asked if you could phone them back."

"Who?"

"Do I look like I have time to remember names? I left a note on your desk, on top of that case file. You know, the one that's still late."

Fixing Emily with a final, withering stare, Erica glided back towards her office and shut the door.

Cringing, Emily headed in the opposite direction. Inside her office, she carefully slipped out of her jacket and hung it up. Her neck was hurting, and she desperately needed more coffee. But first she checked her desk. The case file was there, with the new car keys and insurance forms sitting pointedly on top.

"Subtle," Emily remarked.

Next to the case file was the folded piece of notepaper Erica had also deposited. Emily picked it up and read the message. She frowned.

It was from Carter. But the phone number he'd given Erica wasn't one that Emily recognised. She stared at the notepaper. As far as she could remember, Carter had never called the office. There was no need for him to, not when he could reach her on her mobile phone.

Unease crept over Emily, prickling on her skin. It was the same unexplained sensation she had felt last night at Charing Cross police station.

Reaching for her phone, she dialled Carter's mobile number. When he didn't pick up, she hung up and tried his house phone.

The answer machine kicked in. Emily hung up again and tried the number for Carter's workshop. She chewed her lip as the phone continued to ring. No answer.

Emily stared at the notepaper. She glanced up at the office door, then back at the phone number. Tapping out the digits, she hit the call button and waited for the line to connect. But instead of ringing, a recorded message immediately began to play. When Emily heard the familiar, synthesised voice, her blood froze in her veins.

"Emily Swanson," Cobb said. "You thought you'd won, didn't you? You thought you could beat me. But surprise! There's one last game to play. It's called Kill For Love. You have exactly two hours to put an end to the miserable life of Wilson Peck. He deserves to die for what he's done to me. You deserve to be the one to make it happen. If you fail to comply, someone you love will die. If you contact the police, someone you love will die. And if Peck isn't dead before your time is up, someone you love will die."

Emily's heart smashed against her chest. Cobb's strange, computerised voice continued, brimming with glee.

"I told you I'd win, you pathetic whore. Your two hours start . . . now."

The line went dead. The notepaper slipped from Emily's fingers. She called Carter's mobile number again.

"It's me," she said, when the voicemail activated. "Please call me as soon as you get this. It's urgent."

She tried both the house and workshop numbers again, leaving the same frantic message. She stepped back from the desk, her body trembling, the floor shifting beneath her feet, and opened the office door. Out in the reception area, the desk was still empty.

Emily called Jerome's number. When he didn't pick up, she left him a panicked message, then grabbed the notepaper from the floor. She redialled Cobb's number. Three high-pitched tones hurt her ear, followed by a pre-recorded operator's message: "The number you have dialled has not been recognised. Please hang up and try again."

What did she do?

She couldn't think straight. Her chest heaved up and down as she struggled for breath.

How was Cobb in police custody yet still playing his twisted games?

The wall clock came into view. 9:05 a.m. Which meant she had until eleven to come up with an answer.

She wasn't going to kill Wilson Peck. Or anyone else for that matter. She didn't have that kind of darkness in her. But until she could confirm Carter and Jerome were both safe, she couldn't ignore Cobb's threats either.

What did she do?

The truth was, she didn't know.

Grabbing the key to the new car, she hurried from the office and out through the doors of Braithwaite Investigations, praying that an answer would come to her soon.

CHAPTER 47

Forty minutes later, Emily was weaving in and out of heavy traffic in a black Vauxhall Corsa. Fear gripped her mind, making it difficult to think and to concentrate on the road. She had called Carter several times now on all three numbers, but he still hadn't got back to her. Where the hell was he? She had spoken to him just last night. How the hell had Cobb pulled a stunt like this while he was in police custody?

But as Cobb's recorded message replayed in her head, she reminded herself that this wasn't the first time he'd been in two places at once. The night Jenna Laurent had been murdered, someone had tried to run Emily off the road. Which meant that, while Cobb was stuck in an airless room being interrogated by the police, he still had people under his control. Dangerous people like Rick Frost, who enjoyed the thrill of inflicting pain.

Reaching the outskirts of West Hampstead, Emily swerved the car to the right and parked at the edge of a shabby courtyard, where twisting vines grew up the walls. Carter's workshop was at the far end. She hurried towards it, her neck complaining bitterly, and found two large padlocks securing the door. Cupping her hands to the sides of her face, she peered through a small, dirty window, then twisted around to face the courtyard. There were other workshops here, but no one was around.

Trying to steady her breathing, Emily returned to the car and drove for another five minutes, until she pulled into a residential street lined with large, comfortable-looking homes, and parked in front of Carter's ground floor flat. She knocked on the door then let herself in with her key, calling out Carter's name.

When he didn't answer, she checked each room, finding the kitchen neat and clean, with dishes stacked in the drainer, and the living room furniture recently polished. But no Carter.

She moved to the master bedroom, throwing the door open in a panic. Carter's bed was unmade, the sheets crumpled and pulled back. A table lamp lay on its side on the carpet.

Emily felt the room spin around her. She stared at the lamp, disturbing images taunting her mind.

No, she thought. Cobb was behind bars. This was supposed to be over. Carter was never meant to become embroiled in her work.

Her mind reeling, she backed out of the room and into the hall.

What did she do? The question repeated

itself, over and over. She couldn't do what Cobb was demanding of her. But if she didn't, terrible things would happen to the people she loved.

She took another step back. And sensed the air particles shift.

Someone was here. Behind her.

Slowly, Emily reached inside her jacket pocket and pulled out a small can of pepper spray. She twisted around, finger poised on the nozzle, bolts of pain shooting through her neck.

"Hey, it's me!" Carter cried, hands flying up to his face.

Relief flooded Emily's body. Still gripping the spray can, she hugged him tightly. Then she leaned back and punched him hard in the arm.

"Where the hell have you been?" she growled. "Didn't you get any of my messages?"

Carter rubbed his arm and stared at her. "I decided to take the day off. I wanted to make something special for dinner tonight, so I've been to the supermarket."

"But I've been calling your mobile."

"I left it at home. Is that a crime?"

Emily stared at him as tears sprang from her eyes.

"What is it?" Carter asked. "What's wrong?"

But then Emily's phone was ringing in her pocket. She pulled it out and saw Lee Woodruff was calling.

"You rang?" he said, his deep voice full of cheer. "Hey, yesterday was fun. We made a great team, don't you think?"

"Have you heard from Jerome?" Emily asked him.

"No. I just got into the office and he's not here. What's wrong? You sound a little—"

"I need you to go to his house. I think he's in trouble, but he's not answering his phone."

"Are you sure, he's not—"

"Please, Lee. Cobb's still playing games."

The change in Lee's voice was instant. "I'm leaving right now."

He hung up.

Emily stared at Carter, who was still rubbing his arm.

"Are you going to tell me what's going on?" he said. "You look scared to death."

But Emily wasn't listening. Who else could Cobb have targeted? It was uncomfortable to admit, but Emily had very few people in her life. It hadn't always been that way, and her circle of loved ones was gradually expanding, but as for Cobb's threats. . .

Carter was standing in front of her. Lee was on his way to Jerome's. Emily's elderly neighbour, Harriet Golding, had left her home for the first time in years and was currently enjoying a Mediterranean cruise with her son, Andrew. That only left—

Emily looked up.

"What?" Carter asked, exasperated now.

Emily quickly dialled a number and pressed her phone to her ear. When the call went to voicemail, she hurriedly tried the house phone. Trevor answered.

"She's not here," he told Emily. "Mark

Edelmann texted her early this morning and asked her to come into the office. Said he had something new to discuss about Bridget's case."

Hanging up, Emily dialled the lawyer's office and waited as the receptionist patched her through.

"She's right here," Edelmann said. "Good job, by the way, Ms Swanson. With Cobb in police custody, you may have just helped Bridget's case enormously. Oh, did you want to speak to Angela?"

Emily couldn't breathe. Her head felt light and dizzy. "No," she said. "It doesn't matter."

She hung up.

"Em." Carter placed his hands on her arms. "Tell me what's going on. What can I do to help?"

"It's Jerome," she said. "It has to be Jerome."

Emily stared at Carter. There was nothing he could do. Nothing anyone could do. Because if she refused to kill Wilson Peck, Jerome would die. If she went to the police,

Jerome would die. If she didn't kill Peck in time, Jerome would die.

She had no doubts in her mind now. This wasn't a joke. It was Cobb's final game.

"Em, you're scaring me. Please say something."

Emily reached up and touched Carter's face.

"I love you," she said. Then she kissed him softly.

"I love you too. But—"

She kissed him again, harder this time. "I have to go."

"Go where?"

"Don't leave the house again today. Lock the doors. Don't answer the phone."

"You can't just say something like that and leave. What the hell is going on?"

Emily pulled free from his grip and headed for the front door. She felt numb now, the pain from her injuries suddenly receding.

Carter was following behind and throwing his hands in the air. "Em! For God's sake, where are you going?"

But Emily was heading out of the door, leaving him behind, and hurrying towards her car. Then she was driving, eyes fixed on the road, as she headed towards the South Bank. Towards Wilson Peck's home.

CHAPTER 48

Emily pulled up outside of the house and switched off the engine. She was deathly pale and having trouble breathing. She had tried Jerome's number several times now, and Lee Woodruff had not been in touch. The temptation to call the police was still overwhelming, but until she knew Jerome was safe, it was too great a risk to take. Now, she had just twenty minutes left to kill Wilson Peck.

She stared up at the house, the pain in her neck returning with a vengeance. Tears welled in her eyes, spilling down her cheeks. She couldn't do it. She couldn't take a life.

And yet, if she didn't, Cobb would take Jerome's.

If only she had a way to find him. If only she could get to him before time ran out.

Emily hit the steering wheel with the heel of her hand. Her eyes flew open.

Of course. Why hadn't she thought of it before?

Grabbing her phone from the cup holder, she quickly dialled a number.

"Really?" Carla whined in her ear, without pausing to say hello. "You're just calling me out of the blue now, like we're besties?"

"I don't have time for your bullshit," Emily snapped. "I need your help. Now."

"Well, why didn't you say so? Is it that Cobb guy again?"

"Cobb is in custody, and I have a more urgent problem. If I give you a phone number can you track its location?"

"Yeah, that's easy. You could do it yourself with one of those friends and family apps. I mean, you'd have to invite them to join first, but—"

"Pretty hard to do right now because they're missing." Emily glanced up at Wilson Peck's house again. "Please, Carla. Two lives depend on it."

"So, stop wasting time and give me the damn digits."

Emily read out Jerome's phone number and told her to hurry.

"I'll let you have this one for free, seeing as last time didn't work out so well," Carla sighed. "I'll call you back in five. Oh and Emily?"

"What?"

"Take a pill or something. All that stress will give you a heart attack."

Carla hung up. Emily climbed out of the car.

If Carla could track Jerome's location, there was still a chance for Emily to alert the nearest authorities and find him before time ran out. She didn't want to think about the alternative. But now she had just eighteen minutes left.

Walking on unsteady feet, she made her

way towards Wilson Peck's home and pressed the door buzzer, willing him to be home. Twenty seconds ticked by. Emily pressed the buzzer again.

"One moment!" Wilson Peck's voice called out. A second later, the door opened and his imposing figure appeared.

"Miss Swanson, what a pleasant surprise," he said, staring down at her. "What can I do for you?"

"I have some news," she said, barely able to meet his gaze. "Perhaps I could come in for a moment?"

"Of course. I was just making coffee."

He stepped to one side, his large frame leaving little room for Emily to pass. But she remained on the doorstep, her feet fused to the ground.

Wilson smiled. "Something wrong?"

"No," Emily said. "Still a little sore."

She forced her legs forward, crossing the threshold and squeezing past Wilson, who shut the door then took the lead once more, beckoning Emily with a hand as he strode the length of the long hallway and into the kitchen. It was a large room, with chequered ceramic floor tiles, expensive looking wall units, and a kitchen island in the centre with a rack of pots and pans hanging above it.

Wilson pointed to a breakfast bar on the right. Emily perched on a stool and watched him move to one of the counters, where he added water and ground coffee beans to a silver espresso maker and set it down on the stove.

"I'm assuming the news is about Brian Cobb?" Wilson said, glancing over his shoulder as he lit the hob and fiery blue petals began to heat the coffee.

"That's right." Emily's heart was beating erratically. A large block of kitchen knives sitting on a worktop had caught her attention. "Cobb was arrested yesterday afternoon, thanks to your help. His computers have been seized. I'm hoping they'll tie him to the murders of Wendy Wilson and Jenna Laurent."

"Let's not forget Duncan Scott and Tara. This could be good news for your friend too."

"I hope so." Emily's eyes were glued to the knives. Cobb's recorded message played on repeat in her mind.

"I have to say, I'm deeply saddened by all of this," Wilson said, leaning against the counter. "But I suppose it comes as no shock, not after what I shared with you yesterday. I suppose we should all be thankful that Brian can't hurt anyone else."

Except that he still can, Emily thought. She tore her gaze from the knife block to stare at a cat-shaped clock on the wall. Fourteen minutes left. What was taking Carla so long?

"Emily, are you all right? You've gone very pale."

Wilson was staring at her, his large arms folded across his chest.

"I'm fine."

The knives called to her, luring her gaze back to their sleek handles. Could she do it? Could she grab one of the knives and plunge its blade into an innocent man's chest?

Thirteen minutes.

Her knee began to jig up and down. Her

fingernails dug into her thighs. If she didn't do it, Jerome would die. If she did, Wilson Peck would die and she would spend the rest of her life in prison.

Would it be worth it? To take a life to save another? One of the few people she truly loved?

"I see you're admiring my knife set," Wilson said, following her gaze. "Do you like to cook?"

"When I have time."

"Well, I can highly recommend that set. Kai Shun Nagare. Superior Japanese craftsmanship. The meat just falls away from the bone as if the blade is slicing through butter. They're a complete indulgence, of course, with a price tag to match. But sometimes, the finer things in life will only do, don't you think?"

Emily dragged her gaze away. Wilson was smiling at her. It was a strange smile. Behind him, the coffee began to bubble in the pot.

"Ah," he said. "We're almost ready."

Removing the espresso maker from the

stove, he poured thick black coffee into two bone china cups. Emily hadn't seen him take the cups out. In fact, hadn't they been sitting on the side when she'd entered the kitchen? Almost as if he'd been expecting her?

"It's very sad about Brian," he said, carrying the cups over to the breakfast bar and setting them down. "Such a shame to see extraordinary talent go to waste like that. But in every orchard there's always at least one rotten apple. Milk and sugar?"

"Just milk." Nausea climbed Emily's throat. She watched Peck as he fetched a jug from the fridge. "What do you mean by that? In every orchard?"

Peck returned to the breakfast bar. He poured milk into Emily's cup, then his own. "Well, I suppose, as a mentor, I don't like to see my students fail. I pour my heart and soul into imparting all my knowledge, wisdom, and skill, as a foundation on which to build their own unique trajectory. Brian Cobb took everything I taught him and he twisted it into his own beautiful, dark shape. But he was careless and arrogant. And now he's paid the price."

Emily stared across the breakfast bar, her coffee untouched.

"You sound almost impressed by him," she said. Her eyes drifted to the left, finding the knife block again.

Eleven minutes.

"Are you sure there's nothing wrong?" Wilson asked. "You seem very agitated."

"It's just that I don't think there's anything impressive about killing four people."

Wilson parted his lips, revealing a toothy grin. "What is it about those knives? If I didn't know any better, I'd think you were planning to kill me!"

He threw his head back and laughed. Then his smile faded.

They stared at each other, Emily's hands gripping the edge of the breakfast bar. The air between them growing thick and hot.

Ten minutes.

Emily's phone began to ring in her pocket,

snapping her out of a strange, bewitching spell.

She got to her feet, pulled the phone from her pocket. "Excuse me. I need to take this as a matter of urgency."

She turned to leave, but Wilson held up a hand.

"No, no. You stay right here. I'll step out."

Flashing another smile at Emily, he circled the breakfast bar and strode out of the room, his powerful frame almost filling the doorway.

Emily waited until he was gone then pressed the phone to her ear.

"What took you so damn long?" she hissed.

"Well, excuse me for having a full bladder," Carla said. "Do you want the location or not?"

A surge of relief shot through Emily's veins, but it was short lived. There were just nine minutes left.

"Where is he?"

"Church Road, Battersea."

"What?" Emily's heart caught in her throat. "No, there has to be a mistake."

"Do you know who you're talking to? I don't make mistakes."

Slowly, Emily turned to face the open kitchen door, her eyes fixing on the empty hallway beyond. "But that's where I am right now."

"Well then, why are you—"

Carla's voice suddenly cut out as the line went dead. Emily stared at the phone screen: No Service.

She looked up. She was never meant to kill Wilson Peck. He had lured her here. To die.

Striding over to the kitchen counter, she pulled the largest knife from the block and brandished it in a trembling hand. With the other, she checked the phone screen again. Still no signal. Peck was using some kind of signal jammer to prevent her from calling for help.

Emily hurried towards the far end of the kitchen and the back door. It wouldn't budge and there was no keyhole, which meant the door had electronic locks. Not that she could leave when Jerome was here, somewhere inside the house.

Blood pulsing in her ears, Emily crossed the room, heading for the open door. She leaned out and peered down the length of the hallway. The house was quiet. Wilson Peck was hiding somewhere.

There were four doors on the left of the hallway, with the staircase climbing up on the right. Emily crept forward and reached the first door. She pushed it open, the knife wavering in front of her. Peck's study, where she had sat with him yesterday, was empty. She slid one foot back towards the hall. Then the other.

A sudden crackling filled the air. Emily glanced up and saw a small, round speaker fixed in the ceiling.

"I have a confession to make," Peck said, his voice rumbling through the speaker. "There was a small part of me that didn't think you'd show up today. That I was wrong about you. But here you are."

"Where's Jerome?" Emily cried. "What have you done to him?"

"Oh yes. Mr Miller. The question you should be asking isn't what I've done to him, but why did I choose him in the first place? Because wouldn't the obvious choice have been your beau, Carter West? The one you should love with all your heart?"

Emily crept forward, reaching the next door and pulling it open. Inside was a small closet containing a vacuum cleaner and a box of polishes and sprays.

"Try again," Peck said.

Emily glanced up and saw the red light of a small security camera staring down at her. She moved away. The camera swivelled, following her movements.

"Back to Mr West," Peck said, his disembodied voice filling the hallway. "He was going to be my first choice, until I realised you wouldn't care if he lived or died. You've barely spoken to the man in days. Even when you have, it's been brief at best. Those aren't the actions of someone in love."

"What would you know about love?" Emily hissed, as she hurried to the next door and tugged on the handle. In front of her, a wooden staircase descended into pure darkness.

"Getting warmer," Peck said. "And you're right. I don't know much about love. But I know enough to recognise it when I see it. Like Jenna Laurent. She loved me. Or, at least, the version I projected. And dear, pathetic Bridget. It didn't take much to make her fall head over heels at all."

Emily stared into the darkness of the basement. The knife trembled in her hand.

Peck continued, his strange, metallic voice reverberating around her. "I think you and I are alike, Emily. Having watched you these past few days, I can tell we think the same about people. That, for the most part, they're inherently stupid and easily manipulated. All it takes is a few words here, a few suggestions there, and you can make them do anything you want, like dumb, little meat puppets. You can make them laugh and you can make them cry. You can inflate their egos and then break their hearts. You can make them steal, hurt, kill. You can even make them jump off the roof of a school building . . .”

Startled, Emily looked up.

“That's right,” Peck said. “I know everything about you. As much as you love to condemn people like me, you're just the same. A killer. Devoid of remorse and hungry for violence. That's why you came today, isn't it? Because you felt that desire burning inside you. To hurt. To tear flesh from bone.”

“I'm nothing like you!” Emily screamed. She swayed on the top step, a chill blowing up from below as memories assaulted her mind. Pushing them away, she reached for the light switch. She flicked it, but nothing happened.

“I've been meaning to change that bulb,” Peck said, his voice seemingly everywhere. Emily stared into the darkness and saw another red camera light winking at her from the shadows. Slowly, she began to descend the stairs.

“You and Cobb, you both want to change the world, to bend it to your will. But what you both lack is discipline. Cobb had the potential to be a criminal mastermind, yet his desperate need to control the people around him was ultimately his undoing. It's true what I told you —that he came to me that night. But what I didn't tell you is that he confessed to killing Duncan Scott and that tiresome whore of his. And just like that, in a single instant, Cobb was under my control."

Emily reached the bottom step. The darkness swarmed around her. Taking out her phone, she activated the light, painting tall shelves and stone walls in a pale blue wash.

"Once that happened, I lost all respect for him," Peck said. "People are so disappointing. Take Bridget, for example. I'd barely got started with her and she turns into a blubbering wreck. Then she goes crying to you, a sad, little tell-tale. As for Rick Frost, that Neanderthal barely had two brain cells to rub together. The promise of money and a little stroke to his violent ego was all it took to make his hands bloody. Where's the challenge? I suppose dear Wendy's murder gave me a little thrill, but then like everything else, it grew boring. That's why I went to see Jenna."

Emily shuffled further into the basement. There were more speakers down here. Peck's voice swirled around her, penetrating her skull, until he was speaking inside her mind.

"You know, I'd never killed anyone until then. It seemed like dirty work, something for others to take care of. But to see the life fade from her eyes. To hold her down while the blood oozed from her body—it made me feel powerful. Giddy. I daresay it gave me a taste for it. Which brings me to you."

Emily was half listening as she weaved between the maze of tall shelves, the phone light making shadows dance like dark spirits on the ceiling.

"Jerome?" she hissed. "Are you here?"

Peck's voice rumbled all around her. "You see, you're a complication. An anomaly that I hadn't anticipated. I have to admit you're cleverer than most. But that's why I had to bring you here. One last little game for you to play before you disappear . . ."

Emily cleared the shelves, moving into a rectangular empty space surrounded by shadows. She turned a full circle, knife swinging dangerously in her hand. Silence enveloped the basement.

"Jerome!" she cried, her terrified voice bouncing off the wall.

She spun around, swiping the blade at the darkness. Sucking in dust and mildew.

Jerome wasn't here.

But someone else was.

She felt him behind her. Sneaking through the darkness. The air particles shifting out of his way. Emily turned.

A blood-curdling scream shattered the silence as Wilson Peck's powerful frame burst from the darkness. Spittle flew from his mouth. His face twisted into a grotesque mask. In his hand was a heavy wooden mallet, which he swung at her.

Emily recoiled, dropping the phone and plunging the cellar into darkness. She gripped the knife in both hands.

The force of a speeding train hit her square

on, lifting her off her feet and slamming her into the wall. She felt the knife sink into flesh and scrape against bone.

The world turned white. Then yellow. Then red.

For a moment, she was falling through space, with no awareness of where she was. Then the ground slammed into her back, and an unbearable weight fell on top of her.

Warm wetness seeped through her clothes. A ragged breath rattled in her ear. Wilson Peck grew still.

Gasping for air, Emily squirmed beneath his weight. The smell of blood, sticky and metallic, invaded her senses. She cried out, pushing against his body, dragging herself out, inch by inch. Until she was free.

Clambering to her feet, she stood, swaying in the darkness. Floating in it. She turned and saw a thin, vertical strip of light. A door, left slightly open. She staggered towards it, each footfall weighted with pain. She pulled on the handle, turning the strip of light into an arc that illuminated the basement.

Wilson Peck was flat on his back, his dead eyes staring up at the ceiling. The kitchen knife was plunged deep inside his chest, right up to the hilt. Emily stared at the dark red stain painting his shirt. She had done that. She had taken his life.

Her phone lay on the ground, near her feet. She bent down and scooped it up, before stumbling through the doorway.

The room inside was small and claustrophobic, with a wide desk in the centre filled with computer keyboards, electronic devices, and a jumble of wires all knotted together like a nest of vipers. Rows of computer screens covered the far wall like wallpaper, right up to the ceiling.

Each screen was a secret window into someone else's life. A social media profile. An email account. A hacked webcam, watching the watcher. Cooling fans filled the air with a calming buzz as Emily stared at the screens, transfixed.

A loud ringing tore her from their hypnotic power. She stared numbly at the phone in her hand. Her signal was back. But it wasn't her phone that was ringing.

Her eyes moved down to the desk, where the blue screen of another phone was glowing between the keyboards. She stepped forward and picked it up.

"Hello?" Her voice sounded a million miles away from her ears.

"Em?" The voice was familiar, pushing through the numbness. "Em? Is that you? How the hell do you have my phone?"

Emily frowned. "Jerome?"

"Okay, now I'm confused. Because I was out last night for a few drinks. Okay, maybe more than a few. Some bastard lifted my phone from my pocket. Which meant I didn't have my alarm this morning and I totally overslept. The next thing I know, PI Handsome is breaking down my door and all hell is breaking loose. You want to tell me what's going on?"

Emily shook her head. A bolt of white lightning shot through her neck.

"I'm going to kill you, that's what's going on," she said

But as the words left her mouth, she regretted each one. Because she had killed someone. He was lying dead outside this room. And it hadn't felt exciting or thrilling like Wilson Peck had said. It had made her sick to her stomach and filled with horror.

Kill for kicks. Kill for love. Kill or be killed. It all ended the same—with blood on your hands and ghosts haunting your nightmares for the rest of your life.

Emily's life was already filled with ghosts. She supposed there was always room for one more.

CHAPTER 49

The visitor centre at HMP Eastwood Park was filled with nervous anticipation, as families sat at tables and waited for their loved ones. Angela's gaze flitted from the prison guards standing at the side of the room to the electronic doors in the far wall. Sitting next to her, Emily offered her a comforting smile, but it did little to appease her anxiety. The doors unlocked and a line of female prisoners flanked by more guards were brought in. One by one, the women left the line and moved towards their families, some with open arms, others slipping into empty chairs and regarding their visitors coolly.

Bridget was brought in last. Her appearance was shocking. She had lost weight and her clothes swamped her body. Her skin was pale, her face gaunt and haunted. As she approached the table, Angela jumped to her feet and threw her arms around her sister.

"You're too thin," she said. "Aren't you eating?"

Bridget slipped from Angela's embrace and they both sat down. Angela reached a hand across the table, but Bridget didn't take it. It was as if her body was running on autopilot, her mind someplace else.

"Bridget?" Angela tried again. "How are you coping?"

Now Bridget was staring at Emily, a crease appearing between her eyebrows.

"What happened to your face?" she asked.

Emily reached for her bruised temple. "I had an argument with a tree and lost."

"It looks sore."

"You should see the tree."

"We have some news," Angela said,

leaning forward. "Marc Edelmann will fill you in properly, but he said I could tell you first."

For the first time since she'd entered the room, Bridget looked at her sister. "What news?"

"The man who did this to you," Angela said. "He's dead."

A light switched on in Bridget's eyes. "Dead? How?"

Angela glanced at Emily, waiting for her to explain. But Emily was back in the cold, dank cellar, darkness pushing down her throat, a terrifying, unbridled scream curdling her blood.

"Because I killed him," she whispered.

She began to tell Bridget the whole story. Wilson Peck was a former university lecturer in computer science, who also happened to be a dangerous psychopath with a penchant for vulnerable young women. After taking an 'early retirement', following a stalking allegation made by a former student, Peck took to creating false online personas and stalking women via dating websites. Once he had reeled them in, just like he had done to

Bridget, his true identity was revealed—a cruel and unbalanced man, who enjoyed manipulating and controlling others, forcing them to commit terrible acts for his own personal enjoyment.

"Brian Cobb was a former student of Peck's, whom he'd taken under his wing and mentored. I suspect in more ways than one," Emily explained. "Cobb had his own sociopathic tendencies and a talent for cybercrime. He came to Peck one night, deeply upset, and confessed that he'd killed his business partner and fiancée in a fit of jealous rage. Peck saw an opportunity. He blackmailed Cobb and, just like that, had him under his control.

"Peck had Cobb driving up and down to Somerset, following me around and reporting back. It was Cobb who drove me off the road. Forensics found damage to his car's front bumper, as well as matching soil samples. But it was Wilson Peck who murdered Jenna Laurent, who conned Rick Frost into killing Wendy Wilson, and who forced you into an impossible position. And it was Wilson Peck who lured me to his home."

A little colour had returned to Bridget's complexion. "Brian Cobb," she said. "Peck was going to frame him for . . . for what we did to Wendy? And to that other girl?"

"He must have planned it from the moment Cobb confessed to the hit and run. He planted little seeds along the way, using Cobb's name to catfish both you and Jenna, as well as the name of Cobb's games company. Shyboy Games becomes Shyboy88. When I first turned up at Peck's house, he must have known it wouldn't be long until I caught up with him. So, he put his contingency plan of framing Cobb into action. It wouldn't matter what Cobb told the police about Peck; he'd already committed murder and stolen millions, so why would they believe a word about a crazy, blackmailing ex-university lecturer? It was all neat and tidy. Except for one small problem. Me."

Emily paused, Peck's twisted, demonic face pouncing at her from the shadows of her mind. "I suppose Peck didn't want to take any chances. So, with Cobb out of the picture, he decided to take matters into his own hands. Unfortunately for him, it backfired."

"So what now?" Bridget asked. She was almost animated, her eyes darting back and forth as she stared at Emily.

"Well, the good news is that both Peck and Cobb's computers were retrieved intact. From the little I saw, there's enough incriminating evidence to keep the police busy for months."

"Marc is on the case," Angela said, leaning forward. "He says as soon as the computers have been analysed and the evidence logged, he'll request all the files and go through them with a fine-tooth comb. This could be a chance to prove none of this is your fault. Isn't that right, Em?"

Emily stared at Angela's hopeful eyes, then at Bridget, who looked as if she had lived a hundred lifetimes already while on remand. It would be a miracle if Bridget escaped a prison sentence. But with a sympathetic judge and jury, and enough compelling evidence, perhaps the time she would serve while awaiting trial would appease the courts, and she would be released after the verdict. Bridget would have to live the rest of her life with a criminal record and the weight of Wendy Wilson's murder on her conscience. But she would have a chance to start again. To rebuild on the ruins of what Wilson Peck had destroyed.

"I'm sure they'll find something helpful on those computers," Emily said. It was all she could offer right now.

Bridget nodded silently and stared at the table. Angela exhaled deeply. "Well I think this is good news. Don't you, Bridget?"

"Maybe," her sister said. "But it doesn't change the fact that Wendy is dead because of me. Out of everyone in the world, I chose her. I did that. Not Wilson Peck. Not Rick Frost. Me." She looked up at Emily and smiled sadly. "It doesn't matter what happens to me now. What matters is you stopped that man from hurting anyone else. Thank you."

"It's true, Em," Angela said. "What you've done for us, I can never repay you."

Emily tried to smile, but the pain in her neck was making her nauseous.

"I told you already," she said. "I was just helping out a friend."

CHAPTER 50

Jerome was sitting at the reception desk when Emily pushed through the doors of Braithwaite Investigations. A bright smile spread across his face as he raised his mug of coffee in salute.

"Why, Ms Swanson, good morning. How are we today? Still doing the robot?"

He moved his arms up and down while keeping his neck stiff and still.

Emily rolled her eyes, leaned across the desk, and wrestled the coffee mug from his hands. "You're not funny."

"Yeah, bad joke. How is it? Any better?"

"A little. How are you? Recovered from your hangover?"

"That was almost a week ago. It still makes me shudder to think that Wilson Peck was planning to abduct me. What a psycho."

Emily sipped some coffee. "Well, I suppose he changed his mind when he realised how annoying you are, then went for your phone instead."

Jerome took his mug back. "She may not have the use of her neck, but her tongue is as sharp as ever."

"That reminds me, I need to give you my new number."

"Me too." Jerome stared at her, his eyes softening. "How are you really?"

"Oh, you know." She glanced down at the desk. "Still getting my head around the fact that I killed a man."

"In self defence."

"Still, I think it will take some time for me to be okay with it. How do you even begin to process something like that?"

"I have no idea. But I'm here for you,

whenever you need me. I'll even let you have my coffee. Just this once though. Wouldn't want you developing any more bad habits."

He handed the mug back to her.

"I feel honoured. And grateful to have a friend like you." Emily glanced over Jerome's shoulder. "Where's PI Handsome? I noticed you two have been spending time together outside of work."

"Lee is out in the field. And if you must know, the only reason we've been spending time together is because he's concerned about my safety. I did almost die, you know."

Emily rolled her eyes. "I'm happy for you. He's a good guy."

"I told you, our relationship is strictly professional. At least until I finish up here in a couple of weeks." Jerome flashed her a wicked grin. "By the way, our overlord and master would very much like to see you."

"Really? That's good timing. I need to see her too."

"Oh? What about?"

But Emily did not elaborate. Instead, she

thanked him for the coffee and took a slow, deliberate walk towards Erica Braithwaite's office. Stopping outside, she sucked in a nervous breath, ignored the sudden fluttering in her chest, and knocked on the door.

Erica was sitting at her desk, dressed in one of her many stylish trouser suits. She looked up as Emily entered and offered her a slight smile.

"Emily. Do sit down."

Emily carefully lowered herself into the empty chair and waited for Erica to finish signing a pile of papers. When she was done, she looked up and stared at Emily, like a scientist analysing microbes in a Petri dish.

"How are you now? The bruising seems to have cleared up. Your neck any better?"

"It's getting there."

"Yes, well, I've been reading all about Wilson Peck in the newspapers. It's all very disturbing. Now I understand why it took you so long to complete your last job."

Emily bit her lip and said nothing.

"In any case, the client is happy with the

results," Erica said. "As a matter of fact, I have a new case for you. It's another insurance job, but before you roll your eyes, you might like to know that this is a much bigger and more complex case. Corporate espionage, involving huge sums of missing money. I'm partnering you with Lee Woodruff for this one. But it's an exciting opportunity for you, Emily. One that I know you've been waiting for."

Emily stared at Erica, her throat running dry. She coughed to clear it, then swallowed.

"Well, don't look too excited," Erica said, her eyebrows knitting together. "I've hand-picked this case especially for you. Is there a problem?"

"Actually," Emily began. But the words were stuck halfway down her throat.

Erica leaned forward. "Yes?"

Emily coughed again. "Thank you, Erica. But as grateful as I am, I don't think I can take that case on."

"Nonsense. You've spent the last year proving you're more than capable of working a case like this. You just need the confidence and self-belief to tell yourself you can do it."

"That's not exactly what I meant."

"Then what?"

"I've made the decision to leave Braithwaite Investigations."

Across the desk, Erica grew very still. She stared at Emily for a long while, one eyebrow pointing to the ceiling. Finally, she placed her pen on the desk and leaned back on her chair. "I see. You're quitting. May I ask why?"

"Because I don't think I'm cut out for the world of corporate investigation," Emily said. "I'll always be grateful for your mentorship. You took a chance on me, a novice. You took me under your wing and taught me everything I know. I'll never forget that. But helping insurance companies, taking on cases for big corporations, it's not what I want to do."

Erica was still staring at her with hawk-like intensity. "To be perfectly frank with you, it may not be what you want, but it's the exact kind of work that will put food on your table and money in your pocket."

"I know that. I do. But there is far worse evil in this world than someone pretending to have a bad back, or ripping off some corporation for a few thousand pounds. I'm not discrediting the work. I get that it's important. But it's not where my heart lies."

"And where does it lie?"

"I want to help people," Emily said. "I want to stop bad men from hurting women. I want to find the missing and bring them home. I want to help people like Bridget Jackson, Jessica Harris, Diane Edwards, Alina Engel. Even Becky Briar."

"I don't even know who half of those people are," Erica said, crossing her arms over her stomach.

"People I've helped in the past. People who were in trouble. That's where my heart lies. That's how I want to help."

Emily sat back, her heart thumping, yet filled with certainty.

"Very well," Erica said at last. "If I were speaking to anyone else, I would tell them that this is a grandiose idea formed with their heart and not with their head. But seeing as it's you, I think I'd be wasting my breath." She smiled then, a slight, barely visible curving of her lips. "But I suppose it was also that same drive and aptitude that made you stand out to me in the first place."

"So, you're not mad?" Emily asked.

Erica picked up her pen again. "Disappointed. But no, not mad. I wish you good luck, Emily. And I wish you all the best. Please have your written notice on my desk before the end of the day."

She nodded then and returned to her work.

Meeting adjourned, Emily thought. Standing up, she moved to the door, where she hovered.

"Thank you," she said. "For everything."

Erica did not look up again.

Out in the reception area, Jerome was waiting with a curious smile on his lips. "You're still alive? What happened in there? And why are you looking at me like that?"

"When did you say you finish here?" Emily asked.

"In two weeks. Then I suppose it's back to waiting tables."

"Not necessarily." She stared at him, adrenaline fizzing in her veins. "I may have a job for you."

"A job?" Jerome said. "What kind of a job?"

Emily broke into a grin. "One I think you might like."

CHAPTER 51
FOUR WEEKS LATER

A cold, sunless Monday morning descended over the city, forcing Londoners to collectively groan as they pulled up their collars and zipped up their coats. Emily stood in front of a small sash window, staring down at the street six floors below, where pedestrians hurried by and traffic chugged along the road. She had a strange feeling in her gut, a mixture of nerves and excitement, all bundled together and growing wings. The sound of an electric drill filled her ears, but she barely noticed it.

Had she made the right decision? Breaking away from Braithwaite Investigations to go it alone? After all, she had no client list, no pending cases, and just enough savings in the bank to cover the bills for two more months. But she had to try, didn't she? It was all that mattered.

She turned around, slipping her hands inside her jean pockets. The office was cramped, with just enough room for two desks. The walls were in dire need of repainting, and the heating was temperamental at best, but the rent was cheap by London standards, and it was all that she could afford.

Her eyes shifted to the far-right corner, to the source of all the noise. Carter was busy securing the final bracket to a set of wall shelves, which he'd made with his own hands back at the workshop. Emily smiled as he put down the drill and stepped back to admire his handiwork.

"It's a good job I'm dating a carpenter," she said. "Think of all the money I'm saving."

Carter arched an eyebrow. "Actually, you're dating a furniture maker. And I can think of alternative ways for you to repay me."

494

"Sleaze." Grinning, Emily moved up beside him.

"So, what do you think? Strong enough to hold up those law books of yours?"

"I do believe they are." She kissed his cheek, then rested her forehead against his temple. "Thank you."

Carter wrapped an arm around her waist. "You're very welcome."

He kissed the nape of her neck and nuzzled her ear.

"You better watch yourself," Emily said. "Fraternising with your employer is grounds for dismissal."

"But m'lady, I thought you liked workers with big, rough hands."

He kissed her again, then leaned back a little. "What's the matter?"

"Nothing." Emily stared at the empty shelves. "I suppose I'm a little nervous. I mean, what if this doesn't work out? What if I'm pouring the last of my money into a bottomless pit?"

"Well, I guess, you won't know until you

give it a try. And if it doesn't work out, you'll find a way to fix it. It's your superpower."

"It is?"

"Yeah, you're like a problem-solving ninja, or something."

Carter leaned forward and kissed the tip of Emily's nose.

"I am?" she said.

"Uh huh. You want to see my superpowers?" He grinned wickedly, placing his hands on her hips.

Emily laughed. "I hope you're not going to make a joke about those power tools of yours."

"Well, it's funny you should mention that . . ."

He leaned forward, shifting his hands to the small of her back, gently nudging her towards the desk.

"Oh God, no!" a voice cried behind them.

Emily glanced over Carter's shoulder. Jerome stood in the doorway with three takeaway cups of coffee clamped between his hands and a look of pure disgust on his face.

"I literally spent an hour polishing that desk, which is my desk, by the way," he said. "If you want to do gross and revolting heterosexual things, please do it in the privacy of your own homes. No one needs to see that, least of all me!"

Carter pulled away from Emily, a sheepish grin on his face. He stared at Jerome, who stared right back.

"Well, I guess I'll leave you both to it," he said, collecting up his toolbox, before leaning over to kiss Emily goodbye. "Us mere handymen better get back under the stairs where we belong."

"And you better stay there too," Jerome said, handing him a coffee. "Nice shelves, by the way. Very sturdy. We may hire you again for future fixtures and furnishings."

Carter sipped his coffee. "I'm honoured."

"I'll see you at home," Emily said, shaking her head. "Is seven okay? I'll cook."

"Sounds good."

"You won't be saying that later," Jerome

quipped. "And please shut the door on your way out."

Carter waved goodbye and headed out, a confused expression creasing his face.

"You're so mean to him," Emily said, narrowing her eyes, as Jerome handed her a coffee.

"Just keeping him on his toes. Anyhow, he likes it. He told me I'm funny."

"Funny looking."

Jerome looked around. "Did this room get even smaller while I was out?"

"No. Your head got bigger."

Pulling a face, Jerome sat down at his desk and wiped the surface with his sleeve. Emily heaved her shoulders and took a seat at her own desk. They were quiet then, sipping coffee and drinking in the silence.

"How's it going with you two?" Jerome asked, after a while.

"Good actually. He's staying over a couple of nights and I'm staying at his. I know he'd rather us move in together, but I think this is a good compromise for now. Until I'm ready."

Jerome nodded, his eyes wandering to the stencilled lettering on the smoked glass of the door: Swan Song Investigations.

He cringed. "You really should get that fixed."

"I would, except I can't afford it right now." Emily smiled, then laughed as she stared at the words. "Your first task as office manager and you blew it."

"Hey, it's not my fault the guy was hard of hearing. Anyway, Swan Song Investigations has a ring to it. Don't you think?"

"As a matter of fact, it does."

Jerome stared at the boxes of books on the floor. "Well, I've placed all the ads, the phone line is connected. What do we do now?"

"I suppose we wait."

"I can do that."

Emily sucked in a breath, held it, and let it out again. She stared at the door, quietly waiting. Quietly hoping. As she waited, she thought about how strange her life had become, and about how much it had changed in five short years.

Just as doubt began to fill her mind once more, making her wonder if she'd made a terrible mistake, the phone began to ring.

She glanced at Jerome, her heart beating hard in her chest. He glanced back, his eyes sparkling.

"It's the first call," he said. "You should take it."

Standing on shaky legs, Emily crossed the room towards Jerome's desk. She stared at the ringing phone.

Jerome winked at her. "You've got this."

Emily picked up the receiver and pressed it to her ear.

"Swan Song Investigations," she said. "How can I help?"

DEAR READER

I hope you enjoyed Kill For Love. When coming up with story ideas much of my research involves scouring news archives of violent crimes (which sounds like a disturbing past time now I've written it down). One afternoon, I came across two chilling stories that would go on to inspire this novel.

The first was the 2012 murder of sixteen-year-old Skylar Neese, who snuck out of her house one evening to see her two best friends, Sheila Eddy and Rachel Shoaf. Eddy and Shoaf claimed to have given Skylar a lift back late at night, dropping her off near her home so that she could sneak back in. But Skylar was never seen alive again.

As a search was mounted, suspicion fell on the two best friends, who appeared to be hiding a secret. But it wasn't until a few months later that Rachel Shoaf suffered a nervous breakdown and confessed that she'd helped Sheila Eddy to stab Skylar to death and bury her body in a shallow grave. The two had planned her murder during a biology class. Later, when questioned about the motive for killing the sixteen-year-old, Rachel Shoaf said, "We just didn't like her."

The second and more prominent story to inspire Kill For Love, was that of nineteen-year-old Cynthia Hoffman, who was murdered by her best friend Denali Brehmer and four others. When confessing to the murder, Brehmer claimed that she'd met a millionaire on an online chat site, who offered her $9 million in exchange for pictures and videos of her murdering Cynthia.

Enlisting a group of young friends to help, including two minors, Brehmer lured her friend with the promise of a hike. Cynthia, who had learning difficulties, was tied up, shot in the back of the head, then dumped in a river. When Denali Brehmer and her accomplices were arrested for the murder, Brehmer told detectives about the millionaire's offer. But it turned out that the so-called millionaire was in fact a twenty-one-year-old loner named Darin Shilmiller, who had successfully catfished Brehmer for his own deeply disturbing kicks.

ABOUT THE AUTHOR

Malcolm Richards crafts stories to keep you guessing from the edge of your seat. He is the author of several crime thrillers and mysteries, including the PI Blake Hollow series, the award-nominated Devil's Cove trilogy, and the Emily Swanson series. Many of his books are set in Cornwall, where he was born and raised.

Before becoming a full-time writer, he worked for several years in the special education sector, teaching and supporting children with complex needs. After living in London for two decades, he now lives in the Somerset countryside with his partner and a cat named Sukey.

Get in touch:

malcolm@malcolmrichardsauthor.com

www.malcolmrichardsauthor.com

Printed in Great Britain
by Amazon

21409885R00292